RAG &
BONE MAN

RAG &
BONE MAN

DON DICKINSON

COTEAU BOOKS

Edited by Dave Margoshes
Book designed by Tania Craan
Typeset by Susan Buck
Printed and bound in Canada

LIBRARY AND ARCHIVES CANADA CATALOGUING IN PUBLICATION

Title: Rag & bone man / Don Dickinson.
Other titles: Rag and bone man
Names: Dickinson, Don, author.
Identifiers: Canadiana (print) 20190128615 | Canadiana (ebook) 20190128623 | ISBN 9781550502749

(softcover) | ISBN 9781550502756 (PDF) | ISBN 9781550502763 (HTML) | ISBN 9781550502770 (Kindle)

Classification: LCC PS8557.I324 R34 2019 | DDC C813/.54—dc23

2517 Victoria Avenue
Regina, Saskatchewan
Canada S4P 0T2
www.coteaubooks.com

AVAILABLE IN CANADA FROM:
Publishers Group Canada
2440 Viking Way
Richmond, British Columbia
Canada V6V 1N2

10 9 8 7 6 5 4 3 2 1

Coteau Books gratefully acknowledges the financial support of its publishing program by: the Saskatchewan Arts Board, The Canada Council for the Arts, the Government of Saskatchewan through Creative Saskatchewan, the City of Regina. We further acknowledge the [financial] support of the Government of Canada. Nous reconnaissons l'appui [financier] du gouvernement du Canada.

For Luke

"It is by glorious action
that a man comes by honour in any people.
...But to elude death
is not easy; attempt it who will,
he shall go to the place prepared for each
of the sons of men, the soul-bearers
dwelling on earth, ordained them by fate:
laid fast in that bed, the body shall sleep
when the feast is done."
— from *Beowulf*

"Oh as I was young and easy and in the mercy of his means,
Time held me green and dying
Though I sang in my chains like the sea."
— Dylan Thomas, *Fern Hill*

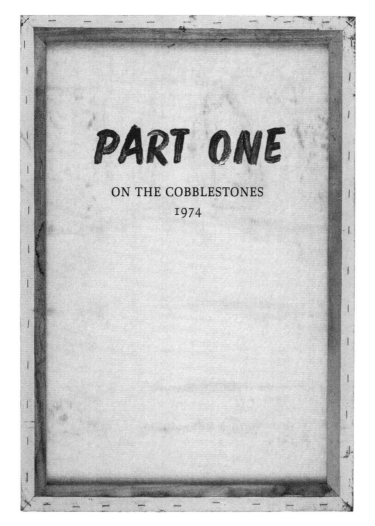

PART ONE

ON THE COBBLESTONES
1974

I'm nine years old when I walk into the Wasagam Souvenir Shop and steal a jackknife that has an Indian chief's head painted on it. Afterwards I run across the street, cut through Minnie Jones's yard towards the beach and climb the hill near the museum. Ashamed. Scared. I bury the knife under a spruce tree.

I promise myself I'll never go back to dig it up. Couple of years later I do.

Solid rust. Indian chief worn off. Won't even open.

1.

A fter the cut, Hendershot went back to his billet to make the calls. To Glasgow, to Cardiff, to Humberside, to Oxford City – even to Brighton where he and Steve Wozniak had started out when they first came over. Where the rink was one hundred and twenty feet long and leaked into the shoe store downstairs and the attendants hung fishing nets to keep the puck from killing spectators. He phoned – no openings. It was the middle of March. Season was nearly over. Rosters full, designated players signed.

His landlady, Mrs. MacGregor, offered tea and comfort. "Dinnae fasch yersel, Rob. You're aye young yet."

"Hockey, Mrs. M., is the one thing I'm good at."

"It's a long road that's no got a turnin'."

"I don't need a turning, Mrs. M. I need hockey."

He left Scotland. Shook hands with his replacement, Gervais – six-two, one ninety-five, a slapshot you could hang laundry on, said goodbye to his teammates, and with his severance pay bought a train ticket and headed to London, where that spring the train station luggage lockers and garbage cans were shut tight against the threat of Irish bombs. Rumours had told him freighters hired non-union deckhands to ship to Southampton and from there back across the Atlantic to Halifax. The rumours lied. The docks had been abandoned to rusty cranes and night watchmen who sat in shacks. They searched his equipment bag for explosives and came up with his jock strap and elbow pads. They laughed and told him to move along. The sun had set on the British Empire a long time ago, they said.

He checked into a railway hotel that had a shared bathroom at the end of the hall and porridge for breakfast with a piece of toast and an apple, if he got to the kitchen early. Then off to the day-labour exchange to deliver beer kegs to pubs, sweep out warehouses or wash windows. He took his blues harp into the tiled stations of the underground on weekends. The tourists were generous and the acoustics great. He knew only one song, the *St. James Infirmary Blues*, his dad's favourite. Classic performance. But the Metro police told him to push off and take his sign with him.

Hand-lettered message on a clean piece of cardboard, a sort of gothic script to catch the eye of the passengers as they hustled to the trains: *Hockey Player, Need Team*. Because at that time he was young enough for hope to spring eternal. Him, his hockey bag, pads, skates. Give them a stick and a team, any team, and they'd give you hard work and loyalty. He was a grinder, a plumber, one of the troops in the trenches. Forecheck, backcheck, bodycheck, penalty kill, drop the gloves if he had to. Once in a while he'd even score. When the knee wasn't acting up, he could skate with the best of them. Or at least most of them. Fans' noses pressed to the glass, the roar of the crowd, a beer and a ploughman's lunch after. Number twenty-three on your program, number one in your heart.

He got no offers. Except one from an old lady with a wig full of lice and a dozen plastic bags belted at her waist, filled with all her worldly goods. She called him Ducky and cried when he played the *St. James*. Best audience he'd ever had besides his father, so he took her to a shop across the road and bought them both ham sandwiches.

When the day-labour jobs thinned out, he dropped the hotel, bought a frying pan and rented a cot in a doss-house until the landlady wanted cash instead of an IOU. When she told him to get out, he pawned a few shirts, a pair of dress shoes and the suit his father had given him to wear when he made the big leagues. Didn't need it. The suit was black and would've looked good on an undertaker.

He bought an army surplus blanket and lived free range – bed on a park bench, stand-up bath in public facilities, one meal a day from his choice of menu: soup, egg-and-chips, tea-and-a-bun. March went out like a lion. Frost. One day, snow. Wandering the city, he came to rest under a bridge, snug in a nest of newspapers and cardboard. He shared the space with two professional drinkers, amateur street performers. One was big and hairy, the other small and one-legged. Christian names Reg and Vic, but he dubbed them Sasquatch and Pogo, respectively. They said they were escape artists, weather permitting. Or when their stock of methylated spirits ran low.

One morning he woke up uncovered, chilled to the bone. Sasquatch and Pogo were gone, as was his blanket, blues harp and hockey equipment. A note pinned to his toque said: *Used gear, Petticoat Lane, Cheers.* He swore for a full minute without repeating himself, rubbed the knee, peed behind a stanchion, then set off to find a cup of tea or a sausage roll, whichever came first.

2.

He reached the river just as Sunday church bells were ringing and it came to him that the note might've been serious. The public market: outdoor booths, trinkets, souvenirs, used clothing, war surplus – everything up for sale. Plus crowds who might be generous to a proffered toque. He imagined his stolen hockey bag set out on a table and the idea got him excited. He saw himself tracking down the tools of his trade, buying them cheap, reviving a career.

He hurried as fast as the knee would allow. Cruciate ligaments, the team trainer had suggested, but Hendershot figured a strained tendon. Along the Embankment under a steady drizzle. Thames the colour of sludge.

He took a shortcut through a square near the Tower where a man on the cobblestones was swallowing a chain, ten feet of half-inch links, the kind used to shackle a mad dog to a kennel-house door. A bus tour crowd had the swallower surrounded and each time a link slid past his pursed blue lips they breathed 'aahhh' and shifted their feet for a better view. A big guy, face like a mop. No worries about rust, road slime or tetanus shots, he simply aimed his beard at heaven. His bobbing Adam's apple did the rest. It took Hendershot a second to recognize Sasquatch because he'd never seen the big guy out of his cardboard, but the man on the ground wrestling to escape a burlap sack and hemp rope was undoubtedly Pogo. Right trouser leg pinned over his pointed shin, torso wrapped up like a flipperless seal, mouth an O every time he sucked in a circle of burlap.

When he finally peeled the sack up over his head Hendershot moved in, leaned over the ferret face. "Where's my bag?"

"Wot bag?"

"My hockey gear."

"Fuck off."

"How much did you get for it?"

"Fuck off."

No confession, but no denial either. Between the two performers, a cloth cap bulged with money tossed there by the crowd. Coins, paper bills. Hendershot picked up the cap and started to do a quick count of what he considered his share, but Pogo warned Sasquatch, "Cunt's got the money, Reg." The chain dangling from his mouth, Sasquatch spun like a hammer thrower and a length of the links caught Hendershot a good one across the chops. Blood in the mouth, ringing bells, adrenaline rush. He wiped his lips, hugged the cap to his chest and took off.

People who saw, lunged. One or two clutched at his sleeves. He dodged and twisted, ran broken-field, ducked a cape swinging a camera, hip-checked a raincoat, nipped around a turban, head-faked a bus driver attached to a tire-iron. Then ran smack into a tray covered in sprigs of heather wrapped in foil. Knocked the vendor flat on her back, her legs kicking the air like a downed beetle. "Fink of the children," she said. He tossed her some coins, vaulted a wrought-iron fence, snagged a pant-leg on a spike, face-planted the grass. Up again, he felt a hand clamp his shoulder. He pistoned his elbow backwards and struck bone. A policeman's whistle shrilled.

When he got to the street, he tucked the cap under his arm and sprinted.

3.

He needed to lose himself in the maze of streets. But to do that he had to get away from the river. Too many people had seen him. He zig-zagged through the traffic and jogged among the passengers spilling out of an underground station. At a corner, two skinheads called him a fucking wanker. He turned right under a green pub sign with gold lettering, *The Lion's* something or other. Farther along, space opened up so he dove between two buildings. Cement on one side, red brick on the other, graffiti-smeared – ERUPT, SUPERGRASS, UP THE IRA.

He followed the rising ground, but didn't know that part of the city well. He was used to lakes, rivers, trees. Give him landmarks like the Great Big Spruce and he'd make it to the creek, the bridge, the place where the horse trail met the road. But here everything was pavement and stone, overcast sky, apartments like a kid's giant building blocks with most of the paint rubbed off. He funneled through the streets like a lab rat. Hoped he was headed north.

His knee grew sloppy. Crossing a street, he was nudged by a car and fell down. Spilled the coins and bills into the gutter. While he scrambled on all fours to pick them up, something smacked him on the rump.

An old man waving a cane. Tattered mac, face hanging from his hat like melted cheese. "I told you lot before, you want to be careful." The old man glared at the whizzing cars, swore and shook his fist at them. Hendershot asked him where he was, which cheered the old man up. He couldn't have been more pleased if the hockey player had been hit by a truck. "Gorn, not lost as well? Yer muvver must've had her hands full. Yer in Whitechapel, mate."

Not north. East.

A sudden rain began to fall. The old man retreated up some stone steps into a doorway where Hendershot joined him. Edwardian building, stone columns, cornices, boarded up windows. Former Bank of Something.

"Taking the lolly out for an airing?" Nodding at the cap.

"Donations for the poor. Where's the nearest underground?"

"Aldgate. Miles away."

The rain fell in front of them like a beaded curtain. Through it, Hendershot saw, across the road, a line of cars between him and them: Sasquatch, arms hanging like King Kong ready to climb buildings. And Pogo, who'd somehow grown a leg.

Hendershot was halfway around the corner when the old man shouted something about a number fifteen bus.

The streets he ran through had names – Tenter, St. Mark's, Alie. And warehouses, their whitewashed walls as yellow as tea-stained teeth. Farther along, rowhouses, stunted fences, water-blown roses. School playgrounds done out in cinders. Rusty fire escapes that petered out ten feet off the ground. More graffiti, ANARCHY RULZ. He smelled cat piss and curry, heard an electric guitar rattle an attic window. Once, for fifty yards, he ran inspired, knees high, arms pumping, until the ligament said goodbye. On his way down, he grabbed at a dustbin and sent it clattering.

They cornered him in a dead-end lane ringed round with corrugated steel doors that were locked tight. *Imperial Raj Import-Export Pty. Ltd.* Dustbins and plastic garbage bags. An opening recently bricked in between two buildings was too slick to climb.

"I don't mind saying we're deeply disappointed," Pogo

said. He nodded to Sasquatch who waltzed Hendershot between brick and steel and tried to snap his spine. Hendershot barely had time to pocket the bridge of his two front teeth before they were into it, down among the orange peels, cigarette butts and used condoms. Sasquatch's weight was close to that of a sperm whale. Below the beard, Hendershot spied a boil on the neck, aimed his thumbs at it, missed. Kneed for balls and struck air.

"Take all the money," he said. "What the hell." Sasquatch flipped him on his back like a burger on a barbeque. Hendershot hammered the guy's kidneys – like punching a mattress. Sasquatch breached, flopped on Hendershot's chest and jammed a forearm into his windpipe. Hendershot's tongue swelled up and his eyes got big. He drifted, his brain turned off. Somewhere water runneled in a drainpipe and after a while a liquid voice said, "Hold him steady, Reg."

"Wojer fink I'm doing?"

"Lively fucker, in't he? That's it, good. Now move yer arm."

A tunnel of light out of which a pink prosthesis peeked from under a lifted trouser leg. The black boot cocked and swung. Pain leapt into his groin, ribs, back, head. He twisted away, curled up and covered his head with his arms. But the boot found him again and again, until a hollowness spread through his bowels. With a sort of gratitude, he relaxed under the wave of it and as he closed his eyes, his brain pitched forward and slid down a long dark trough that collapsed into foam.

4.

The two kids sidled up the alley towards him, like skinny dogs nosing around a butcher's back door. Wet hair plastered to their skulls. The tall one had big ears and a nose like a parsnip snapped off at the tip. The short one was harelipped and sucked at a bulge in his cheek. They might've been on stilts; their heads were level with the chimney pots.

"Havin' a bit of a lie-down, are you mister?" The tall one stepped close, leaned over to look. Long drink of water in a man's overcoat and paratrooper boots.

Noises came out of Hendershot's throat. His left eye hid behind a hill. His lips were inner tubes.

"He's Mutt n' Jeff," the short one said.

"Shuddup." The tall one scowled. "Yer not deaf, are you mister?"

Mister swallowed, licked his lips.

The short one tugged at the tall one's sleeve. "It's no good, Nigel. He's a dead loss. She won't want him."

"Shut it." Nigel nudged Hendershot with his boot. "They done you proper, din't they then?"

Hendershot hawked up blood and spat. "I geth tho."

Nigel grinned, little teeth, big gums. He nodded to his friend. "Told jer."

Nigel was one of life's hopefuls. Under ordinary circumstances he'd have applied a boot to Hendershot's head, frisked his pockets like airline security. He had long fingers. But these weren't ordinary circumstances, so instead he cupped a hand under Hendershot's arm and eased him up until he could sit. "That's the ticket, mister. Upright and breaving."

"Won't do you any good to feel for my wallet."

"Slip of the fingers."

"Thure." Hendershot probed his teeth. The top two were missing but he remembered they'd been missing before. In a game once. In an arena. Had pennants hanging from the rafters. Where were his teeth? Automatically, he patted his front pocket, pulled out his bridge, fitted it into his mouth. A little loose, but it would tighten up. The other thing, though, had him stumped. He couldn't remember where he'd put his hockey equipment. When he asked, they stared.

"Ice hockey." His teeth made talking easier. He took a moment to be impressed. "Skates," he said clearly. "Can. Shin pads."

"All you had was a cap. And them ovver blokes nicked it."

Pictures swam in his head: a boil on a hairy neck, a black boot, a pink leg. He tried for more but his brain wandered. Also, the seat of his pants was sopped. He felt with his hands. A puddle. "Help me up."

They grabbed his arms and unfolded him like a lawn chair. On his feet, he wobbled, rubbed the bad knee through the hole in his jeans. Something hot radiated upwards from his nethers, floated up along his backbone like a bubble in a thermometer and exploded between his ears. The flash behind his one good eye gave him x-ray vision: the two kids glowed a brilliant green so that he could see right through them – white bones, blue veins, red arteries, road maps of nerves. Holding him up, they rippled in a cloud of light. A sourness rose in his throat and swallowing it jarred loose a memory. Himself when he was what ... eight, nine? Jumping off a roof, a wool blanket for a parachute tied to his belt. His little brother, K-Man, looking up, the snowbank taller than he was. How old was Kennie then? ...How old were these kids? He couldn't tell. Both of them thin as knife blades.

Stunted, wizened. When they stepped away from him, he slumped like an arthritic grandpa. An elastic band stretched tight between his groin and collar bone and if he'd straightened up too fast his guts would've dropped out of him like sausages from a split grocery bag.

"I dunno Nigel." The short one shook his head. The hare lip gave him an air of wisdom. "He's got the right wojercallit...am-bee-yonse I s'pose, but look at how he's been knocked about. She won't want him."

"You keep sayin' that, Tony, but we dunno, do we? She'll have ter take a look at him, won't she?"

"Who?" Hendershot asked.

No answer. Tony rubbed his pointed chin. Smartass little bugger. Walked around Hendershot like a buyer checking out a used car. Lifted the hood. Kicked the tires. Even so, Hendershot's ego stood and saluted. He squared his shoulders in imitation of a man with something in reserve. Suspended on a string from the top of his head, as his father, who'd been military, used to say. A question of pride. Ready to take it or dish it out. *Let 'em look you over, son: eye swollen shut, knackers afraid to hang, you're still on two legs. A credit to evolution.*

"I want to thank you guys for scaring off the terrorists. You saved my bacon."

They looked at each other. "You've got ter be joking."

"The department will be grateful."

"Gorn, what department?"

"International in scope, government stuff. I'm not at liberty to say more." Self defense. Maybe if he gave them mystery, he'd be safe. They could have an adventure. Why not ... he was having one. Whoever they wanted to see him couldn't've been much worse than the ones he'd already seen. Besides, he felt sleepy. Maybe they wouldn't have to walk far. Maybe he could lie down.

Nigel sneered. "Department? Pull the ovver one.

Departments don't go in for punch-ups these days. They got codes and guns what look like biros. Computers wiv little whatsitsnames in your teef."

"Implants," Tony said. "Double-oh-seven sort of fing."

"Yer implants."

"Like these?" Hendershot flashed his incisors.

They backed off, whispered together. "She'll want ter see some identity-fication," Tony said. "After what she went through the last time, she won't give you nuffink if you don't have yer Eye Dee."

Hendershot loosened his belt and reached inside his pants. Like a pervert in a park. The kids stepped farther back, conscious of danger yet drawn to it, ready to attack or run, it didn't matter which. They were kids and so would live forever, or at least until they died, which was a long way off. Watching their faces, he was tempted to warn them about time's eyeblink, the sudden drop from youth to age. Twenty-three to eighty-five in one easy lesson. Beyond this alley the city hummed *Beware, boys, beware.* But they didn't hear it, didn't talk. They wanted action and who was he to deny them their dreams? He had dreams of his own. Food, team, someplace where he could sleep for a week.

He fished his passport out of his underwear.

"Canada?" Nigel said.

The lion and the unicorn reared up on the front cover like an illustration from the book of fairy tales his mother used to read them when they were kids. Before the divorce. No Jack the Giant Killer here though, just last year's Hendershot, Robert P., twenty-three years old, grin lopsided, nose broken. Height, weight, hair colour, eye colour, scars – all the particulars that made him particular. But the guy in the passport confused him. He felt alien. The pavement rose and fell under him like a floating dock. The air smelled thick. Somewhere skates rasped the ice, pucks pounded the boards, but he couldn't hear them.

"Here, steady on, mister."

He started to fade. Hitching their bony shoulders under his armpits they set off at a dog-trot, marionetting him between them like thugs shanghaiing a sailor. Laughing up an alley between row houses where dirty windows stared at back gardens. A yard where a woman paused from beating a rug with a stick.

"What you got there, you boys?"

"Rubbish, missis." Dancing a jig on either side, he piggy in the middle, grinning like a drunk in a photograph.

Sirens in his head. An alley, a street, a lamppost. Sitting on a curb, his face between his knees, vomit on his shoes. Underground steps, trickling water. dustbin, a sagging gate. The boys' sharp shoulders under his arms. Cracked cement steps to a door painted a pink so loud it deafened him. A clay gargoyle no bigger than his thumb, chin hanging over a window box. *Kilroy was here.* Smell of paint, wood rot, turpentine. A stubby thick-fingered hand at a curtain. Clank of a door knocker, crowd of brass men riding a brass donkey. A pockmarked face maybe ugly, maybe serene, maybe beautiful.

Her eyes were large and liquid brown.

He fell into them.

5.

"You'd better bring him through."

"Is he a fifty p. or a quid?"

"Mind the cartons."

The hallway was a canyon of cardboard boxes. A gauntlet he couldn't run. He thought *hoarder, secret warehouse.* Over Tony's shoulder he glimpsed the woman, broadhipped in baggy sweatpants and a cardigan, hair as curly as a pot-scrubber, tied with a shoelace at the nape of her neck. *Weight-lifter maybe. Den mother. Pirate.*

The room they entered was roofless. A low grey sky without the rain. Or maybe not. He tipped his head so the good eye could find the ceiling. At the far end of the room light streamed from a skylight. Or maybe a sun porch. All glass and rain-streaked.

The woman turned, rested her hand on his chest. "Wait." Then told the boys to move the canvases and sit him in the big chair. Padded arms, sprung springs. He sat and sank. *Armchair Swallows Hockey Player.*

"A quid or fifty p. Margaret?"

"What is patience, Nigel?"

"Looks like a quid ter me."

Her voice was low and precise, her hand warm on his forearm, her breath soft on his face. "I'm going to fetch some things so I can clean you up. Rest." Her words seemed picked over, the way – who was it, Minnie Jones? – used to pick over things washed up on the beach, bits of worn glass, driftwood. Weaving them into her macramé wall hangings. Like storm-ravaged fishnets pulled from the lake. Something to cling to.

He clung to her words. Then he leaned forward and with the boys watching, threw up. He studied the floor between his feet. Hardwood, shiny with his slobber and something else. Shards of colour – red, blue, green, yellow. As if a rainbow had shattered overhead. "What's this?"

"Paint," Tony said.

The place was cluttered. Sheets of plywood on sawhorses, a work table, a bench, shelves, cans, paint brushes, oily rags, an easel. Canvases stacked face-first against the walls. Photographs, sketches, drawings pinned to a bulletin board. He saw it all as if through popcorn glass. All of it there and somehow alive. His temples throbbed but it didn't matter. It was a big room; his head would fit. He fumbled for something to mop up the slimy bits of toast and sausage at his feet. Nothing. Except for his passport, his pockets were empty.

He spoke to a bowl of soapy water. "Sorry, I couldn't hold it."

"It's not the first time for this floor." She tucked her hand under his chin, tipped his face up to the washcloth. Gentle. Matronly even. Dabbed the sore spots, murmuring. Patted his face dry.

She stood. Seated, he was nearly her height. What was she, four-foot nine – ten, tops? He wondered if this was what is meant by "coming down in the world". Because he felt low. In himself. Bagged, useless, sleepy. Whereas she was compact energy.

She took his head between her hands. Her fingertips grazed the shape of his face before moving along his neck, his shoulders, his arms. She roamed his body and he let her. Welcomed her gentle squeezing, bending, probing. A clinical tenderness. "Does that hurt? That? There's a contusion here ... here as well." Brailled his injuries – ribs, stomach, chest, back, thighs, groin.

"Swollen if I'm not mistaken."

"The guy kicked a field goal."

She held up a penlight. "Look to your right. Good. Now left." The light snapped off. "Pupils look normal," she said. "One eye at least. A good sign."

"Are you a nurse?"

She and the boys laughed. "Not in my wildest. First-aid training at the hands of nuns a hundred and twenty-three years ago. Before," she added.

"I'm a hockey player," he said, as if it explained something. "Ice hockey." He could've added *before*, but didn't know if this was *before*. He thought it was still *now*. *I'm a hockey player. It's what I do. Not right this minute but...* With this woman...this...Margaret...now was *now*. She was too intense for a past or a future. She filled the room with her nowness.

"Nothing broken," she said. "At least from what I can see. They'll know better at the hospital."

"No hospital."

"X-rays. It's all on the national health."

"No hospital. No cops either. If you don't mind."

Cocking her head, she folded her arms across her middle. Behind her Nigel and Tony closed ranks. Her breasts were noticeable; they announced themselves. He wondered where else to look and found her eyes. Darker than when she'd first opened the door. "So," she said, "no medicine, no law."

"If that's not okay, I can leave."

"Oh yes. And where would you go?" Because those eyes saw right through him. Which puzzled him later, considering what happened. But right then this short, almost midget Margaret with her amateur first aid had him pegged. She knew desperation when she saw it and why not? She wasn't blind. She had the artist's eye. His soiled running shoes, torn jeans, dirty fingernails, greasy hair – anybody could see those. What she saw was different. Some quality he wasn't aware of but hoped he possessed. Her eyes gathered him in; she approved.

And smiled. Big white teeth against skin as red as sunburn. Placing her hands on her knees she bent close, her face filling his one good eye. Some genetic blunder had crammed her hips, breasts and head onto her sawed-off frame. She owned the parts of a bigger person but if that was nature's joke, she was willing to go along with it. "I need your face. I need your body." She was serious. Without moving her eyes from his she said over her shoulder, "I expect he is a quid, Nigel."

6.

After a while, he yawned. The strength drained out the soles of his feet as it did sometimes after a hard and unprofitable game. Where every shift you're no better than a pylon, set up for the other team to skate around. Back on the bench, you tell yourself next time you'll move your feet, you'll want the puck, you'll go for the net. But you don't, and before you know it, the game's over.

Loss hangs over everybody in the dressing room. Heads down, quiet, because they know what loss is and it shames them. And then somebody feeds somebody else a line, "Jeez man, you keep playing like that and we're gonna buy you a lobotomy for Christmas," and gets answered, "Oh no, I'm not going through that again." Because they have to laugh. Because there's always a next time. Has to be, or what's the point?

Half awake, he asked Margaret if he'd had a pair of skates with him when he came into her house. She said no, her head cocked like a bird's. "That's it," she said, "keep looking down. Don't move. I shan't be a minute." She darted away, came back with a sketchbook and pencil. Pulled up the worn footstool so their knees touched. Drew him from all angles. Feverish, the pencil racing across one page, then another and another.

Nigel said, "You got classical ligaments, mister."

"Linny-ments," Tony said.

"Shuddup, Tony. Don't 'e look all classical-like, Margaret? Worf more than a quid, I shouldn't wonder."

But she didn't answer. His face had got into her hand and was pouring off her pencil, no stopping it. He sat as still as a potted plant and let the life seep back into him. The nearness of her. The roar of her pencil. His body being shaped. His face. Because he could see it, upside down, through one eye. Himself, through her. His *whole* self. Rolling off the end of her arm onto the paper so that he thought, *This is art.* Who'd never thought of art before. Who'd worried about tendons, muscles, training, diet, the twists and patterns of the game. Suddenly there on the page, if not the real him then at least Margaret's real him. Bruised, beat up, eye like a ripe plum, jaw off-kilter, scars like train tracks on his face, like grins on his knuckles. All the marks of him. The marks of his *art*...if that's what it was.

He decided then that whatever it took he'd get back on the ice. He promised himself this. But he had to be patient, thinking, *Don't make your move too soon. Hang onto the puck. Wait till the goalie goes down. Choose your shot, high stick side, low stick side, between the pads...*

...or something.

His head ached.

Nigel said, "He's got a passport, Margaret. Government stuff," he tittered, "international in scope. We're not allowed ter say more."

Tony said, "Double-oh-seven sort of fing."

"Shush you two." Margaret set down her pencil and sketchbook. Led the two boys back down the hallway. Murmurs, laughter, coins clinking. Then "Cheers, mister!" and the door slammed. Silence, except for the wind moaning in the sun porch and water dripping from the eaves.

He sat quietly. Kept his mouth shut. Didn't want to scare her off. His brain ticked through pictures like long ago memory. Fading in and out. Tourists, bus driver, Pogo's boot. He'd assaulted somebody ...hadn't he? Stolen money? Heard a policeman's whistle, heard it even now, two inches behind his eyeballs.

When Margaret returned, she held the sketchbook at arm's length, her eyes unfocussed. Like that early morning stare people get sometimes, so far past the cornflakes box that they're hardly in this world at all.

Her voice jolted him back to himself. "I pay my models."

"How much?"

"One pound an hour."

"Is that good?"

"You tell me."

"That's forty pounds a week."

"I shouldn't think so."

"Why not?"

"It's not full time."

"What time is it?"

"One-pound-an-hour time."

"What would I have to do?"

"Pose. Sit still."

"Dressed or nude?"

"Maybe both."

"Would naked pay extra?"

"Ten per cent."

Which got him calculating. One pound per hour, two or three hours a day, that'd be fifteen to twenty pounds a week. Minus food, rent – fifty per cent? Leaving him enough to buy some equipment. His own, now maybe in a pawnshop or on a table at a street market. He tried to remember having his hockey stick, but couldn't. It must've been stolen. But teams often provided the sticks. That left pads and skates. Pads? – anything was possible. When he was a kid he wore Saturday Evening Posts on his shins. Held there by canning jar rings. A goaltender he once knew protected his legs with slabs cut from a horsehair mattress and a belly pad that'd been a rug. You could rig up something for the pads. But that still left the skates. He wanted his. His father had bought them for him. The blades had been replaced a couple of times, but the boots knew his feet, as personal as fingerprints. Stolen, but not lost forever. He'd find them because who in that country of soccer players and cricketers wanted or needed hockey skates?

"You've got a deal," he said.

They shook on it. Her grip was firm, full of meaning. Of what he wasn't sure, but he believed in it. Trusted in it. Because it was Margaret. There was that: Margaret. Even later, when everything else was falling apart.

But that would be later. Now he was very tired. He had posed for her for ten minutes...or maybe two hours...he wasn't certain. And somehow, she was holding his passport, which he didn't remember giving her. Asked if she should call him Robert and he gave her a choice: Rob, Robbie, Hen, Hennie, Henster – nicknames that'd dogged him on the ice. "Hockey players," he mumbled through his fatigue. "The little kid names keep us on the bounce."

"I didn't know we had ice hockey players in Britain."

"Endangered species."

Which in his case was true, because he felt himself disappearing. Like a doper on the nod. There was stuff he needed. A toilet, for instance. Food, drink and a flat surface where he could lay his head. Margaret offered him her hands, hauled him out of the chair and helped him to the WC. Waited until he came out and while he swayed in the bathroom doorway, she fitted the plug in the tub and turned on the taps. "While you get cleaned up, I'll fix something for our tea. Can you manage?"

"Yeah. Thanks."

"If you leave your clothes outside the door, I'll find you something clean to wear." Before she closed the door, he asked her if he was a quid or a fifty p. She said a quid, no question. Was she sure? "I have standards," she said.

Undressing, he found two five-pound notes in his sock.

He couldn't remember putting them there, but he slipped them under the insole in his shoe.

7.

The tub was old-fashioned with claw feet and high sides. He hoisted himself over the edge, like a burglar climbing through a window. His last bath had been a stand-up job in a men's can where he dried himself off with paper towels. A bath gave him a chance to take stock. The face he already knew about, likewise the testicles, the knee, the knuckles. The bruise on the left thigh wasn't a surprise, nor was the pain near the breastbone. He figured a cracked rib. He'd had one before. A slight twinge when he coughed. In the WC he'd peed straight urine, yellow, no blood, so the kidneys were okay.

But he ached – face, knees, elbows, butt, back. And stank. His armpits could've melted tin. Clipped to the tub's edge was a wire basket with soap and one of those deep-sea scrubber doohickeys he couldn't remember the name of. In fact, his memory faded in and out like bad radio reception, so he ignored it. Lathered, scrubbed, rinsed, lathered again, lay back. The tub was good, the soap was good, the water was good. He considered bathing as a career.

We have a galvanized tub. Mum heats the water in the copper boiler on the stove. Dad comes in from patrol. Snow on his warden's cap. Frost boiling through the open door. We four kids take turns, youngest first. By the time Mum and Dad have theirs, the water's scummy, like porridge. Mum's English voice: "We're living like barbarians." Dad's Canadian: "Barbarians don't use soap."

The tap dripped until its noise turned into footsteps outside the bathroom window. A woman's voice: "Obsessed wiv it, he is. Sits all day in that bleedin' chair and when he's not staring out the window and writing notes to himself, he's got his nose in the newspapers working himself into a state over this IRA business. I tell him ter leave off, he's got to watch his heart, but he won't listen. Against his principles, he says. Wot principles, I asks. He looks at me queer and says, Morals. Vengeance. Justice. I dunno what he's on about. Enough ter drive you barmy. So last night I went round to my sister's and she told me to pack it in. Pack it in, Muriel, she says, there's no need for that nonsense, I'll put a word in for you at the factory. So that's it then, he's on his own. I tried to get hold of his mate, but..."

The voice drifted away. He lay back in the tub. Closed his eyes and listened to his head. High-pitched whine. Like the time he dropped down to block a slapshot. Broken nose, black eyes, and a big space where the second period should've been. But this time he was remembering things, so it wasn't a concussion exactly. Just got his bell rung, that's all.

Night time. Two strands of lights, one above each blue line. Snow banks higher than the boards. I'm ten years old, alone on the ice stickhandling through chunks of firewood laid out the length of the ice. Play-by-play in my head. "Hendershot breaks in over the blue line, cuts to the middle..."

The firewood jumps up and starts to clap...

Margaret's voice through the closed door: "Are you still alive?"

"Pretty close." The water was cold. He was shivering.

"I've left some clothes out here. I don't mean to rush you but my husband's just rung up. He'll be here in a bit."

Husband scared him. Sounded grown-up. Somebody who'd taken his lumps and given them back. Like his father. Ex-husband to his mother. Divorced after hammering each other until they split in two. *Husband* could've meant anything, but it got him dried and dressed. Argyle socks and boxer shorts. Shirt and waistcoat. Tweed trousers with two legs that he climbed into one at a time while resting his head against the door. The pants were short in the leg and big in the waist, saved by his own belt. He fumbled with buttons, snagged a shirt-tail on the fly. Combed his hair with his fingers. Looking back at him in the bathroom mirror was a head waiter who'd just been on a bender.

As he stooped to rinse out the tub, his bones creaked.

8.

The husband stood in the studio in a puddle he'd made from the raincoat over his arm. When he took his hat off, his white hair was just long enough to look like it was blowing in the wind. Sleepy face, sharp eyes, black-rimmed glasses. Nice suit, hint of a paunch. Manly grip when they shook hands. Name: Trevor Tayleur-Stocking. "So, you're the epic hero," he said. His accent sounded like education and money. "Interesting choice of clothing, Margaret. I didn't know I'd left anything of that sort behind."

"The trunk."

"Of course. I'd quite forgot."

"You were rushed."

"Indeed." Trevor watched Hendershot. Department store dick sizing up a shoplifter. "You'll do the bruises. Authentic. I'm in two minds about the beard, however. Bit scruffy. And the posture – vintage corner boy slouch if you don't mind my saying." He gave Hendershot a thin smile, maybe the only kind he had. He asked if the hockey player was *ailing*. The last one had been *ailing*.

"I straighten up when they play the national anthem," Hendershot said.

Tayleur-Stocking brightened. Moved directly in front of Hendershot, raindrops on his glasses. Eyes glittering behind the lenses like guns in the moonlight. "I'm sorry, what are you called again?" Hendershot told him. "What am I to make of you, Rob? Not a professional model, are you?"

"Not yet."

"But a specimen of some historical or social significance. The borrowed clothes, the borrowed house, the borrowed wife – "

"Trevor," Margaret said.

"Free speech, my dear. An Englishman's home, castle, etc." He waved a hand. All this was nothing. "The rent, you know, Rob. Roof, four walls, household expenses and, I might add, the model's fee. The true price of art. So you don't mind if the husband – the villain of the piece, if Margaret hasn't already told you – has his say? Do you? Rob?"

"Hey, I'll lend you my ears."

"Ha!" Short bark. As if he'd been goosed, a cheap shot that made Hendershot feel smarter than it should have, and open to retaliation. But Trevor turned on Margaret. "You may have done better than I expected. Certainly better than the Rumanian."

"Csongor was Hungarian."

Trevor shrugged. "Disadvantaged at any rate. My wife," he confided, "is what one might call a painter of lame ducks. You're her latest bird. And judging by your feathers – borrowed clothes, flat vowels, bristled chin – I suggest the tedious North American, the latter-day wandering Jew, partially comatose – no, my dear, let me finish – comatose or at the very least hermetically sealed against a classical influence or a good strong beer. I'm surprised there's no rucksack. You do have a rucksack? Haven't you? *Rob?*"

"I left it in your other suit." Because Hendershot was enjoying the guy, and wondered if he should let him take off his glasses before popping him in the mouth.

"Rucksack," he was saying, "although by your general appearance one is reminded more of a –"

"– rag-and-bone man," Margaret finished for him.

Which stopped him cold.

She paced the room, around the sagging armchair, the easels, the workbench, the stacks of canvases. Her voice imitated her husband's exactly as she went on a rant about civilization slouching towards annihilation sporting a black eye and carrying a sack bulging with the detritus of a bleak and mindless century. She mentioned cracked tea pots, old photos, button shoes, clothes mangles, gas masks, OBE's, and ration coupons. Her voice never faltered, scarcely paused for breath, attacked among other things *Top of the Pops*, and oh god, television documentaries narrated by washed-out actors from the National Theatre. When she stopped, Trevor said, "You do that well, Margaret." She said she'd studied the original. "Oh no. Some touches are all your own." She told him all his boxes were stacked in the hall, and that she and Rob had to discuss the project.

Trevor hesitated, looked around as if for a place to sit down but couldn't seem to find one worthy. Put on his hat, shrugged into his raincoat and headed for the hallway. Paused. "Incidentally, I'm back at the college full-time."

Margaret said, "Now you and Angelica can drive to the college together."

"She's rather an intelligent girl, you know."

"Girls of her type and age usually are."

They faced each other. Stand-off. Like the time Hendershot was driving with his father on patrol during hunting season. Looking for poachers. Rounded a bend and in the middle of the road crouched a badger. On guard in front of her den, dug deep into the gravel. The badger warned them off, chattered her teeth. His father had said, "She shall not be moved," and waited in the truck for the badger to signal the all-clear.

Margaret the badger, Trevor the truck. Trevor took half a step, said he'd get those papers and come for the rest later. Then added: "If Lionel should ask, what do I tell him?"

"I'll have the preliminary sketches by week's end."

"The committee is getting on at him at the moment. They're expecting it in time for the opening."

"I've got my model now."

"*Todo por el arte*, then."

"Yes."

He took Margaret's hand and bowing, kissed it. Said "*Bueno sombra, mi filomela*,". She followed him and a good thing too. Hendershot's knee gave out. He had to sit down. Shock, he supposed. From the hand-kissing.

When Margaret came back, he asked if he was fired.

She told him not to be absurd.

9.

Big fry-ups. Eggs, bacon, potatoes, tomatoes – though she said she was kosher. Mopped up with fried bread. Washed down with milky tea, followed by slabs of chocolate. Heart attack on a plate, she called it. That first time, he ate two helpings.

She had less than a month to complete the commission that Trevor had arranged. Her soon-to-be ex-husband was also her agent, soon to be agent only. Two frown lines appeared on her forehead just above the bridge of her nose. She said it'd been a year since she'd been awarded the commission and with no portrait in sight, she'd been afraid her muse had left the building.

"But now you're here. Your portrait is one of six scheduled to hang in the Manuscripts and Rare Book Reading Room at University College."

"*My* portrait?" Hendershot couldn't help but feel the thrill. Immortality. He should've been in hockey uniform, on his skates, stick in hand, turned sideways spraying ice, big grin for the fans. *Number twenty-three on your program, number one in your –*

"Oh, not you, per se."

"Who then?"

"From a poem a thousand years old," she said. "Beowulf."

Kennie and I lie in bed under the covers with the flashlight, so I can read the comic books to him. Batman, Superman, Spiderman,

Flash. And those Classics Illustrated, the ones Stephie left wrapped in plastic after she won the scholarship to the girls' college. Robin Hood. The Deerslayer. The Three Musketeers.

When Kennie finds out he's sailing away with Mum, he has nightmares. Men with swords live on the ship. Monsters hide in the ocean. "Don't worry," I tell him, "it'll be okay. If any of them try to hurt you, I'll punch 'em." From his bed on the other side of the room Lyle laughs. "How you gonna do that, big man? You think you're going with them?"

When he told Margaret he didn't know much about Beowulf, she said, "Read this," and handed him a skinny paperback.

His head ached. He poured himself another cup of tea, stretched his fingers like tentacles. Noticed the tabletop had sprouted green leaves. If he could've rested his cheek against them for a few minutes, smelled the earth, he would've been fine. Margaret said he could sleep on the chesterfield in her studio. He thought that was fine too.

The last thing he remembered was her hoisting him out of the chair. Her head no higher than his chest. Her arm around his waist, breasts below his ribs.

Later in the dark, nudged awake. Her voice so close he felt her breath on his cheek. A light swung past the window outside, her face flared, disappeared. "What's your name?"

"Rob."

"Rob who?"

"Hendershot."

"What's my name?"

"Margaret Low . . ."

"Lowenstein."

He told her his birthday, counted backwards from a hundred.

"You were talking in your sleep. You said a name: K-man."

"My brother."

"Oh."

"Did I say anything else?"

"No. Why K-man?"

"I called him that when he was little. His name was Kennie. K-man was just a thing."

She patted his shoulder. "Sleep now." And left him.

But sleep would not come. As he lay and attempted to identify the shadows that lurked in the room – the trestle tables, the easels, the armchair – memory suddenly ambushed him. He whispered the name to himself, simply to hear if it could be accommodated by the strangeness all around him. "Kenneth John Hendershot," he said. The room listened. "Kennie. K-man."

10.

That first season in Brighton, Hendershot kept the address in his wallet, his mother's handwriting on the envelope his father had taped inside the cupboard over the sink where the liquor was kept. Hendershot had thought he'd warn them he was coming, but it'd been twelve years since he'd seen them last and he was afraid they wouldn't want to see him. Or even if they did, they wouldn't recognize him.

In the movies inside his head, they always showed up at one of his games. In Sunderland, say, or one of the northern towns, so they wouldn't have to travel far. They'd sit behind the players' bench and watch him at his work. Cheer for him. Show him there were no hard feelings.

After the game he'd take them for tea and they'd study the photograph he carried in his wallet. They'd laugh at his mother's old-fashioned hair and Kennie's sailor suit. He'd tell them the rock they'd sat on was still there on the banks of the Wasagam. And before he climbed back on the team bus, they'd invite him for Christmas. And Kennie would be tall by then and have an English accent and Hendershot would ask him if he remembered how they'd read comics under the covers and how he'd called Kennie K-man.

But they didn't show up at a game. The Christmas card he sent to the address his father had given him got no answer. So after the team didn't make the playoffs and Woz went up to Scotland to visit Elspeth and Hendershot was left sitting in his Brighton billet staring at the oily sea, he bought a train ticket north. All-day trip. London, Birmingham, Warrington Quay, rain all the way. At Windemere station, he arrived in the dark, too late for a bus. Draped his poncho over his head and backpack, hitched a ride to Ambleside in a lorry hauling a pottery kiln.

Stone house, two stories high, across the road from the churchyard. The sign said Loughrigg Guest House No Vacancy but he rang the bell anyway. A red-haired woman with a Scottish accent answered the door. He asked if Mrs. Hardacre was at home. The woman invited him in to wait and disappeared down the hall while he dripped on the carpet. The foyer was clean and had an umbrella stand and cobbler's bench shaped like a frying pan.

The red-haired woman returned with her husband. Roly-poly guy in rimless glasses. He asked, "What do you want with Mrs. Hardacre?" and Hendershot said, "I'm her son. From Canada. I'm Kennie Hardacre's brother."

The woman wrung her hands and the husband said in his gentle way that he was afraid the Hardacres didn't own Loughrigg House anymore, they hadn't owned it for years. He took off his glasses and cleaned them on his shirt and when he put them back on, he said he was sorry to say this, you'd have thought someone would've informed the family. There had been a terrible accident, one of those huge articulated lorries from the continent. The Hardacres and their son never had a chance.

"They're buried in St. Mary's churchyard," the man said. "Just opposite. Across the road."

The lady wondered if Hendershot had a place to stay. She telephoned a friend at another guest house and gave him instructions how to get there.

In the morning, he visited the graveyard – tombstones, crosses. The Hardacres had modern markers: granite stones set flush with the ground. Hardacre, William Thomas. Hardacre, Megan Rose. Hardacre, Kenneth John.

He tore away the grass so the names weren't hidden. Hardacre. He remembered trying to teach K-man to write his name *Kennie Hendershot*. He got no further than Kennie H. And there he was, still Kennie H. Still with his mum.

He bought a map, went hiking. Lines of stone fences draped over the hills like black string. Sheep dotted the fields. He watched a kestrel hover over the green and brown hills. The bird hunched, wheeled, hovered again, looking for mice. Later on, rain clouds dragged themselves over the mountains, trailing sheets of rain. He hunkered behind a stone fence to eat bread and cheese. Slithered back down in the rain and freezing wind. All around the sheep grazed; he thought what it'd be like to be a shepherd in that country.

When he phoned his father and told him about Kennie and his mother, his father went quiet for a long time. Finally he said, "Age will not wither them nor the years condemn. You think that's true, son?"

Hendershot wasn't sure, but he said yes anyway.

11.

He slept on Margaret's couch for three days, ate her food, sat for her while she struggled to get him down on paper. Posing, he was a tree stump. Sometimes the only thing he knew for sure was that his neck was cold and his backside had seized up. He considered death by pneumonia, with cramped-ass complications. Decided against it. Instead he'd simply fall over. Tragic. Tasteful. But she'd probably say, "Good, great, perfect. Stay dead like that while I get the line of your shoulder where it meets your back..."

When she wasn't drawing him, she was on the phone. "Yes, it's going well. No, not yet. I'll let you know when. Well, I've been away. Oh, don't say that. We have an understanding."

Judging from her side of the phone calls, he pieced together what he imagined was the life of an artist. Constant hustle. Picture frames to choose; canvases, brushes, paints to buy; exhibitions to arrange; commissions to fulfill; luncheons to attend; grants to win. Gallery owners, Trevor, Lionel, critics. Her excitement bothered him, mainly because it was hers and not his. She was in motion while he wasn't. He was benched. Not placed on waivers, not sent down to the farm team (there *was* no farm team) but cut, severed, amputated.

"You know where the food is," she said one day on her way out. "Spoil yourself."

Toasted bagels and tea at mid-morning. Soup and sardines for lunch. Chicken, rice and veg for supper. Beowulf he was not. He'd read the book. Twice. You wouldn't catch Beowulf stretched out on a couch stuffing his face with tea biscuits.

One day she came home and said, "I have a friend coming to stay. I shan't be needing you for a few days. Not to worry though. I've arranged for your accommodation."

12.

Mister Green lived in the flat upstairs. Five-foot-three in carpet slippers, silver hair shooting out of his head like forked lightning. Narrow shoulders slabbed with muscle, legs short and bandy, a boxer's torso on a shore-bird's pins. If he'd been a hockey player the question would've been: *Are those your legs or are you riding a chicken?*

After Margaret left them together, Mister Green gave him the tour, starting at the back, in the kitchen, where the sloped ceiling brushed the top of Hendershot's head. Midget stove, bar-size fridge, wooden table and two wooden chairs. One greasy window overlooking a weedy allotment. Little tin shed out there for garden tools. "At one time, I grew vegetables and the like." Mister Green pointed to the stove. "Gas cooker. Oven's a bit tricky, but it does the job. You cook?"

"Meat and potatoes, bacon and eggs, toasted cheese sandwiches."

"Never mind." He tapped his skull. "I got recipes in 'ere. Fry-ups, of course. Bubble and squeak, fish and chips, bangers and mash. Anyfink Eyetie – spaghetti, linguini, lasagne. But I do a nice lamb curry as well. Change of pace."

"My grandmother taught me roast beef and gravy. I boarded with her when I left home to play hockey."

"You'll never make a bob playing ice hockey in this country."

A shot. Hendershot blocked it. "She was seventy-five, my grannie. I was sixteen."

"I'm eighty-three."

Mister Green showed him the bathroom. Toilet jammed up hard against the tub. "Where my wife done herself in. Slipped while she was having a bath. Banged her head on the taps." Mister Green said he'd been out at the time. When he got home even the water was cold. He hauled her out, dried her off, got her into her night dress and put her to bed. "Bit of a prude was old Maeve. She wouldn't have wanted strangers ter find her starkers in the bath." In the morning he'd phoned the authorities. Hendershot asked how long he'd been married. "All my bleedin' life it seemed. Still, if there's a heaven, she's in it. It'll be endless cups of tea and digestive bickies for the old gel now."

Living room: worn couch, two overstuffed chairs, TV, radio, shelf of books, fold-up cot along a back wall. Fireplace with gas heat and a coin box for the meter. One picture, a spider's web of cracked glass. Hendershot looked at it through the good eye: not a picture after all, but a spread of military medals. "Highland Light Infantry," Mister Green said. "Corporal. The Great War, mate. Bloody great cock-up." He turned suddenly to the cot. "You can set that up. I got a curtain to hang from them hooks. Private-like. Sheets, pillow, blankets – the lot. Five pound a week, grub included. Margaret's paid you up for the next two weeks. She does that sometimes. You're one of the lucky ones. Provided you keep the place tidy. You can be the lady-wot-does. Yer grand-maw teach you anyfink about that?"

"Enough to get by."

"Not allergic to tomartoes are you? The last one of Margaret's was Hungarian. Bloody stupid being allergic ter tomartoes. I think he done it out of spite."

"I'm not allergic to anything."

Mister Green confessed he'd fired the woman who'd come in once a week to cook his meals and clean his flat. "Used cayenne pepper in everyfink. 'Good for yer blood pressure,' she says. 'That's as may be,' I says, 'but it wreaks havoc on my arse 'ole.' Like a bleedin' gasworks, I was – smell so bad you could hear it in the street. Muriel Mickelthwaite...there's a mouthful for you. Didn't like my politics as she called 'em. You know, the Irish and the Troubles and that. Said it wouldn't surprise her if the boys from the IRA came 'round ter take me away. Serve me right and all. I told her ter piss off..."

Muriel – the voice outside Margaret's bathroom.

Mister Green listed Muriel's other flaws and his rambling took Hendershot back to his stay with his grandmother. Grannie Hendershot. Five-foot-nothing. Backbone of steel. She had left England with all her belongings in a wicker suitcase, settled in a city where the streets were mud. Married his grandfather and given birth to seven children. Four of them lived, one of them Hendershot's father. In return for doing odd jobs – the garden, the lawn, the leaves, the storm windows, the snow, the trips on the bus downtown with her to buy groceries – she'd taught him things she said he'd need all his life. How to cook, wash clothes, run a sewing machine and bend to the will of an old woman who wasn't about to treat him like a baby. "Your mother may have left your father and the rest of you, but there are worse things in life, so you'd better get used to them." One of Hendershot's uncles regularly mailed her the Jehovah Witness *Watchtower* which predicted the end of the world and which she regularly pitched into the garbage. Hendershot pulled them out and read her articles about beating swords into ploughshares. But she had her own views on the planet and how to live on it. His stay with her had been enjoyable because One, he loved her, and Two, nothing lasts forever.

Mister Green wasn't his grandmother, but he had all the old-timer symptoms Hendershot had learned to respect. Even so, he was startled when the old man suddenly dropped into an armchair and ordered him to fetch the binoculars from the kitchen.

Hendershot stood next to the chair as Mister Green focussed the binocs out the window, pausing to scribble in a notebook he kept in his cardigan pocket.

"Bird watching?" Hendershot's National Park Warden father was a birder. Liked watching them while he sat next to a bottle of scotch.

"Irish linnet."

"Don't know that one."

"Or a kestrel."

"Isn't a kestrel –"

"Bird of prey."

Hendershot stepped to the window to take a look. Mister Green pulled him back. "Stand behind the curtain. Tell me what you see."

In the street two kids dribbled a soccer ball. On the corner a man smoked outside the tobacconist's shop and talked to a woman wearing rubber boots. Three workmen in blue coveralls bent over a storm grate. Striding away a big guy, all back and shoulders.

"Now then," Mister Green said, "turn away from the window."

Hendershot turned. "What for?"

"The woman in the wellies. What was she holding in her hand?"

"What's this – quiz night?"

"What was she holding?"

"A purse – no, wait. A string bag."

"That's right. The big bloke: what colour was his hair?"

"He didn't have hair."

"What colour?"

"He wore a hat."

"What sort of hat?"

"Cap. Cloth cap." He saw it in his mind. "Blond. He was blond."

"Well done."

"Also, one of the workers had his coveralls unzipped to the waist. Do I win a prize?"

"Not at the moment. But you got yer wits about you, I'll grant you that."

"What good does that do me?"

"You noticed him, didn't you? Big bloke, cloth cap."

"Yeah. Who's he?"

"Irishman. Connor Mack."

Hendershot didn't find the name familiar.

"Margaret's fancy man," Mister Green elaborated. "He's back."

"Oh yeah?" Hendershot was puzzled. Felt vaguely betrayed. "What's he do?"

"He makes bombs."

"What?"

"Bombs, mate. Boom, boom."

"Are you serious?"

"He would say he doesn't. He would say he's a working man. But I know the truth, don't I?" Mister Green's watery blue eyes took Hendershot in. "What do you know about the Irish?"

"Whiskey, shamrocks, leprechauns. And bombs...I guess."

Mister Green went to the book shelf, brought back a photograph album. Newspaper clippings. Photographs. Not the explosions themselves but of the aftermath. Burnt-out cars, shattered windows, rubble scattered in the street. Bodies. Some curled up alone, others scattered like tree branches after a storm. The dead tossed aside, the living left stunned. A woman holding a child, limp against her middle. A man on his hands and knees amongst the wreckage.

And then the people who'd been arrested. Not gangsters in cheap suits, but ordinary guys in jeans and windbreakers. Climbing out of police vans on their way to courthouse back doors, jackets pulled over their heads. Or a surprised face staring into the camera: *Am I the guy? Are you sure?* Or belligerent: *I'm the guy and guess what? – Fuck you.*

Hendershot had thumbed through the album, closed the cover, sat with it in his lap. "There's four years of reporting in here," he said.

"The Troubles have been going on a lot longer than that, mate," Mister Green said stoutly. "Longer than either of us has been alive. But it's got ter stop."

Hendershot thought, *It's a hobby, that's what it is. An old man's hobby. Grannie used to do needlework.*

Mister Green stood, set the album in its place on the bookshelf. "And it will stop, mate. I guarantee it."

"If you say so," Hendershot said.

13.

Spiders' webs. Rusty tools, dirt floor. Cracked flowerpots, moldy seed packets and cigarette butts. On the workbench made of rotted two-by-fours Hendershot found a burred file and used it to hone edges on the fork, the hoe and the shovel. He turned the soil as the April sun came up. Mister Green called him in for a cup of tea but he declined. He was into the work by then, grateful for the mindlessness. Weeds as high as his waist. He worked up a sweat for the first time in weeks.

Because the allotment was around the corner, he had to wander towards the fence to see who came out of Margaret's flat. He heard him first. Big voice, big laugh. Then the man himself: head like a bullet with a fringe of blond hair. Hendershot thought, *No wonder he wears the cloth cap. Give him a couple of years and he'll be as bald as a snake.* Connor Mack was wearing the same jacket he'd had on when Hendershot had seen him from Mister Green's window. And he had shoulders, all right. So heavy he could hardly hold them up. Wrestler, maybe. Bouncer.

Grendel.

"I piled the weeds," Hendershot said when he came in for supper. "Thought we could burn them."

Mister Green wasn't having it. "Council's got rules and regulations. I used ter fling 'em in the dustbin but they weren't keen on that. What I done was bury the lot: makes good compost if you don't mind the seeds. Now then, wash yer hands. I've done eggs, chips, peas. Got meat pies and a blood pudding from the butcher's. And a bit of Swiss roll for afters. You can do the washing up, but for now lay yer teef into that. Proper ploughman's grub, that is."

He didn't answer Hendershot's question until they were sprawled digesting in front of the TV. "That Connor," he said. "Been going on for years, that has. Connor shows up, he and Margaret have a jolly old Friar Tuck, then it's back to work for the both of 'em."

"Oh yeah?" Trying to hide his jealousy. "What's *he* actually do for a living, besides bombs?"

"He would say he's a stonemason."

"What would you say?"

Mister G rolled a cigarette as thin as a straw. Watched Hendershot over a curl of smoke while the quiz show host on TV spun the wheel. The old man had a habit of going quiet, as if he were rehearsing in his head what to say out loud. As if he were alone on his own personal rink, practising his moves. "I would say, that *he* would say, that he's a stonemason, which he is." The cigarette hung from his lower lip, quivering. Signal that he was changing the subject. "Margaret will want you ter pose for her in the next few days."

"You sure of that?"

"You needn't mention Connor. But you might ask her about two gentlemen named MacAleer and O'Shea."

"I think I smell a grudge."

"You do."

"Why shouldn't I mention Connor?"

"Margaret's sensitive on that subject. The Hungarian found that out. I shouldn't want ter put yer job at risk."

"You must know Margaret pretty well."

"She's lived in that flat seven years. But we don't really know other people, do we? Not really. But Margaret – well, she's an artist, in't she then?"

"Seems like one to me. I've never met one before."

"Yer lucky mate. I've known artists all me life. My father fancied himself an artist."

According to Mister Green, his father used to paint pub-signs, murals in restaurants, coats of arms for the carriage trade, portraits of merchants and their wives. "He done well for a time." As a boy, Mister Green's job was to stack gold sovereigns on the dining room table so they could be counted. They lived in a house just off Clerkenwell Road. "Then the old man decided he was a *real* artist. Started doing oils. *Thames at Midnight. Hampstead Heath at Dawn.* That sort of thing. And him wiv a wife and three kiddies."

Mister Green gazed at Hendershot fiercely. The rooms they rented grew progressively smaller, as did the pile of sovereigns, he said. In the end, they crowded into the back of an Italian restaurant's warehouse. "When he had a few pictures, the old man used ter take me along wiv 'im down the West End. Barefoot I was. We'd prop the pictures against the railings round Russell Square. One day a clergyman come out. 'I'll take two of them,' he says. 'Do you like 'em?' my dad says. 'I'm offering to buy them,' the clergyman says. He's looking at me, see. Me bare feet. My father sees this and packs up. 'My art's not charity,' he says. Stupid gitt. His art wasn't steak-and-kidney pie, neivver. We went home empty-handed. Empty-bellied, as you might say. Mind you, he always found money for his paints. My sisters mixed 'em for him. The paint come in cakes, see, and the girls ground 'em up wiv a mortar and pestle. Added the oil. After years of this, their gums and fingernails turned blue. Lead poisoning. Killed 'em both in the end. Broke my muvver's heart, that did." His eyes dared Hendershot to contradict him.

Mister Green said, "My mum was Irish. Lost her whole family to the potato blight, so you'd have thought she'd be used ter life's little tragedies." He drew on his cigarette, thoughtful. "When Margaret calls you in, remember, *caution's* the word when it comes to Connor."

14.

Two days later, she was sketching Hendershot in charcoal on a huge sheet of brown paper spread over the trestle plywood. Broad strokes, her body moving like an orchestra conductor. "Strange?" she said. "In what way strange?"

"He told me about his wife's accident. The bathroom. Putting her body in bed."

"Yes." She kept drawing. "Well. Something hit her on the head."

"He mentioned a couple of guys, MacAleer and O'Shea."

She straightened, charcoal in her hand like a magic wand. "Is he on about that again?"

"I don't know. Is he?"

She'd stopped drawing. "MacAleer and O'Shea lived next door but one. They put it about that Mister Green had brained Maeve with a skillet and cleaned her up to throw the police off. Stupid. They meant it as a joke. Mister Green denied it, of course. He accused them of belonging to the IRA. There were enquiries all round, but nothing ever came of it." She looked at him with those clear brown eyes. Too big, too bright, sometimes. "A word to the wise," she said. "You'll want to be skeptical about what George Green tells you."

"Why's that?"

"He's an old man. A dear friend...but he has his own view on things. Please," she said, bending over the paper, "try not to fidget. If you can hold your right arm like that..." She stood very still, her eyes glazed over – fuzzing them, she called it.

"You don't think..."

"Don't speak," she said. "Don't move."

Her breathing when she drew was full of secret grunts and sighs. Involuntary murmurs. Barely audible groans, moans, breath-exertion-release. Like exercise. Like sex. The sounds worked their way into his ears, warmed his chest and set fire to his groin. Her presence filled him. Even without looking, he could see her, feel her. The baggy pants draped over her hips, the cardigan hugging her breasts, the tangled hair on the back of her neck. Under her clothes her body threw off a great heat. He wanted her, but more than that. He wanted her to want *him* – her eyes, her hands, the way she looked at him and allowed him to flow onto the paper. He had no idea how old she was – older than he was, for sure, but he didn't care. He was falling into the present; the future was still hockey but it seemed a long way off. Though he didn't know the guy, he envied Connor Mack and wished him a sudden and early death. That he was Irish was obvious to Hendershot, and that Mister Green held that fact against him was certain. But none of that had anything to do with Margaret.

When she'd finished sketching him and put the drawings away, he asked her if she thought Mister Green was crazy. She said he was passionate, which wasn't the same thing. "I don't believe he was trying to hide anything by putting Maeve to bed," she said. "I think he was trying to show something."

"Like what?"

"Love," she said.

15.

One day after the third or fourth session posing for Margaret, Hendershot went for a walk in the neighbourhood. Old brick rowhouses, blocks of soot-stained flats three storeys high. Victorian housing, according to Mister Green. Chimney pots like top hats. Narrow streets. Wrought-iron fences, iron capstans to wrack his shins. Smell of diesel fuel, coal smoke, boiled cabbage. Corner shops.

One street was an open-air market, crowded as a circus. Used clothes, old records, stuff made of plastic. No hockey equipment though. At the end of a lane, he found two pence and on impulse went to the nearest phone box where he dialed Steve Wozniak's number in Dunfermline. Morning practise would be over and Woz would be home for lunch.

But he wasn't. His wife, Elspeth, said he was at a team promotion with the local gas board. "I can give him a message though, Rob." Hendershot imagined her leaning on the kitchen door-jamb, hand on her belly. How many weeks was she now – sixteen? "How are you, Elsie?" She laughed. "Bigger. Steve and my dad are building a bassinet. It'll be ready by the time this bairn's three years old. And how're you getting on, Rob? Are you all right?"

He considered lying but what would be the point? He explained the situation and asked if Woz could put out some feelers for him. "A team, Elsie. Or coaching kids – anything on a rink." She promised to let Steve know and he knew she would because she was Elsie. When she asked for a phone number, he told her he'd phone back in a week or so, since Mister Green was in the process of getting a new phone. He left the phone box lighter than he'd felt in weeks. Close to giddy, for no other reason than knowing Woz and Elsie were on the job. In the street, a crowd of kids including Nigel and Tony were playing soccer between parked cars, so he jumped into the game as a goalie, made five stops, let in two goals and eventually was told to piss off because he was too old and too tall.

But the game had got his blood going and his hopes up. Apart from an odd twinge, the knee knew when to bend and when to straighten. The bruises on his face were healing and though the testicles and ribs were tender, his overall in-shape-o-meter was climbing to a seven out of ten. By the time he got back to Mister Green's he was practically bouncing.

"What's got inter you?" asked Mister Green.

"Carry on regardless," Hendershot said.

"Where'd you hear that?"

Hendershot launched into World War Two, Lancaster bombers, rear gunners and his father. The abridged version. How Jake Hendershot was wounded over Berlin, given a DFC and sent off to a secret location where he guinea-pigged for aeronautics engineers, who were developing a new kind of tracer bullet to estimate distances. How Jake married Meg, the woman who would become Hendershot's mother, an RAF radio operator stationed at the same aerodrome. Hendershot's father was twenty-three when he was wounded on April 23rd, while serving in the 23rd Squadron. His wife had been born in 1923, and they were married on February 23rd. "I'm twenty-three," Hendershot told Mister Green. "Number twenty-three on your program, number one in your hearts."

"Yer off yer nut," the old man said, but he was smiling and his wild hair looked delighted. "What's it all got ter do wiv the price of tea in China?"

"I don't know – maybe nothing. But it's got to be lucky. I yam what I yam."

16.

"You am what you am," Mister Green mused. He paused to study his war medals in their fractured frame. "Your dad pin his medals on a wall?"

"No, he keeps them in his sock drawer. Takes them out on Remembrance Day."

"Hm," Mister Green said.

"Why's the glass broken?" Hendershot ventured.

"Oh, this?" Mister Green ran his finger over the fracture lines. "Civil disobedience, mate. Whenever the government done somefink stupid, I flung this lot in the dustbin. My Maeve used ter fish it out." He grew thoughtful. He went to sit at the kitchen table, where a pot of tea was waiting. Poured them each a cup. An invitation Hendershot felt rude to decline.

Mister Green settled in his chair. "I joined up in 1914. Lord Kitchener, see. He wanted me. Free trip to France. Me and my mate, Paddy Cahoon. Rank Irishman. Rank as rancid butter. No one could put up wiv him but me. He was me best china."

"Where is he now?"

"Dead, mate. 1917. Artillery shell. He went, as the saying goes, all ter pieces. All over me, as it happens." Mister Green looked at Hendershot square on. Pale blue eyes, older than the rest of him.

Hendershot wasn't sure what to say. "And you?"

"Woke up in a manor house in Kent. Striped pajamas, wicker chair, doing like this." He bobbed his head. A somnambulant woodpecker. "Place was full of blokes, doing like this. Shell-shocked. Barmy."

"You must've come out of it."

"Put on me slippers, and leapt the garden wall. They dragged me back, brought me 'round and sent me back ter France." The old man was proud in his bitterness. Proof that he was alive.

After France, he joined the Black and Tans, shipped to Ireland to guard the Dublin Post Office. A two-mile march from the barracks. Each morning, the soldiers left spit-and-polish, and arrived covered in horse dung and slops. "The Irish hated us. Can't blame 'em, really." He sent a note to Paddy Cahoon's mother. Wanted to tell her that her boy had been a good bloke. A good mate. "But she wrote back, saying I shouldn't come 'round. Me being a British soldier and all. British soldier! What did she think Paddy had been, scotch mist?" He remembered, "It was Paddy named me Scrounger. I was good at finding things the French had hid after Jerry had shattered their houses. Potatoes. Onions. I'd ask myself, 'If I lived here, where would I hide the necessary?' And that's where I'd look." He sipped his tea. "Paddy Cahoon. You'd never find him stuffing bombs in a postbox."

"But you think that's what Connor does?"

"I know he's got somefink ter do wiv it. What I'm trying to work out is how he manages it."

"I wouldn't know."

"Aren't you even a *bit* curious?"

"Maybe. But what's the point?"

"I'll wager I know what yer dad would say the point is. 'Carry on regardless.' That's the point."

"I don't know about that."

"'Course he would." Mister Green aimed his chin at Hendershot, like a man who had no doubt.

I am four, maybe five. K-man is a baby in his crib by the door. Lyle sleeps next to me in the bed. Stephie has the little room off ours, divided by a curtain. I am sleeping, then I am awake. In the dark a man is shouting. "No, no! My legs, Meg, it's my legs! They got my –" *A woman murmurs,* "It's all right Jake, it's all right. I'm here. I'm here. You're all right."

"Oh Christ, Meg," *my dad says.* "Oh Jesus."

I listen. After a while their voices fade. But I lie awake waiting. The house creaks. I hold my breath. The dark starts right where my eyes begin. Next to me Lyle must be breathing, but I can't hear him.

The house keeps creaking. I won't sleep until it stops.

17.

He started early in the mornings when the roads were still wet from the street cleaners and his breath steamed in the early spring damp. Except for a few lorries and delivery vans, the city was asleep. Most days he jogged in the dark down the middle of deserted streets like the last man on earth.

There were no signs of life until he reached the market, where people who were bundled up against the dawn readied themselves for the day's business of flogging vegetables. Joking, swearing, smoking, drinking mugs of tea, they rolled out their barrows and tarps and waited for the market garden trucks to arrive. Seeing those people up before the sun gave him energy. He picked up his pace, pumped his arms. One old porter took to calling out to him, "That's it, mate, keep yer left up!" so that Hendershot shadow-boxed the length of the street, prize-fighter extraordinaire if that's what the old guy wanted.

Sometimes, at the bottom of the road, he'd turn into an alley, passing a corner newsagent's where the kid who lived above it, if he was awake, would flash Hendershot the two-finger salute and yell, "Faster, you wanker!"

He loved those mornings. The way the ache in his knee gradually dissolved under the tensor bandage he'd fashioned out of a pair of elastic stockings Mister Green salvaged from his wife's cast-offs. The warmth of the hooded sweatsuit he'd bought at Saul's Used Clothing, around the corner from Mister Green's flat. The feeling of purpose, of being back in training.

At a schoolyard, he jumped the fence and rope-climbed the swings, did incline push-ups on the teeter-totters, chin-ups on the soccer goal posts. Every now and then he thought of Margaret, saw himself reflected in her eyes, a bona fide epic hero. Stalwart and strong. Possibly even noble.

The notion allowed him to finish a workout feeling purified. But one day, on his run back through the fog, he bumped into a man carrying a canvas sack and a large toolbox. In the mist, the man wasn't much more than a lump on legs, but when he shoved past Hendershot to get into a waiting van, Hendershot glimpsed the bullet head and apologized to it. "Watch yerself next time, boyo." By the van's light, Connor Mack looked Hendershot full in the face before he slammed the door. The van roared away. Hendershot watched it until the winking tail lights were swallowed up.

18.

He would never be sure how Mister Green fed him the information. A little at a time, he supposed. Whether or not Hendershot believed the old man at first was beside the point. In the end he took it all in.

Mister Green jotted down his observations in a wire-bound pocket notebook that he carried everywhere he went. To the greengrocer's, the butcher's, the park, the pub. To the abandoned docks where he used to work. Once, on a bus to a churchyard where Maeve Green was buried, they saw Connor loading boxes into a van similar to the one Hendershot had seen the Irishman climb into that foggy morning. When Hendershot told Mister Green, the old man noted the time, place, date and licence number. His hand-writing was small and neat and the charts and statistics he compiled at home were precise and mathematical. Like the geometry theorems Hendershot used to copy in his note-book at school.

Some dates were check-marked, others x'd, still others asterisked. The old man wrote beside each date where and when an explosion had taken place. *Oct. 16, Tottenham Road, post box, 20:10; Dec. 3, Shepherd's Bush, Sailor's Arm Pub, 22:23; Jan 6, Victoria Stn, dustbin, 13:05.* And so on. Pages of the stuff, going back years. Footnotes, distances, meticulously hand-drawn street maps. He'd invented codes for establishing connections. Graphs drawn in coloured pencil to show if and where the Irishman intersected with the explosions. Connor's movements in green, explosions in red, police investigations in blue. Mister Green's own movements in yellow. All orderly. Accurate. On some level, convincing.

But Hendershot was skeptical. "Why don't you go to the police?"

"I have done, mate. Not about Connor – but about them ovver blokes."

"What other blokes?"

"MacAleer and O'Shea. Not what I'd call trustworthy, so I grassed 'em up."

"So, you've done this kind of thing before."

He lifted his chin. "On occasion."

"How many occasions?"

"Five. No, I tell a lie. Six."

"You've been to the police six times?"

"That's right."

"For six different people?"

"That's right."

"And you told them every one of them was a bomber?"

"That's right."

"How many arrests did the police make?"

"None."

"Then you haven't been right about any of the guys you turned in."

"Not as such." Mister Green held steady. "But just because there were no arrests, don't mean they weren't bombers."

"The police must be tickled when you show up."

"I don't go round there these days."

"Why's that?"

"They're rude. They put me off." His gaze was unflinching. "We could find out things, you and me. Undercover, like."

Hendershot admired his tenacity. At the same time, he wondered if the old guy was nuts. The thing was, Mister Green didn't look insane. He leaned back in his chair, stuck out his bony chest. "I'm laying a trap for him," he said. "If he's guilty, he'll be caught. If he's not, he won't. You could help me."

"Let me think about it," Hendershot said.

He went for a walk. Down the street, around the corner. No Margaret in sight, but the streets were filling with kids on their way home from school. Labourers, clerks, salesgirls and charwomen coming home from work. He was swept along with them, hands in his pockets. He wondered how Mister Green would trail Connor through this river of people, how he would find him , how he would trap him.

The crowd washed Hendershot up in a small square where a derelict stone church sat behind wooden barriers. A signboard named the company in charge of its demolition. Crumbling stone steps. Pitted columns. He stepped around a barrier, went up the steps and sat with his back against a column. A panhandler appeared and asked for spare change and Hendershot managed 50 pence. Above them, pigeons fluttered around the cornice. "Cheers, mate," the guy said and left him alone to consider Mister Green.

He grappled with the unreality of it. This was the country where his parents had met and from where they went to war. Those photographs at home of them in their uniforms, outside historical buildings, hiking in the Lake District, standing on bombed-out streets. This was their youth, and to Hendershot it was fixed, permanent. But his youth? His was temporary. He was just passing through. What Mister Green intended seemed eccentric, but at the same time not unreasonable. Hendershot was short on achievements, and Mister Green was offering him opportunity. To do something.

He sat with the pigeons at the church until dusk, when the streetlights came on.

The trap my dad has hitched to his truck is a converted steel culvert, eight feet long, four feet in diameter, mounted on wheels.

There's one way in: a barred door that's raised like a portcullis on a spring release. A prison on wheels, painted the same green as Dad's truck, the same green as his uniform. NPC stenciled on it: National Parks Canada.

My dad tells me the bear climbed through the open door, grabbed the bait, a sack of bacon suspended on the hook, and thus sprang the trip wire so that the door slammed shut behind him. Inside the trap, the bear huffs and grumbles. Paces in circles in the small space. Musty smell, like a wet fur coat. Through the bars I see its dark puzzled eyes. Back and shoulders like a man's.

Dad has spray-painted it behind the head. White, first-time offender. Two more colours to go: yellow, second-time offender and red, third time offender. Animals marked red are shot.

We drive the bear out into the bush to let it go. I stand on top of the trap to lift the door. Below me the bear charges out, stops, turns. Huffs and paws the ground. "Go, go!" I yell and Dad roars us out of there. The bear chases the truck a short distance just to make sure we're gone.

Less than twenty-four hours later he's back in the campground tearing apart a woman's tent to get at a bag of chips. He has walked fifty miles in one night.

19.

Hendershot spent several evenings poring over Mister Green's notebooks (there was more than one), and his archive of IRA atrocities. Most of the bombs were set on timers; a delivery took place – package, sports bag, suitcase, once a baby carriage; the bomb was placed – in a post box, on a step, under a table, under a car, on a bus, at a train station, in a dustbin; the bomb went off – while people were shopping, standing in a queue, having a beer, going to work, catching a train. The end result of all this stealth was there all right. What Hendershot couldn't see was how that much damage could be caused by so few people. Surely, they all had been caught. The newspapers listed the arrests.

"But there's more of 'em all the time," Mister Green explained. "You've seen 'em in them photos. Ordinary blokes."

Hendershot looked up from one of the albums. In Mister Green's flat, the ordinary whispered from every corner: from the worn chairs, threadbare rugs, and fly-specked windows. Cramped, drab, collecting dust. How could the man who lived in it know anything beyond its walls?

"They're not stupid, the IRA," Mister Green said. "They get stuck in – part of the landscape, like. Sleepers. Take Connor. Shows up one day, friend of Margaret's. For a time, he's what's new. People talk about him. Who is he? What's his name? What's he after? Well – he's Margaret's fancy man. Stonemason. Looking for work. So, after a bit, people pay him no never-mind. He goes down the pub. Down the shops. Sets off ter work in the morning. Gets a girlfriend. When he meets an old bloke like me in the street, he chats away nineteen ter the dozen. But he's sleeping, see. Waiting ter do a mischief."

"How do you know that?"

"Look at them days I've put ticks beside. See there? What day of the week do you think most of them is? Fridays. Same day he comes ter see Margaret, as a rule. When do them bombs go off? Fridays. Not all of them, I grant you. But enough ter raise suspicion."

"But he's with Margaret."

"Course he is. That's how he does it. He's got them bombs on the clock. Scarpers before the timer goes off. The minute the bomb goes up, he's wiv Margaret having a good old Friar Tuck. Perfeck alibi, that is."

Hendershot studied the columns of figures, the coloured graphs. He had to hand it to Mister Green, the statistics were first class. Since Connor's arrival, the number of attacks had risen. But it wasn't only statistics that worked on Hendershot. One night he wakened to unmistakable moaning from the apartment downstairs. Instant jealousy, followed by anger. Margaret, Margaret. But when he told Mister Green what he'd heard, the old man merely shrugged. "Bit on the side, I expect."

Mere opinion, but Mister Green had seen more of the world than Hendershot had. In general, Hendershot respected the opinions of old people. When he was a kid, people had said old Millie Jones was crazy. But when his best friend Eugene drowned, it was Millie who had helped Hendershot build a raft out of the top of an old picnic table in honour of Eugene's passing. Hendershot's grandmother had exhibited her own brand of loopiness. On downtown shopping trips, she kept herself alive at intersections by untelescoping a white curtain rod like a cane from the Institute for the Blind, a real traffic stopper. Beneath both

Millie's and his grannie's airy dementia lay a bedrock practicality.

And so with Mister Green. Who suggested Hendershot should meet Connor Mack face to face before he made up his mind about the Irishman. "But we'll stop in at the greengrocer's first," he said. "He's got apples on terday."

20.

Scaffolding masked one side of the art gallery's entrance and above Hendershot and Green, workers moved to and fro along the cat walks. As they stood on the pavement, Mister Green said that the Gallery was Whitechapel's monument to social democracy and that in 1939 he'd brought his wife along to see Picasso's Guernica. "The Jerries bombing the Spaniards. Bloody huge it was. You seen it? No? There's this bloke dying down in front wiv his arms flung out. And a horse screaming at the sky, a lady on fire, that sort of thing. 'Course they don't look real – it's Picasso. But a beautiful piece of work. I said so to the missis. 'That's a beautiful piece of work, Maeve,' I says. 'Don't be daft, George,' she says, 'it's horrid. Look, it's all in black and white for a kick-off. There's no happiness to it.' 'It's war, Maeve,' I says. 'War?' she says, 'that's not what I call war.' 'You don't know, old gel, you've never been.'" Mister Green stuffed his bag of apples under one arm. "But not long after, old Hitler started the Blitz. So she did get ter see one after all."

A tarp on the scaffold parted and a man's head and shoulders poked through. "George," the man called down, "What're yeh doin' here? Have yeh lost yourself?"

"Connor." Despite his hip, Mister Green stepped nimbly forward. "I din't know you was working today, mate. Have you met our Canadian?"

"I have not." Connor said this so straight-faced that Hendershot might've believed him, had there not been that light when the van door had opened on that foggy morning.

Watch yerself next time, Boyo. "Connor Mack," the man said. "You must be Rob. Ice hockey, isn't it?" He leaned his elbows on a rail. "Ice hockey is descended from the Irish game of hurley, you know, or so the scholars say. Everything from the telephone to original sin had their beginnings on the Auld Sod." He laughed. Strong white teeth, broad face, friendly sprinkle of freckles. The face of the good-natured lad he'd once been and still was. No sign of having recognized Hendershot. "How are yeh getting on?"

"Mister Green's helping me out. Giving me the tour."

"Yeh couldn't be in better hands. A grand host and keen observer of the human condition is our George." Connor Mack made everything sound like fact. "Have yis heard the news? Margaret's to have a showing. Right here. Can yeh beat that? After all these years. It's brilliant. Her work's to be shown in the main gallery, along with two other painters' in the smaller rooms."

Mister Green was caught off-balance. "I din't know that. I don't see Margaret much these days."

"News to me," Hendershot said. Because it was.

Connor's face flushed – glowed actually. Pleasure and pride. "Tis a grand thing she's done. The work it takes. The dedication. I know. I fancied bein' a sculptor meself till the old laziness got the better of me."

A barked order, from behind the tarp. Connor lowered his tone and talked fast. "She's a grand painter, yeh know. Feckin' brilliant. I've seen a good bit of work come through these doors and I can tell yis, hers is the real thing. An exhibition no less. It's no more than she deserves. The husband's arranged it, and fair play to him. Whatever he is, your man knows genius when he sees it." He seemed defensive and belligerent.

The voice shouted again.

"Back to work." Connor tipped his head in Hendershot's direction. "Have George bring yeh along to the pub Friday night. I'll stand the both of yis to a pint." He ducked back behind the tarp.

"He's crazy about Margaret," Hendershot said when they reached the corner.

"That's what I've been on about." Mister Green was limping. "They get stuck in."

"Maybe he's just a guy who loves art. And artists."

"If he's an art lover," Mister Green said, "I'm the king of England."

They walked for a while without speaking. Eventually the hitch in Mister Green's hip made Hendershot drape Mister Green's arm over his shoulders so he could ease him along. The two of them strolling like army pals caused a young couple to smirk. Hendershot remembered one Christmas when his father came to the city where Hendershot played hockey. While shopping, the two of them walked linked in the same way down an avenue, where a girl from Hendershot's English class spotted them and giggled uncontrollably. Mister Green might've had a premonition of that scene. When a policeman stopped them and asked, "Are you all right, George?" the old man said, "Never better, mate. This is Rob, from Canada, come to see his old granddad."

When they got back to the flat Hendershot told Mister Green about having bumped into Connor in the fog, and how Connor had seen his face. "And yet just now he pretended not to know me."

"He pretends a lot of things," Mister Green said. "I expect he's planning to do a mischief this Friday. We'll have ter try and keep our eye on him."

Hendershot admitted to himself he wasn't completely surprised. "Oh *we* will, will *we*?"

The old man gave him the look of a recruiter. Confident. Ace-up-the-sleeve. "Let me show you somefink," he said.

21.

Mister Green kept a stack of newspapers under the kitchen window. *The Library*, he called it. Most had already been cut up with scissors, articles for his collection. Others were there 'on spec', their contents waiting to see if they gathered pertinence to any future news items. He rustled through the pile, found what he was looking for. Handed it to Hendershot.

A tabloid paper, almost two weeks old. First few pages shredded, but further in, on page 4, past the girl in the bikini called *Smile of the Day*, and the story about the vicar and the privet hedge that looked like Jesus, he spotted the photograph. Grainy, but clear enough. The caption: *Oops!*

Himself. In his jeans and jacket. Plummeting nose-first over the wrought-iron fence, stop-action'd in mid-air above the grass. A pin-wheeling clown, frozen into farce. In the foreground the cobblestones, the tour bus.

He stared at the picture, entranced and mortified. Bruised vanity, mingled with shame. The person in the photo was an idiot. He folded the paper, but the picture stayed with him and insisted he think of something he'd never thought of before: that crime was crime. That even though he was small potatoes, fourth-page jokester filler, he'd made the news. Just like those guys who'd been arrested for planting bombs. Those guys everybody thought were guilty. (Hell, *Hendershot* thought they were guilty.) Now, in some unspecified, B-league revelation he couldn't understand, *he* was one of those guys.

Mister Green produced a pair of scissors. "You can save it, if you like. But I don't think you will. Whatever yer doing in that photo, mate, is not important. There are far more important things going on in the world, than what you're doing in that photo."

"How did you know it was me?"

"He's wearing yer jacket. And yer shoes. Them white trainers. As well, I had a little chat with Nigel and Tony. What I call the Spelman Street Irregulars. They seen and heard you fighting them two blokes. You showed them yer passport."

"I needed shelter," Hendershot said. "They told me Margaret would want to see it." *Schmuck*, he thought to himself.

"And so she would," Mister Green went on. "She had a bit of a turn-up with the Hungarian. Thieving bugger. Left no last name. But you? All above board," he tapped the newspaper, "except for this. And in spite of it all... here you are, then."

Hendershot lifted his cup, and surrendered to his chair. "Here I am," he said.

Twenty-three is old. I know this because in the photograph of the Lancaster bomber, the bombing crew is standing in front of the plane and my dad is the tallest one there. He's the oldest, he's twenty-three, and the others call him The Old Man because they are all younger than he is. And shorter. In the picture they all look old, but they really aren't. And of all of them, my dad is the only one who gets wounded. So he's the oldest. And the wisest. Because when you turn twenty-three and you're wounded, you're a man and you're wise.

But when I tell my dad this, he says twenty-three is too young to be wise, and at the same time it's too old to be stupid. He says twenty-three is just twenty-three, and only for a short time.

22.

Margaret was depressed and Hendershot couldn't understand why. A commission, an exhibition and her boyfriend back in town? She was on a roll. But instead of sketching him, she stood hugging herself. A fisherman's wife left forlorn on a windswept dock.

"Margaret?"

She didn't look at him, but talked to her feet. "The committee doesn't like any of my drawings. They're considering offering the commission to somebody else. As for the exhibition, none of the paintings selected is new. They're ones from long ago." And the boyfriend? "Connor's a bit old for 'boyfriend,' wouldn't you say?"

The passageway had been cleared of the boxes. Several paintings that'd been stacked against the studio walls were gone. "Trevor's trying to sell them," she said, but her voice was flat.

Hendershot was sitting on his usual posing perch, a wooden bench. No shirt, no heat and a fresh crop of goosebumps. Still, he wanted her to pull herself out of the gloom. "Connor's working at the art gallery," he said. "Mister Green tells me he's from Belfast."

"Dublin, actually, as many Irish people are." By the tone of her voice, he knew he was close to whatever line in the sand she'd drawn between them.

"I'm only saying."

"I *know* what you're saying. I told you before, you'll want to be skeptical about what George Green tells you."

"He's honest."

"Just because people are honest about things doesn't mean they're right."

He had no answer to that one. He started to shiver, so pulled on his sweatshirt. "I'm sorry about your drawings."

She stood perfectly motionless. The contradiction of the woman. So small and yet so solid. As if gravity held her to the earth with more force than it held other people. Hendershot waited. When she spoke, her voice was gentle.

"When I was a bit younger than you," she said slowly, "I got pregnant. The father didn't want me to have the child. Being young and practical, I had an abortion. Now I sometimes consider my paintings my only children. And yet ... I sell them." She walked the studio, touched the easel, the stretched canvases, the trestle table and its spatters of paint. When she reached him, she said, "If I don't finish this commission, I won't be paid. I might have to leave this flat. I doubt Trevor will want to pay the rent for an ex-wife unable to meet her artistic commitments."

"But you're having an exhibition."

"Oh yes. People come to see, but not often to buy."

He told her he'd phoned a friend to find a team he could play for.

"Oh?" Her head jerked upwards and her surprise gave him secret satisfaction. He thought he wanted to hurt her, but it wasn't that. He wanted to jolt her. Bring her back to being the Margaret he'd first met: the husband-fighter, the one-track artist who'd drawn him for two hours straight without saying a word. "Where would you go?"

"Wherever the team is."

She stared at him. "I mean if you were to leave this minute, where would you go? With your bad leg and without any of your hockey kit – where would you go?"

He was shocked. And a little frightened. "I don't know. This city has a lot of bridges." Brave words from the tough guy who'd been out in all weathers with his hunter-father. But sleeping rough under bridges wasn't like setting up camp in the bush. He'd tried bridges and he'd tried bush. Bush was better. Besides, he was beginning to add to the nest egg in his shoe. Twenty-two pounds, seventy-three pence at last count. Under a bridge was the last place he wanted to be.

He was standing, by then. She moved in front of him, looking up, studying his face. He felt the movement of her eyes as he'd felt her fingertips that first day – tracing his forehead, cheeks, jaw. As always, he felt her heat. He was drawn to her like a freezing man to a stove. "Sooner or later," she said, "we all have to Beowulf our Grendels." She spoke with the finality of somebody who'd seen all the rituals, the patterns, the compositions. Her eyes saw the arrangement of things, and their loss. He wondered if he could trust her. Her regret for her lost baby, her having married Trevor Tayleur-Stocking, her having Connor Mack.

She laid her hand on his forearm. "I want you to stay," she said.

Her head reached no higher than his chest, yet when she pressed her cheek against him and wrapped her arms around his waist, the generosity of her flesh felt like protection. Without moving he held her, rested his mouth against her tangled hair which smelled like paint and was flecked with grey.

They stood like that for the time it took a brotherly hug to start becoming something else. Which was when she placed her hands on his chest and pushed him gently away. Over her head, he glimpsed her bedroom: iron bedstead, quilt, drawings tacked to the walls. He thought, *this is as close as I'll ever get.* He asked her how she planned on making her drawings different so that the committee would see that *she* was the artist, not them.

"I'm not going to make them different," she said fiercely. "I'm going to make them *better.*"

In her kitchen, she brewed them a pot of tea. At the same time, she told him she'd instructed Nigel and Tony to scour the street markets for any kind of ice hockey equipment.

"They like that sort of thing," she said.

23.

The Angel's Arms was narrow and dim. Wood-paneled walls darkened by a hundred years of pipe and cigarette smoke. Five construction workers sat at two tables they'd pushed together, their faces and shoulders dusted with lime. At the bar, two young fellows in shiny suits and pimples eyed a couple of min-skirted girls giggling in a corner. His back to the window, a man in a torn suit jacket curled his forearms around a pint while a woman, shapeless in a tattered raincoat, blew cigarette smoke at his glass.

When Connor arrived late, Mister Green looked at Hendershot knowingly before he jovially slipped into rhyming Cockney slang, "I'll shout the first round. Three pigs' ears." When the beers came, he took a sip and informed them that most of the real Cockneys had moved to Essex. "The war done 'em in. Them the Jerries didn't get, the Docks Development will soon see off." He blamed the container ships for the death of the docks. "They draw too much water," he said. "There's no life down here now."

Connor disagreed. Hadn't he seen Mister Green just the other day at the greengrocer's bartering away like a mad eejit? "Dancin about the man, yeh were! Yeh nearly drove him mad." He himself, he told them, was a great one for the bargains. The week before, he'd gone 'round to Joe the Pole's and seen a jugged hare hanging in the butcher's window, with bits of lint stuck all over itself like an old mattress. "'By God, Joe,' I says, 'is that maggots?' And for a few pence I took it off his hands."

And then Connor and Mister Green were off, swapping stories to establish who was the thrift champion of the world, until Hendershot found himself admiring both of them. If they didn't like each other, they didn't show it. They sat at the table like old friends, while he sat between them – centerman between two wingers.

Mister Green told them about seeing his first murder when he was eight years old and lived with his family in a warehouse in Mile End. One morning he got up early, put on his father's boots and walked through the dark all the way to Covent Garden where he helped a fish monger set up his stall and in return got a mackerel as long as his leg. On his way home, he took a shortcut through a narrow lane, where two Italians – one big, one little – were having an argument which ended when the "little bloke slit the big bloke's throat." The murderer scarpered, leaving Mister Green to wait in a doorway until the knifed man stopped twitching. "I tip-toed round him, blood laying about like a bathing pool. Went along ter a lamppost and wiped the blood off Dad's boots wiv the newspaper the fish was wrapped in. The old man would've 'ad my guts for garters if I'd come home wiv blood all over 'is daisy roots."

"That's gas, George," Connor said and described his childhood home, a rat-infested two-room flat where seven people slept in two beds, while at night his father sat near the hole with the fire-poker and brained any rat that ventured into the room. One rat escaped with a scalping like a monk's tonsure. Connor named him Saint Francis and planned to keep him as a pet. "When Mam got wind of it, she shrieked to God and all his Holy Saints she'd not sleep another night under a roof that sheltered rodents. So Da brained St. Francis." He drank. "Ah, grand times they were, George. In their way."

Their conversation was like a competition, and so not to be left behind, Hendershot told them about the time his father sprinkled wheat seeds on the basement floor and sat with his kids, a bottle of scotch, a flashlight and a .22 repeater on the dark stairs. When the rats' claws scuttled on the cement, his father yelled, "Now!", the flashlight snapped on, and the shots pinged off the cast-iron furnace, one of them missing their heads and punching a hole through the basement door. His father moved the calendar down to hide the bullet hole, but when their mother came home, she knew something was up because you don't hang a calendar a foot off the floor for nothing.

They finished their beers laughing, and though Mister Green didn't say so, Hendershot understood that they weren't just telling stories. They were sizing each other up.

The next day, the newspapers reported that a bomb blast under the Holborn Viaduct had injured seven people. The bomb had gone off at 10:33 pm., exactly the time when Mister Green, Connor Mack and Hendershot were getting ready to leave the Angel's Arms and where – Mister Green calculated – they'd been sitting for two hours and forty minutes.

My dad wades across the flooded road in his rubber boots. Finds solid ground that'll lead him to the pond. In one hand he carries the dynamite taped to a long pole, in the other the tamping rod. A roll of fuse in his pocket. Halfway across the dam he stops, crimps the cap, attaches the fuse, jams the dynamite down into the mud and logs. Lights the fuse, walks back. We hunker down behind the road's far shoulder to wait. The air smells like wet grass. It holds its breath. Settles in my chest.

When the dynamite goes off, the noise and ground are one thing, the mud and logs another. Dad tells me to keep my head down, but I look anyway. Mud and branches shoot high against the sky, give up, fall like wounded birds.

When I ask him, Dad says the beavers are in their lodge at the far end of the pond. They're safe, he says. In a few days – maybe even tonight - they'll start building the dam again.

24.

"And you say Connor's responsible."

"Course he is."

"I'm not so sure."

"I'm not saying he's not a good bloke. But good blokes can do bad things. Me and Paddy done bad things."

"During a war."

"Still and all, bad things. And what about you, mate? That money, them two blokes."

"That's true."

"Look, I've got a friend I can ring up. A good mate. Knows the in's and out's of things, knows how ter use his loaf." He tapped his head. "You'll see. He'll set you right."

"If you say so."

In the meantime, Hendershot posed for Margaret every morning and left her every afternoon to cull through her drawings, which looked to be in the hundreds. One day, he told her what going through a slump was like. When your passes are off and your hands turn to stone and your skating is crap. How when you try to play harder, you only play worse. How you get scared because once you had the magic and now it's gone and you're so tense you're afraid you'll never get it back.

She gave him a stony look. "A sports analogy," she said. "How marvelous. But you bravely soldier on."

"Or goof off."

"Meaning?"

"Relax. Have fun."

She went back to sorting drawings. "I'll see you tomorrow," she said.

He used some of those afternoons to wander the streets, every neighbourhood a different country. Different people, clothes, food, names, smells, language. Homberg hats to turbans. Yiddish to Hindi. Head scarves. Saris. Bagels, rice and curry. He haunted pawn shops and outdoor markets. Trolled used sporting goods tables for some sign that real hockey had reached those foreign shores. But it hadn't. Vendors showed him field hockey sticks, cricket bats, football boots, roller skates and once a pair of massive shoulder pads guaranteed *genuine American gridiron.* "Ice hockey? Naow, mate. Not much call for it 'round 'ere." It occurred to him that even guys selling gridiron shoulder pads could be targets for terrorist bombs, but that all of them seemed unperturbed. Mister Green had told him Connor lived in a flat above a shop in Spitalfields, but whenever he jogged by the place Hendershot saw no sign of him. After a while his wandering slipped into pure tourism. Spitalfields, Whitechapel – once across the river to Bermondsey.

Sections of some streets were derelict, the buildings brick shells whose windows were blinded with sheets of plywood, their doors kicked in: a squat for junkies, methheads, alcoholics, the homeless, the unwanted, the mentally ill. Sometimes squatters approached him asking for money or cigarettes or if he knew Dave or Nicole or Ahmed. As if he were a missing persons bureau. He offered them small change, told them he didn't smoke, apologized for not knowing their friends, their hang-outs, their memories. When he walked by their squats he smelled urine, shit, mouldy mattresses. He wondered at the graffiti: *Fuck the wogs, Pakis go home,* a swastika, and underneath, *We're back!*

And yet, two blocks over, a different street bustled with life – full of kids, all shapes, sizes, colours. Chasing each other up and down sidewalks, swearing, smoking, spitting, wrestling, laughing. Playing soccer in the street while old biddies leaned out windows and yelled at them, *Bloody kids, do you want to get yerselves killed?* and they yelled back, *Put a stool under it, you old cow.*

One day in a vacant lot, he found a bristleless broom and a tennis ball. From a pile of rubbish, he dug out a strip of old linoleum, flattened it over the weeds and practised slapshots against a wall. The ball still had some bounce in it and as he moved in for a tip-in, he saw Connor Mack at the end of the street.

Connor was carrying a suitcase and walking near a warehouse. As he rounded the corner, he looked back at Hendershot. Looked back, didn't wave, didn't stop.

Hendershot ran. But when he got to the lane, Connor had disappeared. Nothing but a line of locked doors; storage rentals according to the signs. A few garbage cans and one man in an army greatcoat pushing a wooden barrow of empty bottles, garbage bags, blankets and cardboard. Hendershot asked him if he'd seen a man carrying a suitcase. The barrow man peered out from under bushy eyebrows and pronounced with perfect rationality, "Rash-cash-cunt," and walked on.

You have to be patient. My dad tells me this. You just have to wait and see. There's no use getting in a tizz-wozz. That's a word Mum uses: tizz-wozz. It's a funny word but what she's doing isn't funny. She's moving away. To England. With K-man. She takes her leather suitcase and the tin trunk and the big suitcase with the wooden handles out of the closet and packs all her clothes and K-man's, except their parkas and snow boots. They won't need them, she says.

They're going on the train to Montreal and then on a ship called the Empress of Britain, and then they get on a train in

Liverpool and after that I don't know. In the atlas, I draw a line with blue crayon as far as they're going and I measure it with my ruler using the scale at the bottom of the map. They are travelling five thousand three hundred and one miles. And they're not coming back.

Or maybe they will. You never know. Be patient, Dad says. Nobody ever knows what's going to happen. Until it happens.

25.

The attacks had occurred outside of London. Sometimes weeks apart, sometimes days. An explosion at a Royal Engineer depot in Yorkshire blinded the only person present in the base canteen, a fifty-two-year-old manageress. A bus carrying soldiers up the M62 motorway blew up, killing nine infantrymen, along with a mother and her two children. An incendiary in a Manchester sporting goods store badly burned a clerk and a teen-age customer who was trying on football boots.

Mister Green clipped the latest reports out of the newspapers, noted them, correlated them with past incidents, and Connor's absences. He dragged Hendershot along to the Spitalfields market near where Connor lived. The trucks were gone and the market was scattered with paper, cardboard, broken wooden pallets. Split wooden crates spilled vegetables and fruit. People pushing baby carriages or shopping carts sifted through the spillage and Mister Green took pride in whittling down prices from the casual curbside vendors. He showed Hendershot how he bartered, trading five pounds of potatoes, say, for a fistful of carrots, two eggplants and three mangoes. All the while on the lookout for Connor Mack. "I want ter know the minute he comes back."

The knock came as they were putting away the groceries. Hendershot opened the door to a tall raw-boned man in a worn tweed suit. Under his cloth cap his ancient face was carved out of stone. He scowled. "Who are you?"

Mister Green said, "He's my grandson, Arthur."

Arthur stepped forward and shut the door. "You don't have a grandson, George."

"He's come all the way from Canada to visit his old granddad."

"No, he hasn't, George."

"My daughter's boy. Jean's boy."

"Your Jean was killed on August 11th, 1941," Arthur said bluntly. "This boy's too young to have been born then, even if she'd had him."

"If Jean were alive, she'd be very disappointed to hear that."

"Nark it, George. It's not working."

"It already has done, Arthur. I used it on the local constabulary."

Arthur looked at Hendershot. "Now then, let's try again. Who are *you?*"

"Who are you?" Hendershot asked.

"Bloody hell." Having removed his cloth cap, Arthur pulled up a chair, sat down, set his cap on his knee. His cropped hair lay against his skull like iron filings. "Arthur de Largo," he said. And turned to Mister Green. "I wish you'd conference with me, George, before you go off half-cocked."

"I couldn't get hold of you, Arthur. Telephone's on the blink. I've had ter use the box opposite the tobacconist."

"That may make communication awkward, but not impossible." Pinching the cloth between big-knuckled fingers, de Largo lifted his cap delicately from his knee and set it down again. His voice rumbled in his chest. "Now then: what are you playing at, George?"

In his easy chair, Mister Green rubbed his hands over the worn arm rests. "He can be of help to us, Arthur."

"And how might that be, George?"

"He's working as her model. He's read everything in the little blue book. He's in training – he's run 'round to the residence of the subject in question."

"Was that wise?"

"Was it wise for us to keep the Hungarian in the dark?"

De Largo turned his pale eyes on Hendershot. "What do you think?"

Hendershot saw the man was serious. The stone face never wavered. "The stuff Mister Green showed me in his book is pretty convincing, but..."

"But what?"

"We had a couple of beers with Connor and he seemed like an okay guy."

"Ah," Arthur de Largo said. "*Seemed.*" He glanced at Mister Green. "It's always *seemed*, isn't it, George?"

"Always, Arthur."

The big man studied Hendershot from head to foot. "Canadian," he said. "That's a recommendation, is it?"

"Ice hockey player," Mister Green said.

The bony old man shifted in his chair. "Do you know how to keep your eyes open and your mouth shut?"

"I have so far."

Mister Green interrupted. "His father flew in a Lanc during the war. Rear gunner."

"Ah." The big man lifted his cap from his knee, let it fall. "That's George's way of telling you my son flew in Lancs. Until Hamburg. Then his number came up." He shaped the cap over his knee. "Wireless operator. Do you know what his job was? To maintain radio silence."

Hendershot was at a loss. "My dad was wounded. He doesn't talk about the war much."

Mister Green said, as if announcing gold star credentials, "Arthur was a special constable during the war."

"That's right," the big man rumbled. "On the docks, same as where George worked. I made my nightly rounds. Kept an eye on things. Made sure nothing went amiss."

"Firm but fair, that was Arthur," Mister Green said. "There was no looting or messing about wiv Arthur on duty.

Carried a torch and a cosh. Show him, Arthur."

De Largo reached inside his coat. Special pocket sewn in. The nightstick was a foot and a half long, black walnut filled with lead. Knurled at one end with finger grips and fitted with a leather thong. "You hold it like this." He passed his big hand through the leather strap so that he gripped the thong and the club at the same time. "Gives the wrist a bit of leverage."

Hendershot couldn't have been more startled if de Largo had pulled out a grenade launcher. "You still carry it?"

"On particular occasions." He laid the club gently in his palm. "You don't want to overdo things. But you *do* have to be prepared." He paused. "Now then, Rob. George and I would like a little chat – in private."

"I'll go for a walk," Hendershot said.

26.

On his way downstairs he pictured de Largo swinging the nightstick. Christ, the guy had hands on him like Christmas turkeys. *Like Dad's,* he thought suddenly, seeing his father's fist wrapped around a bottle, imagining it, as he often did, gripping the handles of the Browning machine guns in the plane's rear turret. Shooting at night fighters with one hand because the other one, on its wounded arm, wouldn't work. Shrapnel severing his oxygen hose. Perspex shattering around his feet.

Bombs. Those old guys upstairs. What were they doing? Inventing their own war?

Margaret wasn't home, so he went around the back, hauled out his linoleum, tennis ball and broom. Slap shots demanded timing and shifting his weight from good knee to bad. De Largo had put him in a conscientious mood and the rhythm of shooting a ball pushed him into a meditative if not mindless state, where only his body required monitoring. He was working up a sweat when Nigel and Tony arrived. Watched him for a while.

Nigel said, "Cricket's a game for toffs."

"Ice hockey," Hendershot wheezed.

"Gorn." Nigel had a cut over his left eye. "Wiv that?"

"I need a stick." He slapped the ball knee high, tipped in the rebound.

"You need a *game.*" Nigel was in a mood. "Football. Bobby Charlton. Greatest footballer in the world."

Hendershot stopped. "What's up, boys?"

Tony stuffed his hands in his pockets. "Ice hockey. Skates and gear and that."

A kick-start to his heart. "You know where I can find some?"

Nigel grunted. "Possible. Very possible. Provided you got a quid or two."

"How many do I need?"

"One." Tony vacuumed out his cheek where his salivary glands worked overtime. "Each." The scar on his harelip turned blue.

"For the whatsitsname," Nigel prodded.

"Commission," Tony said.

"Commission," Nigel said.

Hendershot asked if there was anything they didn't do for a commission.

Nigel thought. "I shouldn't fink so."

"Where'd you see this stuff?"

"Well..." Nigel's eyes narrowed. "That's the question, innit?"

He tried to talk them down to 50 p. each but they wouldn't budge. They suggested he pay for a bus ride but he balked. Thanks to Margaret, the money in his shoe had multiplied but he wasn't ready to binge. Tony said the walk wasn't far and that it wouldn't kill them and Nigel snarled that no, he didn't fucking suppose it fucking would and anyway that wasn't what he fucking said, was it? "Sometimes Tony," he said, "I fink the docs should've done yer ears as well as yer lip."

Tony's mouth went tight but he said nothing as Nigel stalked away. Hustling after him, Hendershot asked, "What's with him?"

"His dad come home last night," Tony said. "Been in the nick for six months. Smacked Nigel and his mum about a bit."

As they turned north, the streets filled with people. Like

a parade. Or a carnival. Hendershot said, "You guys and your commissions. Smooth operators. Sharp. I'm amazed you don't carry guns."

At the notion, Nigel, who'd been brooding, cheered up. He grinned, or at least showed his teeth. "Gorn," he said. "Wojer fink this is – the fucking wild west?"

27.

The street was jammed on both sides. Stalls and booths roofed with bright plastic tarps. Fruits and vegetables laid out in tiers, fish packed in ice. A sign hanging from wires: *Definitely the only kosher poultry shop in the market.* Past the food stalls, vendors displayed long-handled bed warming pans, ceramic beer mugs, model cars, watercolours of the Thames, used school uniforms and anything else that was worth the money if you needed it. Pop music blared from cracked speakers, swinging London's greatest hits. Crowds shuffled, stopped, bought or moved on.

"How come I've never seen this place before?" Hendershot asked.

Nigel rolled his eyes. "They only let the booths in on the first day of each month, don't they then? Today's May first. International whatsitsname's day."

"Workers' day," Tony said.

"Yeah." Nigel growled. "All them communists on the fucking dole."

Tony touched Hendershot's arm. "You don't want ter show an interest," he advised when they got close. "You're just having a look round."

The table was loaded with used sports equipment: tennis rackets, chipped golf clubs, cricket bats, soccer balls, a polo mallet, snorkel and fins. No hockey sticks. But at the far end, the pads spread out like spilled guts, Hendershot's hockey bag. The vendor, a Sikh – tall, turbaned and bearded – allowed Hendershot to swing a jai alai scoop. Offered him three tennis balls for the price of two. Pointed out the croquet set.

Pieces were missing. Shoulder pads gone. Only one elbow pad. Jockstrap but no cup. Laces taken out of the skates, but his number still painted on the heels.

"Tony," Hendershot said, "smell this." Held up the pants. Stench that could have killed a cockroach.

Nigel sniffed from a distance. "Fuck me. The pong from that."

The vendor leaned in and suggested thorough laundering. Hendershot told him the stuff couldn't be washed. Used his locker-room voice. "It's gotta be sprayed with bleach and hung in the sun for two weeks. And look at these skates. They're rusty." And so on. Talking too much, his hands practically shaking with the thrill. Even his practise jersey was there. Old home week, which gave the seller an opening. "How much?" he asked.

"Did I say I was interested?"

The vendor smiled and tipped his head a couple of times: let the games begin. He started at fifteen pounds, Hendershot offered him six. And so it went, Tony and Nigel watching from the peanut gallery. Hendershot felt shrewd, the vendor probably shrewder. When they finally settled on nine pounds fifty, they shook hands and Hendershot slung the bag over his right shoulder and basked under its familiar weight, its clumsy bump against his leg.

"Fucking wog," Nigel said as they walked away.

"The guy gave me a good deal. No, a *great* deal. A *fantastic* deal." Hendershot was pumped. If that market had been hit by a sudden ice age, he'd have jumped into his skates, laces or no laces, and sprinted to the edge of the world. Missing elbow pad? – He could cut a plastic cup lengthwise, stuff it with old socks and tensor-bandage it to his arm. Hockey stick? Whittle one out of a tree branch. Why, here they were, marching three abreast, the other pedestrians opening up, streaming around them. The music. The barrow vendors singing their pitches...*must be mad to sell at these prices, barmy, off me nut...*

They were out of the market passing the greengrocer's, the baker's, the hole-in-the-wall that sold jellied eels. Ahead of them, some kids with drums and guitars rattled on a corner, a juggler flipped Indian clubs, two girls on the arms of soldiers slipped into a pub, heroes all. Life was good. At the intersection, he tap-danced while the boys stared.

"You guys still don't get it, do you? I got my equipment! *My* equipment. Christ, this is like a breakaway with a man short. This is as good as a natural hat trick."

"The world's yer oyster sort of fing," Tony said.

"You got it." He wanted to know how two kids found his equipment when his search had turned up nothing. Tony grinned, said they were his guardian angels. Nigel said, "A bleedin' miracle is what we done. Worf more than a quid each by my reckoning." Hendershot pointed across the street to a fish and chip take-away, and offered to buy them lunch.

"Smell that grease, boys. That salt, that vinegar. Know what that is? The sweet smell of success. Let's go. Order anything you want."

For a minute there, as they stepped into the street, he felt like a dad.

28.

At the first shock, he dove for the gutter and took the two kids with him, burrowed their heads under his equipment bag as the smoke and grit broke over them. The pub down the street didn't so much blow *up* as *out*. Lying there he could feel the ground grumble against his guts. Later, he saw the crumbled bricks, shattered windows, shredded tarps from the market. But while it was happening, all he wanted was to crawl in out of the wind. Shove those kids under the bag. Because it was a storm. As if everything – all the air, glass and dirt – had been crammed into a ball and sent roaring down the street.

When the wind eased, he lifted his head. People staggered through the smoke. A tipped-over baby carriage. Somebody's purse. A man in a bloody shirt headfirst in a barrow. A woman, arms stiff at her sides, mouth open as if she was screaming. A long shard of glass sticking out of her eye.

"Help me with this thing," he told the boys. Or thought he did. His voice was under water. His arm tangled in the bag's strap. Nigel and Tony stunned and coughing. Then the three of them up and scrambling toward the screaming woman and the fallen man.

The air was dust and smoke. Tasted like soot. There were noises. Alarms maybe, sirens, he wasn't sure. His ears weren't quite right. Something was wrong with his ears. Later, he'd wake up in the dark, thinking he heard something. Not the explosion, but a rumble. Like rocks falling.

He'd shake his head and the rocks'd go thump. But that would be later.

Now he saw the man in the barrow was dead. Oranges scattered around his feet. One in his hand. He'd died holding an orange.

The shard of glass in the woman's eye was shaped like a knife. Blood ran down one side of her face, into her mouth, onto her neck. The eyeball bulged over the edge of the glass. Her arms were shaking. Hendershot took off his jacket and wrapped it around her but she couldn't stop shivering. She seemed to want him to pull the glass out of her eye but he couldn't. What if the glass snapped off? What if it wouldn't let go of her eyeball? What if –

He sat her down on the curb. Put his arm around her. She was sobbing. He couldn't hear her clearly but saw her lips move. She was asking him to take the pain away. He held her. "It's all right, ma'am. Hold on. The ambulance will be here soon."

But it wasn't. The ambulance took a long time. He and the boys stayed with her until the two attendants led her away.

After the medics had checked them over, they walked home. A few minor cuts. Tony and Nigel were quiet at first – then argued. *"You were scared," "No I wasn't," "Soiled yerself," "Piss off."* Hendershot wanted them to stay calm. "Shut up," he said.

Because he could still feel the woman's thin arms, her bony shoulders. Because he didn't want the boys to know that he'd been wrong. He'd always thought that disaster was some huge and shapeless force. A storm that roared across the lake, an explosion that blew up beaver dams, shrapnel that blasted rear gunners out of the sky, trucks that killed little brothers. But the woman with the glass in her eye had straightened him out. Disaster wasn't huge. It was small and mean.

Personal.

At the corner, he said goodbye to the boys. Dusk was falling. In a doorway a mother yelled at her kid that he'd better get up them apples right this minute or she'd know the reason why. Hendershot wanted to climb the his own set of stairs. Dump his hockey bag. Fall exhausted onto the bed. Maybe a cup of cocoa. Then sleep. Wake up to a new world.

But when he stepped into Mister Green's flat, Arthur de Largo was still there.

29.

They were sitting at the kitchen table like poker players. Mister Green with his notebook open, de Largo spreading out a street map as big as a tablecloth. When he saw Hendershot Mister Green leapt up, grabbed him by the shoulders. "We heard," he said. "Are you all right, mate?"

"Tired, that's all."

"I'm not surprised. But you're fit and a good job too."

Mister Green's energy an antidote to Hendershot's lethargy. The old man set the bag in the corner, dragged a chair in from the living room. "Pull up a pew," he said. Poured a mug of tea, filled a plate from the frying pan on the stove. "Bubble and squeak ternight. Sticks to yer ribs." De Largo smoothed the map and they both hitched their chairs closer. As if their excitement was tugging them forward.

"Now then," de Largo said while Hendershot tried to eat, "we've got a job for you."

"I feel like I've already had one, thanks."

"Course you do," de Largo said. "But all we ask is that you watch and listen. For now. You don't have to be blatant. You don't have to interfere. Just watch and listen. That's the key."

"Watch and listen for what?" The rocks in his head were settling. His hearing sharpened.

"His comings and goings," de Largo said. "If he talks to anyone. Or if he doesn't. You've got to get a feel for the ordinary." He shifted so Hendershot could see the map clearly. Some of the streets had been traced with different coloured pencils. Woven like threads.

"Now," de Largo said. "George says you train every morning. Show me where you run."

"It's not always the same route. Depends on how I feel. My knee. What the traffic's like."

"Your usual route then," de Largo said kindly, "the one you like to do."

Hendershot traced his run through the penciled streets. "This one I have to do really early in the morning. Before all the trucks get to the market."

"Spitalfields." De Largo lifted an eyebrow.

"It's like I told you, Arthur," Mister Green said.

"Fortuitous." De Largo nodded. "Now then," his big finger pointed, "right along here, beyond the market, there's a little shop. Sells all-sorts. *Prescott's*, it's called. Green sign, white lettering. *Prescott's.*"

"The newsstand. There's a kid upstairs. Calls me a wanker."

"Hm," de Largo grunted, frowning, "but *Prescott's* has got four windows above that sign. The fourth one over – not the window on the corner, mind, but the one to the far right along the street, is Connor Mack's."

"There's a door below it, opens onto the street."

"That's the one. Inside, the door opens onto a staircase up to his rooms."

"Sometimes there's a car parked outside there. Little rust bucket."

"A Cortina," Mister Green said.

"I guess."

"Back seat's been taken out."

"I never looked."

"Burgundy colour," de Largo said.

"Yeah. Well, dirty red."

"That's his vehicle." De Largo wrote letters and numbers on a slip of paper. "That's his number plate."

"And if he leaves in it, you want me to run after him."

Mister Green cleared his throat. "Don't be daft."

Hendershot looked at them. Weary. "What good is any of this going to do?"

Arthur de Largo spoke carefully. "All you have to do is take your exercise as usual, and when you return tell George if this vehicle," he pointed to the number plate he'd written down, "is there or not there."

"That's it?"

"That's all. For the moment."

"Doesn't seem like much somehow."

De Largo's eyes were calm. "Is the car there or isn't it."

"Watch and listen," Hendershot said.

"That's right."

He looked from one old guy to another. Were they playing a game? Was this all just a game to them?

"Okay," he said, though his limbs had grown impossibly heavy. "I can do that."

30.

The next morning, he wasn't so sure. But ran the route anyway. Head up, ears open.

Nothing. No Connor Mack, no burgundy Cortina, no van. But the kid at the newsagent's yelled *wanker*. And the peddlers at the market were on the job. And the old guy told him to keep his left up as he ran past. Business as usual. The explosion had been blocks away. Here life continued as if the bomb had never happened.

Yet at the schoolyard where he did his exercises, a mist hung over the playground. Silent as death. During push-ups, he found himself remembering hunting with his father. Grouse in the fall. Birch leaves as gold as coins. Deer after the first snowfall, muskeg frozen over. That time he shot his first buck. Bleeding in the snow, its frightened eyes fading into a distance he could only guess at. The deer lay still until the lights went out. For his father, the death meant meat: steaks, roasts, short ribs, hamburger, stew meat. The hide to Grannie Ahenakew on the reserve in return for a pair of smoke-tanned moccasins.

But that buck. Hendershot had cried soundlessly. He was sixteen. "I know, son," his father had said. And then showed the boy how to gut an animal without piercing the bladder.

It should've calmed him, that memory. The irrefutable lesson of it: do what you have to do even if it hurts. *But*, he wondered now, *how do you know what you have to do?*

31.

He showed up at Margaret's at the usual time. Newly stretched canvas. Base-coated. Paints on the palette, brushes in a custard tin. She laid her hand on his shoulder, asked him how he was. He said fine. He didn't want to talk. Had his own pictures in his head. "You look exhausted," she said.

Painting, she swayed behind the easel like a dancer. From time to time she stopped, stood back, unfocussed her eyes. To look past the details. Find the lights and shadows. Discover the line. While he did his part: sat. Impersonal as furniture. Thought about the woman with the glass in her eye. He should've got her name. Was she alive? Was she blind? He considered Connor Mack. Where was he sitting now? What was he thinking about?

When Margaret took a break, he asked, "Have you ever killed anything, Margaret?"

"Pardon me?"

"Shot something. Stabbed it. Slit its throat."

"My god." She stared. Hurt. This pleased him. She considered. "Insects," she said. "Flies, silverfish, cockroaches, lice."

"Lice? When did you get lice?"

"When I was a kid." She stood with her weight on one leg. Hip-jutted. "I grew up not far from here. My father was a furrier – stitched fur coats. Sam Lowenstein. Jewish from his Homberg hat to his sensible shoes. But he didn't observe. Never went to synagogue. No mezuzah outside our door, no menorah on the sideboard cupboard. Still, he was what

Mister Green would call a proper tin lid. Drank his tea from a glass. Liked his chicken kosher."

"And your mum?"

"Irish Catholic. Went to mass every Sunday. Dragged me along until I was old enough to refuse." She dabbed at the canvas. "My parents' marriage was a declaration of war – against the world and each other. That's not to say my childhood was unhappy. It was *eventful*. Gave me practice for when the real war came along."

"You're not old enough to remember the war."

She cocked her head. "Such an idealist. So many illusions. What about you? Have you killed things?"

He told her how when he was eight, he found a hare in a leg-hold trap, its back legs broken. When he picked it up, it screamed, exactly like a baby. He'd tried to strangle it. He'd prayed to God to make it die. "But he didn't," he said. "I had to bash his head against a tree. I didn't have a knife. Didn't know what else to do."

She gazed at him for a long time. Told him she was seven at the outbreak of the war. She remembered the bombing, sheltering in the tube station. Imagining giants stomping above in big boots. One morning after a raid, they came up to find their street was rubble. "I saw my first dead person. Mrs. Mankewicz, the shoemaker's wife. Lying in a puddle. My mum told me not to look but I did. Someone had put a coat over her but you could see her white legs poking out of her dress. She was wearing one shoe."

Her father moved them to lodgings above a laundry, but the steam press gave her mother a cough. Her mother did piece-work at home. Sewed ladies' underthings. They moved again, got bombed out, started to argue. "They roared around me like a hurricane. But they never touched me. Their little Margaret, drawing at the kitchen table. I think my parents thought my small body was a judgment on their having loved each other. It didn't surprise them that bombs came from heaven. What surprised them was the damage. It made them disappointed. Not in God – I think they accepted that God is a proper bastard – but in people. It was terrible what people did to each other during the war."

"It's not so great what they do to each other now." Giving her an opening.

But she merely nodded. So lost in memory she looked like the little girl she must've been. "When the Germans dropped firebombs, my father shipped us off to Mum's people in Ireland. County Wicklow. I cried all the way on the ferry over. But the Dominions were good people. Country folk. My grandparents spoiled me. They hoped I'd been released from damnation. My grandfather asked my mother, 'You're not a Jewess then, Kathleen?' and crossed himself when she said no. He went out of his way to show me round the farm. Everything fascinated me. I loved watching him milk the cows and squirt milk at the cats who lined up waiting for a drink. We had fresh cream every day. Butter. We ate real eggs."

She went to the village school, taught by nuns. "Actually, that's where I met Connor. On my first day at school, some big boys picked me up and left me on the garden shed roof. I couldn't get down. Sister Agnes came out to ring the bell and everyone went in. It was Connor who stayed behind and held out his arms to me. He was new there, too. 'I'm Connor Mack,' he said. 'Jump. I'll catch you.' And he did. We were late getting in and when Sister Agnes asked us why, he told her about the big boys. 'They're night and day a shower o' bastards, Sister,' he said. She kept him after school and made him kneel in a corner with a pencil under each knee while he prayed to the Holy Virgin to clean up his tongue."

He could see she was painting him a picture: Happy Valley, down on the farm. Irish bog-trotter with a heart of gold. Any minute now they'd sing the *Rose of Tralee*. When all he could hear was boom and see smoke in the streets.

"Haven't seen Connor around lately," he said. Casual. Drawling. "Since a few days before the bomb."

She stared at him. Shock. Or anger. "Are you being absurd?"

"I didn't find it all that funny."

"He was in Ireland. His uncle died." Her words almost choked her. "He wasn't here."

"But what if that's the whole point?" He got up and started pacing. "What if every time he's here nothing happens, and every time he isn't something does?"

"My god," she said. "Listen to yourself."

"All right." He stopped moving. Spread his hands to show her at least he was unarmed. "You tell me. How can you be sure he's got nothing to do with it?"

She scowled. "I've known him for thirty-six years."

"My dad knew my mum for twenty. She still managed to keep her little secrets from him."

"What's that got to do with...," she shook her head. "Sometimes I forget how young you are."

"There was a lady with a piece of glass rammed into her eyeball. And I did nothing about it. If I was as old as you or Connor, could I have done something?"

She gazed at Hendershot steadily. "It's not him."

He started pacing again. When his father had talked about the war, he had ignored what was fair and what wasn't. You got shot because *your number came up.* Death was a bingo game. Hendershot said, "I can't believe you people. How you put up with this shit. Even Nigel and Tony. They were scared, but afterwards they joked about it. Know what Nigel said? 'That's the last time I go to that takeaway for fish and chips.' Jesus Christ, you English. Tally-ho and stiff upper lip. Everything's a joke."

"I warned you about listening to George Green," she said.

"Yeah, I know, he's nuts. But at least he cares."

She coloured. "And I don't?"

A question he didn't want to answer.

"Come here," she said.

"That's not going to work."

She opened her arms. "Come."

It wouldn't be the first time he'd chastise himself. When she laid her cheek against his chest her words fluttered against his ribs. "You say we put up with it. That's not entirely true. We don't accept violence. We endure it."

"Christ." Philosophy. "What's the difference?"

"Maybe nothing. But we've endured before. And survived."

"There's got to be something better than that."

"Oh, there is. Art. Beauty." She took a breath. "Love."

He snorted. "You forgot hockey."

"That too."

Without moving, he held her. Hoped she was right. *Wanted* her to be right. He felt rather than thought this. She was older, wiser, wasn't she? An artist. World unto herself. A full round globe of a woman whose single-mindedness insulated her from the things that got in the way of what needed to be done. He admired her. He was lean and hard but where his skin was thinnest his joy or rage seeped out and slammed him nose-first into whatever was out there. And what was out there? One Irishman. That he'd talked about. To Margaret. After Mister Green had warned him not to. He thought, *you've blown your cover, stupid.*

"I can't pose for you any more today."

"Yes, you can."

"Not today."

"Tomorrow then."

"Yeah. Maybe tomorrow."

He left her standing in her studio and walked straight down the street to the corner phone box. Plugged his loose change into the slot, listened to the pips, dialed the number.

"Woz," he said.

"Hennie." Woz didn't sound surprised. "What's happening, man?"

32.

Steve Wozniak; nickname, Woz. Used to be called Squeak after a slapshot to the throat bumped his voice box into the upper registers. Sounded like he was being perpetually strangled. He was still Squeak when they'd roomed together after Junior B, but once they got to Britain he insisted on Woz. It suited him. Solid defenceman. Head up, stick on the ice, hip check at the ready. Woz the Wise. You could tell him anything, and Hendershot did. About Mister Green, Margaret, Connor Mack, the bomb, the woman with the glass in her eye. When he finished, Woz stayed quiet. Then he said, "Sounds dangerous, Hen. If I was you, I'd haul my ass out of there."

"But if it's this guy, Woz, I want to get him."

"And if it isn't?"

"Then it isn't. But if it is... "

"Not your best option, man."

Hendershot listened to Woz thinking. Forehead puckered, scar over his right eye as red as a teacher's check mark. "Look," Woz said. "This is only a rumour, okay? Word is the league is letting in a new team. Swindon in Wiltshire. A guy from British Gas let it slip. They got a sponsor, arena, rec centre. Big plans for hockey programs for kids. Could be room for you on the ground floor, Hen. Player, coach – hell, director of hockey operations. A title and a paycheque. Thing is, you gotta be alive to apply."

"Fits in with my plans, Woz."

"How's the knee?"

"I'm running on it. It can be strapped."

"Be a week or more before I'll know anything for sure. Meantime I can wire you some cash if you need it."

"No need, Woz. I'm earning. Artist's model, you know?"

"I mean it, man. Elsie and I talked it over. Just say the word."

"I'm okay. How is Elspeth by the way?"

"She's got that glow. Looks good on her."

"And you? I read Sheffield beat you out in the finals."

"Overtime in the last game. But we got the bonus and they signed me to another three years. So I'm still cranked. Must be the fatherhood thing. My universe is expanding, man. We're picking out wallpaper. Looking at those do-hickeys you hang over cribs."

"Mobiles."

"Sure, mobiles."

"I'm happy for you, Woz. Not sure how to thank you."

"For what, man?"

"For this. I fink yer me best china."

Woz laughed. "Where do you pick up this shit, man?"

"I get around," Hendershot lied.

"Phone me in about ten days," Woz said. "We'll see what we get."

As he stepped out of the phone box, Hendershot felt lighter. Bounce in his step. Woz's promise the ace up his sleeve. At the mouth of an alley, he met three kids of different sizes in identically frayed, striped jerseys. Little boy carrying bread, little girl a grocery bag, big boy a box marked MARGARINE. He told them they looked like they were on the way to a feast.

"Fuck off," the biggest kid said.

Advice from all sides.

It's winter. Snowing. I'm standing on the roof of the Lakeshore

Hotel, *one foot on either side of the peak. Shingles coated in ice. Four corners of the wool blanket are tied to my belt. Below me the others look up, faces like medallions. Waiting. For the blanket to open up, me to float down. "Jump," they yell. "Jump."*

I look across the lake. Falling snow, far shore invisible. The snowbank below dirty on top. My feet in my moccasins. My bent knees...Now! – no, not now. Okay... Now –

Blanket doesn't open. Curls up like a wool sausage. I don't float, I plummet. The snowbank is deep, with a hard crust. And a forty-foot drop is a forty-foot drop. My ankles sing. Are they broken?

They're not. Only sprained. So I become him: the kid who parachuted off the Lakeshore Hotel.

33.

Well sure, he thought, *it's easy to take a chance when you're ten and don't know any better and have a neck-deep snowbank to break your fall. But work with bombers and you work without a net.* Also, he'd given Margaret a tip-off that she might pass along to Connor Mack. It would've helped if he'd kept his mouth shut. As Mister Green pointed out when he confessed to him his mistake. They tossed around that topic between them until they both agreed it was a dumb move and Hendershot apologized for being an idiot. Mister Green cheered up at this, and set about looking for a silver lining. "All's not lost, mate. I've been through this sort o' thing before."

Csongor the Hungarian had posed for Margaret, slept with Margaret, got jealous of Connor and probably would've gone to the police with bomber accusations, if one day, while Margaret was out, he hadn't broken into her studio and taken off with four paintings under his arm. Never to be seen again. What Csonger left behind, though, were observations about Connor Mack that filled in the blanks in Mister Green's notebook.

Which he showed Hendershot yet again on the off-chance he hadn't noticed them the six other times he'd looked them over.

"It's all 'ere in black and white," Mister Green said. "Any time a bomb goes off in the London area, he goes to ground for several days. Then he pops up again. Like a bad penny. But always casual-like. Wiv a tale ter tell. He's been off on a job, or his car broke down, or a relative has got the plague. All that kind o' caper. Very sincere, he is. Butter wouldn't melt. You'll see when we find him."

An invitation to do something interesting. Or at least useful. One part of Hendershot thought wandering the streets with Mister Green would be a good time-filler. Something to do until Woz came up with an escape plan. Because in spite of everything – or because of it – he still had hopes. He had most of his equipment. Was almost in shape. Had his skates which he could lace up. Get on the ice. Feel the balance come back into his feet.

Another part of him thought that finding Connor Mack with Mister Green would be an achievement. A test of his something-or-other. Like killing a penalty, say. Get possession, rag the puck. Make the other team come to you and when they do – dump it. Or pass it. Or hedge your bets for a breakaway. Or if *they* get it, check 'em. Above all, keep your head up. Stick on the ice. Thinking this, he became pleased with himself. Seeing life as hockey kept it simple.

But then it got complicated. On their outings, Mister Green had trouble walking and requested frequent stops. Leaned on lampposts or in doorways. Found benches where he could sit and massage his hip, give his ticker a rest. "Arthritis," he said. "Heart congestion."

Their trips had to be planned so they could either search for Connor Mack, shop for groceries, or both. Corner shops flogged frozen chips and soggy meat pies, but fresh meat and vegetables lay further afield. Sometimes as far as Commercial Road where Hendershot hiked the distance alone, leaving Mister Green in a pub with a pint. When Hendershot returned with the food, Mister Green paid for a bus home. A matter of pride. At his best, on foot, he was good for a six-block radius. Gave Hendershot the Connor Mack tour: this was where the Irishman bet on the nags, this where he bought his bread, this where he had his tea.

Bookies, pubs, sandwich bars, cafes. The rest was housing estates, shops, schools, churches, parks the size of tennis courts. Public conveniences. "Give us tuppence," Mister Green would say as he entered the Gents'. "I got ter take a Jimmy Riddle."

So went their afternoons. Mornings remained the same. Training run, breakfast, posing for Margaret.

She was working in oils by then. Had him sitting on a wooden bench. Holding a pig's leg in his fist. Which was Hendershot's idea: a peace offering after the argument. Beowulf clutching Grendel's arm and shoulder, torn out at the socket. He scrounged it from Mister Green's butcher, Joe the Pole, a sawed-off wood block of a man, dressed in a blue and white striped apron. Carried a meat cleaver. The pig leg was in pretty good shape. Haunch to trotter hung with bristled skin and shreds of flesh. "Very human-like," Joe said when he was told what it was for.

"The artist is Jewish," Hendershot said. "You got anything off a cow?"

"I'll trim the trotter. She'll never know."

She knew, but appreciated the gesture. They didn't mention Connor Mack and her acceptance of the ham hock was gracious. Bygones be bygones. A tribute to their tolerance, she said, theirs was not to judge. Seen that way, Hendershot could keep the relationship professional and his work with Mister Green secret. Whether or not she knew what Connor Mack was up to was beside the point. Her knowing or not knowing didn't change Connor's doing or not doing. Didn't change her, didn't change Hendershot. Didn't change Beowulf holding Grendel's arm.

Didn't stop his wanting her.

He fidgeted on the bench. Seeing his discomfort, she laid down her brush, put a record on her portable player. Classical music. Pachelbel's gigue, she said. To him, a blues fan who didn't know Pachelbel from Sonny Terry and

Brownie McGee. Or what a gigue was. But the music soaked into him. The rise and fall, joy and sorrow, beauty and pain. Oh, she played other, longer, pieces. By all the big names: Beethoven, Brahms, Mozart, Elgar. All first-round draft picks, all-stars to a man. Pachelbel was B-league. A kind of fourth-liner. Centre, maybe. But that was okay. For Hendershot, Pachelbel was the guy. He asked for him again and again.

She painted without speaking. Until late in the afternoon she laid down her brush. "That's all for today."

He asked her if he could see the painting, but she said it wasn't finished. "I won't look at the unfinished bits," he said.

"You won't be looking at any of it. Not yet."

"How do I know you haven't given me two heads?"

"You want me to break a rule..."

"Is it written down?"

"...to go against my policy."

"Hey, take a chance."

"It's an impression, you know. It's not photography."

"Are you kidding me?"

"I can't show it to you. Not yet."

She was facing him. Her smock paint-smattered, her hair as wild as frayed rope. Around her all the tools of her trade – canvases, paint, brushes, palette – a collection that must've taken years. He had to wonder at the expense. Not just the supplies, rent, food, models, but the other stuff. Her childhood, her parents, her sex, her religion, the war, poverty, failed commissions, disappeared husbands, lost baby.

Connor Mack.

As a hockey player he knew some of the costs. Bruises; broken teeth, noses, fingers; stitches; scoring slumps; bad-tempered managers, bus trips, cheap hotels, sadistic coaches, fickle fans. Yet every time he tightened his skates, grabbed his stick and stepped through the gate onto the ice, the old thrill always hit him. He was fourteen years old, he was ten, he was eight. The game made him every age he'd ever been.

He considered that maybe it was something like that for her. Maybe in the same way he skated on a rink with a hockey stick in his hands, so she picked up a pencil or a brush or a piece of charcoal.

"Superstition," he said. "This policy you've got."

"Something like that."

"I get it."

"Do you?"

"You're talking to a hockey player."

"I'm afraid I don't know what that means."

"Give us a sack of rabbits' feet and four-leaf clovers and it's still not enough. Luck? We'll take anything. A horseshoe up the ass."

"And that's good, is it?"

"It's excellent. Especially for goalies. Hockey players have more superstitions than witch doctors."

She was smiling now. "Such as?"

"Where you sit in the dressing room. The order you put your pads on. How you tape your stick. What you do before the game starts. Like after the warm-up. You skate over to your goalie and do your good luck moves. Pat his head. Slap his blocker or his catching glove. Slap his pads with your stick. Or the posts. All kinds of stuff. But whatever you do it's got to be in the right sequence. Take me. I'm a left-handed shot." He showed her. "I skate in from left to right. Forehand slap his right pad, backhand slap his left pad, bump foreheads with him" – he bumped her forehead – "and say, 'Let's do it, man.'" He paused. Embarrassed. "That's it. But I've got to do it. Same way, every game. If I don't, I'm not in that place."

"What place?"

"The place I've got to be in to play well."

She watched him, looking, so he thought, for that door –

gate – whatever-it-was, that would lead them both to that place, her art, his hockey. And he remembered his father, after his mother and Kennie left and Lyle joined the air force and Stephie won her scholarship, so it was just him, his father and his father's bottle of scotch. That his father visited regularly while he pulled out the toffee tin that held some of his wartime momentoes – coins, buttons, shoulder flashes, a piece of Perspex from his shattered turret. And a little woolen lapel pin. Black kid with big eyes and a red mouth. His golliwog. Made by a woman in the NAFFI for each man in the air crew. Good luck charm. Racist rendering of little black Sambo off a jam jar label. Nobody flew without their Golly, he explained to Margaret. On one flight his father forgot his, rode back to the hut on his bike to get it, otherwise his skipper refused to take off. "That was the flight when he got wounded," Hendershot said. "He said if he hadn't gone back for his Golly, he'd have been killed."

"And so?"

He leaned close, rested his hands on her shoulders. "My dad was twenty-three when his number came up. I'm twenty-three. I don't know if I've been wounded yet."

"I'm forty-one and I have." She stood very still. "Besides, forty-one minus twenty-three is eighteen."

"Not such a big difference."

"It is for me,' she said."

"Why?"

"Because right now I need it to be."

He pulled her to him. Her breasts plumped his stomach. Blood to his groin. Reaching, she stroked his cheek before she stepped away. "Connor Mack is my golliwog," she said.

Her eyes held him. He wished he was older, wished he knew when he was being suckered. Chances were, she'd stood like that with a lot of men she'd wanted to draw. Whereas he'd never stood like that with a woman who wanted to draw *him*.

It was the standing that got to him. Feeling his limbs tingle. Like lining up on the blue line for the national anthem when all you want to do is move. Shuffle from one foot to the other. Slide your stick back and forth. Come on, come on. Drop the puck. Drop it.

"I'll see you tomorrow then," he said at last.

"Yes, you will." Her. Revealing nothing.

"Okay."

Having already decided what he'd do.

34.

Mister Green gave Hendershot his blessing. The Green Light, he called it. For a laugh. "You'll have ter *lurk*," he said. As if lurking was a real thing. Hendershot made himself a sandwich and a flask of tea. Then out into the drizzly dark. Streets blurred from mist off the river. Air raw and damp.

In Spitalfields, he picked out a doorway in an abandoned building, huddled in the shadows for a view of Connor's flat. No car parked outside, no light in the window. Down the street under a jenny-rigged plastic tarp, two men sat on wooden crates in front of a fire in a metal bucket. Homey orange glow while they passed a bottle back and forth and broke wooden slats over their thighs to feed the flames. Laughed, sang. In a half-hour, accomplished six times as much as Hendershot did.

After an hour or two, he ate the sandwich, drank the tea, stamped his feet for circulation. Tried to recall who played who in the Stanley Cup playoffs 1954 to 1973. In the meantime, the drinkers had gone. Ran out of firewood, booze, or both. Carried their bucket with them, leaving him feeling damp, cold and foolish. The blood was pooling in his legs.

He was about to stagger home when the van pulled up outside Connor's door. The Irishman himself stepped out of the passenger side, towing a woman. Her laugh echoed along the empty street. She was blonde and leaned her hair into Connor's shoulder while he spoke to the driver. Exhaust from the tailpipe hugged the ground. When the van drove away, Connor slung his arm around the woman's waist so she wouldn't get lost on the way to his door. Hendershot watched until the light in the window went on, and a few minutes later went off. He waited another forty minutes. When he finally slipped away, Hendershot imagined Connor in the darkened room, peering out from behind the curtains.

"Good," Mister Green said when Hendershot got back. His eyes sparkling cold and excited, as if they'd been hit by hoarfrost. "He's back. He's got the woman as an alibi. That's his *modus operandy*. Now we can get on him in earnest. I'll ring up Arthur de Largo first thing in the morning and let him know."

35.

Mister Green set up a schedule that reminded Hendershot of his grandmother. A time and place for everything. Milk bottles on the step every Wednesday by 8 a.m. Last Friday of the month, the meter man. Mondays, laundry. Tuesdays, shopping downtown for the specials.

"But how will we know where *he* is?"

"Recky-noitre, mate. Recky-noitre."

Which they did. Every afternoon. And saw Connor from a distance: at the end of a bottlenecked crowd or passing a bus queue, on the other side of the street. Always with some obstacle between him and them. School kids, road crews, snarled traffic. Connor's round head and heavy shoulders just out of shouting distance. Slipping around corners, muscling through doorways, ducking into waiting cars.

"That's *his* car," Hendershot said once, "but who's the guy driving?"

Mister Green squinted. "I dunno." Stopping to rest his hip. Wheezing like a water pump. Spirit willing, flesh weak. When Hendershot suggested he go home to rest, he said he wasn't quite ready to pack it in, gallant words that took Hendershot back to the time he got home from practice and found his grandmother lying at the foot of the basement stairs. He'd placed a pillow under her broken leg, called the ambulance, and while it was on its way, listened to her lecture about how the stove worked, how not to use too much hot water, how there were leftovers in the freezer to keep him from starving until they let her out of hospital.

So they tailed Connor Mack, which Hendershot often considered if not a lost cause, then a fruitless one. As if the Irishman knew he was being followed and in spurts of competition wild-goosed them through lanes and car parks, lost them, then reappeared with a bag of vegetables or a package of meat. Always surprised to meet them, his grin like a wedge of cheese. "Ah," he'd say, "there they are then, the lads, out and about." Laying on the Irish as thick as Darby O'Gill. "And what are yis after, traipsing about like a couple of snot-nosed corner boys no better than meself?" Teetering somewhere between good buddy and smarm, so that Hendershot played along. "Connor. What's happening, man?"

Which amused Connor. His eyes narrowed as he filled them in on his whereabouts and work plans. After his work at the gallery ("Isn't it grand Margaret's show coming up within the month?"), he'd finished a garden wall in Kensington, laid a patio in St. John's Wood and was about to do a renovation in Covent Garden in a flat owned by Americans. Cash under the table. Working with his brother-in-law, Jimmy the joiner. Had they met Jimmy? No? Jimmy was a gas. Lived in North London and Sunday last went down to the local and sang in drag, mustache, hairy legs and all. Lady O'Grady he called himself and Connor's sister promised to strangle the mad eejit if she could ever stop laughing. Oh, he was prime, was Jimmy. Wore a red-haired wig and one of Gina's frocks and not a bother on him. Doesn't give a shite, does Jimmy.

Nor did Connor. Give a shite, that is. Watch me, his eyes seemed to say. Watch me all yis like. You'll not learn a thing. "I gave Jimmy the Cortina," he said. "Steering's gone and it needs the guts pulled out of it. But Jimmy says he can put it right. Good with his hands, is Jimmy. Or so me sister says." Winking.

As if you could set off a bomb that killed one person,

wounded eleven and severely burned two more and not have it show in your face.

Or maybe you could. Mister Green thought so. As did Arthur de Largo when he showed up the next day with three bottles of stout. "After you phoned," he told Mister Green, "I went 'round and had a chat with Mayhew."

"Oh yes?" Mister Green was suspicious. Though it didn't stop him from taking a pull at the stout and wiping his mouth with the back of his hand. "At the station?"

"No. He was off-duty. We met in a park. I'm nothing if not discreet, George."

"Mayhew," Mister Green grumbled. "Was it before or after you sat on the bench that he told you ter piss off?"

"He did not tell me to piss off." De Largo was offended. "In actual fact he showed an abiding interest in the information to which I made him privy."

"Speak English, Arthur."

De Largo's Adam's apple dove into his collar as he swallowed his stout. "Mayhew says that his governor appreciates our initiative but in his official capacity he cannot condone our involvement. 'Too dangerous,' is how his governor puts it, 'bordering on harassment.' In Mayhew's governor's opinion, we're to leave it alone. Let the Met do the investigating."

"You're packing it in, Arthur."

"No, I'm not."

"Removing yourself from the situation."

"Now George," de Largo held up his hand, "I knew you'd go off half-cocked, so listen. *Listen.* This is off the record now. Mayhew thinks we may be on to something. In his opinion – which by the way, he did not impart to me directly – we are *not* to stand down. We are to remain vigilant and come to him any time we've got something substantial. But we've got to tread carefully, George. Circumspect. If Connor is up to something, we don't want to scare him off. And you needn't look like that. It's sound advice. M.I.5's on this one, I shouldn't wonder. Scotland Yard. Army Intelligence. The lot, George."

"Did you tell Mayhew that Rob had seen him the day before that bomb? Carrying a suitcase, he was. And before that, I seen him go off wiv a bloody great sack."

"Tools, George. I made enquiries. Hammers, chisels, trowels. Tools of his trade."

"It's a dodge, Arthur."

"That's as may be. But we've got to prove it, George. Stay sharp. Look for details. You take that Corsair that was parked outside Scotland Yard. It was an ordinary copper who noticed that the fixing holes on the number plate didn't line up with the bolts holding it on. Solid police work, that was. Bomb squad got on it straight away. Saved untold lives, I shouldn't wonder." De Largo drained his stout. "Mayhew says leave the police work to the professionals, but at the same time keep our eyes open. No unnecessary risks. No false accusations. We don't want to be charged with obstruction of justice."

"Obstruction?" Mister Green said. "Justice?"

"We've got to be inconspicuous, George."

Mister Green lifted his bottle, gauged its level, drained it. "I expect you're right."

"Course I am."

But when de Largo had gone, Mister Green said, "Arthur's gone soft."

"Maybe he just got smart."

"He's always been an intellectual, Arthur. Very nearly a communist when he was younger, till he found out they wasn't Church of England. Give him a day or two. He'll come round – you'll see." He rummaged through his note-book until he found the fixing holes in the number plate incident. "He's got a good memory," he said, and the way he recited the description of the bomb squad diffusing the explosives made Hendershot wonder if Mister Green's obsession with Connor Mack had as much to do with saving himself as with saving the world. He wanted to be useful. Spying on Connor would fill more pages in his notebook. That along with planning his garden, scrounging for food and gathering news went a long way to fit whatever octogenarian bill he'd dreamed up for himself. But it fit Hendershot's as well. After the pub blast, he'd phoned six different hospitals to ask about the woman with the glass in her eye, but the nurses claimed they weren't allowed to give out such information. Nothing in the news report said anyone but the man selling oranges had died in the explosion, so at least she was alive. Even so, if Mister Green was right about Connor being a terrorist, Hendershot figured to cash in on some revenge. Get the satisfaction of showing Margaret that he'd helped nail at least one bloodthirsty sonofabitch.

So when Mister Green announced, "We need to step up operations, like. Double duty and all that kind o' caper," Hendershot was all for it.

"Let's do it, man," he said.

36.

Nights and days of monsoon rain. Leaden skies hurled down water that bounced off the pavement, overflowed the gutters. In his flat, Mister Green chain-smoked and read the newspapers. A lull in violence. Due to weather. A bomb had been set off outside the telephone exchange, but only a lamppost got hurt. "Still," Mister Green said, "it went off. The same fox-and-hounds game he plays. Cunning. Here today, gone termorrow. He'll have laid low for a bit. Had a bit of crumpet." Drawing on his cigarette, suddenly wracked with coughing. Hacked and burbled, hands on knees. Gasping, "Bloody chest'll interfere wiv my natural death if I'm not careful." He got his breath. "Like as not, Connor's come out of his hole, taking stock. We'd best be off, have a look round."

"Your cough. Besides, it's wet out there."

"A little France and Spain never stopped the Greenwich clock. We'll go out for a bit. You can wear my old mac. I got a new one last year."

"I saw an umbrella in the closet."

But Mister Green scorned such luxury. The umbrella had been his wife's, a gift from her sister who lived in the suburbs and only wanted to show off. An umbrella would only draw attention to them: "People will think we're poofs."

The rain pelted them. Gusts of wind soaked their trousers. Except for a handful of people scurrying for shelter, the streets were empty. Within a few blocks, Mister Green was gasping. "Bloody hell," he wheezed, on some thin level gratified. "It never rains but it pours."

They sheltered in a doorway. Mister Green's face paled, his lips went blue.

The door was boarded shut. Hendershot felt the stirrings of panic. He remembered his grandmother's other collapse that time, her frail legs oddly twisted on the kitchen linoleum, the cushion he'd slipped behind her neck hoping it would help her breathe. The way his finger shook as he dialed the phone. Now he looked up and down the street for a phone box, but there was none.

"I've got to get you somewhere," he told the old man.

"I'll be all right, mate. Just give me half a mo'."

Hugging him under the arms, Hendershot lowered him to a sitting position. Loosened his collar, felt for a pulse along his neck: it thrummed against his fingers, fast but steady. "Relax," he said. "Breathe in through your nose, out through your mouth. That's it." Mister Green slumped sideways in the doorway. Hendershot opened his own raincoat over him. "We should've brought a couple of hard-boiled eggs. Could've had a picnic."

Mister Green smiled weakly, leaned the back of his head against the door.

After a while, his colour returned. "Right," he said.

Heads down, collars up, they ploughed on. At a curb's edge Hendershot plunged one foot up to the ankle in an icy stream. A block further, skirting a puddle, they bumped into a man coming out of the Angel's Arms.

"There they are then," Connor Mack said, ducking back into the shelter of the pub's doorway. "The lads, out and about. By God, this rain would peel the skin off a duck." He was tipsy. "Are yeh for a drink, George? Yeh look as if yeh could use the water o' life. And you too, boyo."

"Mister Green's had a turn," Hendershot said, more as a reminder to the old man than an explanation. The openness of Connor's face, his freckled friendliness and broad grin made him wonder what it'd be like to punch the bastard in the mouth. Though he warned it not to, Hendershot's face stiffened. "We were just on our way to..." he searched for the word "...an appointment."

"It's early days." Mister Green, soaked, in a kind of shock. Whether from his turn or from Connor, Hendershot wasn't sure.

Connor's eyes were rimmed red. "A small whiskey wouldn't go amiss, George, the weather being what it is. Look at yis. Come in out of the wet."

The pub was quiet. Two old women sat at a back table, nursing shandies, while at the bar two men who'd been working on the council drains held pints and discussed hair.

"He said it was tree roots," one of them was saying, "until I pointed out to him there are no trees in the area. Hair it was, black, a whole bale of it, big as both my fists. The bloke says, 'I can't think where it come from' – and him standing there with his nig-nog wife and seven little kiddies, every one of 'em with a head like a bottle brush." He laughed. "What about you?"

"Bacon fat," the other said. "Right through the whole building. I smell like a bleedin' fry-up."

Carrying three whiskeys, Connor threaded his way to the table. "I've been meaning to talk to yis," he said when he'd sat down. He dealt the whiskeys like a dealer doling out cards in a poker game he already knew he'd win. Smug. Man with a plan. "Raise your glasses now."

"What's this?" Mister Green had shrunk inside his rain-coat.

"It's good-bye and good luck, George."

"What are you on about? Where are you off to?"

"Government job, George. I'm to be in the employ of Her Majesty." Grin like a crack in a piss-pot. Chest huffed out like Mr. America. "All right?"

"You?"

"Sure, and why not? I've the skill. I've the knowledge. It's the stone, yeh see. I'm good with the stone. It finds its shape when it's under me hands. I may not qualify for the giro, but I'm what they're lookin for in the stone department. I filled in the application and just the other day it came through."

"For what?"

"Tower of London."

Mr. Green was stunned. "Ter do what?"

"Repairs and renovations. Stairwells and archways. Turret walls and buttresses, parapets and quoin stones. Very old they are, George. Some have got to be replaced and repointed. There's a crying need for a lime-based mortar, yeh see. It's the decay and rot because of your sulphation and atmospheric pollutants. Highly specialized work. They're bringing in stonemasons from all over the map. Taffies, Geordies, even Germans and a Frog or two. By God, the police security checks alone made me eyes water. But it'll be a gas, George. Fecken brilliant. It's what I've wanted for years."

"So, you're moving out of the area then?"

"I've given me landlord notice. I'll be away by the week's end to be closer to me work. I've been round the whole Tower to have a look, don't yeh know. Engineers took a crowd of us on an architectural tour."

Like a crazed hockey fan with a head full of statistics – games played, won and lost, goals and assists, players traded, number of saves, averages, records, players' heights, weights. All the numbers – Connor detailed the reno that would be needed on the old fortress. But somewhere between the rusty clamps on the window surrounds and the hard pointing on the door lintels, Hendershot's brain put up its hands and surrendered. The guy was sincere – wasn't he? Or was it a scam? To fool the engineers, the security, the stonemasons' union.

Connor drained his glass, rose stiff and deliberate. Old

world dignity. "All the best to yis." Pumping Mister Green's hand. "And you too, boyo." Turning to Hendershot. Firm grip. Like arm wrestling. "I leave it to you to take care of Margaret." Winking. "As for yerself, I'll see your face hanging in the gallery, wha?" And left, shutting the door behind him, sucking the air out of the place.

Which was why Hendershot couldn't think of anything to say other than "Well, shit." But Mister Green, spurred on by the whiskey, slapped money on the table and told him to fetch Vera Lynns – gins – and pigs' ears – beers – from the barman. But it wasn't a celebration, he said. More of a wake. A gin and a beer did Hendershot; four did Mister Green. Who grieved in the pub and later all the way home.

Flat on his back on his bed while Hendershot unlaced his shoes, the old man grumbled. "Tower of London. Trust a Provo ter blow up the Tower. Stands to reason. It's a whatsitsname, cornerstone of the nation. The ravens, fate of the kingdom, etcetera."

"Go to sleep."

"Them coppers need ter do what they do but they don't." His words slurred. "Evidence? Bloody plods. Staring them in the face." His eyes opened. "I dunno how he does it." Squinting at the ceiling, voice fading in and out of memory. "The king. All of us on parade, spit and polish. After six weeks on the front line. Dead on our feet. His Royal Mam – Mamesty on a white horse. And he fell off. Laugh? I thought I'd wet meself. Whilst behind us, all along the line, the sergeant-major jabbing our backs wiv 'is rifle-butt. 'Shut up you lot, that's your king.'" Fisting his eyes as he lay back.

Hendershot covered him with the quilt. Tip-toed to the door, turned off the light.

Mister Green's voice came from the dark. "A king can't do nuffink. It's the blokes in the trenches." He coughed. "Arthur de Largo. If anyone can sort through this lot, it's Arthur."

37.

Rain hammered roof slates, pinged off chimney caps, overflowed drainpipes. Mister Green kept to his bed. In her studio, Margaret set up extra lamps and cursed the light.

"Shadows," she said, stepping back from the canvas. "Chiaroscuro. I'm turning into Rembrandt."

Hendershot didn't know what she meant, didn't ask. Connor's farewell had convinced him to play dumb. Dumb was easy, because what did he know? Connor took a woman up to his flat. Lights went out. That same night a bomb was found outside the telephone exchange. Forty minutes away by car. Connor, woman, telephone exchange. Connection or coincidence?

At the same time, there was Margaret. Lunging at the canvas: swordfight with destiny. Or standing dreamily. Eyes cloudy. Forehead furrowed. How much did she know? Or care? Hendershot posed all afternoon. Without speaking. The rain outside. Pachelbel on the record player. Over and over. Until, laying down her brush: "Come and see."

Beowulf on a bench. Exhausted. Half his body in shadow, half in light. Head turned to one side, looking down. Grendel's arm and shoulder in his hand. As if he didn't know it was there. The strands of flesh. Strings of ligament, tendon. Blood. Beowulf's knuckles skinned and swollen. Forearm raked and bloody. Bare shoulder through his torn tunic, gash in the deltoid above the triceps. He was Hendershot, worn down. Hendershot felt him. Aching joints, stiffened bruises. His body.

But the face: no nose, no lips, no eyes.

"What's this?"

"It's not finished."

"But you're letting me see it."

"Yes."

"Why?"

She wiped her hands on a rag. Raised her head. Her eyes brimmed with tears. "He's so sad," she said. "He can see it's not over but he knows how it will end. He'll win – but he's so sad. Why? Why should he be sad?"

"I don't know." Hendershot felt miserable.

Without warning she clung to him. Shuddering in his arms. "What is it, Margaret?"

Reaching up, she cradled his face in her hands. As if it was fragile and worth something, before she pulled him down to her. Her kisses long and slow, salty with tears. It was all he could do to swallow her sobs.

"I wasn't going to do this," she said.

Her bedroom was smaller than he'd expected, but room enough for two. They undressed slowly and when she wrapped her arms around his neck, he lifted her gently onto himself so that, standing, they swung there, watched by her bed, the quilt, the drawings pinned to the walls. He couldn't tell where she ended and he began. In a while nothing mattered but their breathing.

Afterwards they lay in bed, her head on his chest, her breasts flattened against his ribs. Heavy leg slung over his belly. With his free hand he reached down to stroke the length of her. The arch of her foot. Her calf, her thigh, buttocks, hips. The dip at her waist, the swag of her belly. He kissed the top of her head. Grey hairs in her scalp. Years of tenderness and generosity. He wished he was an artist. To create the line of her, the shape, the composition. She was woman, a whole world, complete in herself. She laughed when he told her. "It's called fat," she said. He traced her hands, arms, breasts, shoulders. Worried that someone else had already said the words he wanted to say. That she was miraculous. That just as her hands had shaped him, his would shape her. But he didn't have the words, so kissed her instead. And because he was young and grateful, they made love again until all he could say was her name over and over.

They lay as if washed up on a beach. He held her while outside the traffic whispered in the road. Her lips against his throat. "Tell me something you've never told anyone else before," she said.

"Like what?"

"A secret."

"Don't know if I have any."

"One you haven't even told yourself."

Which frightened him. Somewhere in his guts, something dropped. Stomach, heart, liver. Like they did after his mother and brother had left. When the trees lost all their leaves and the air smelled of snow.

He turned on his side, pulled Margaret to him so they lay face to face. So he could look into hers. So that when he spoke, it would be to her, and not just to himself.

38.

" I was eleven," he said. "Late November, maybe December, one day Dad told us. It was in a light blue airmail letter Mum had sent. She loved us, but. She missed us, but. Maybe some day, but. My big brother Lyle said he didn't care, good riddance, he was going to quit school anyway, join the air force. My sister Stephie cried, hugged me and went up to her room to write poems in her journal. Dad poured himself a drink.

"I left one Saturday morning when they were still asleep. Packed a cheese sandwich, a chocolate bar and the thermos from my school lunch kit into the haversack Mum had used during the war to carry her gas mask. At the main dock, I hung my moccasins on a post, put on my skates. From far away, the ice looked black. But up close it was as clear as glass. Weeds waved under there.

"The snowdrifts were spaced like fingers. Packed hard. Tripped me up when I tried to skate through, so I jumped them. Or went around. Took longer, but the wind was at my back. Feet and hands were warm. Ahead of me this low blue line. Seemed like the edge of the world. The Narrows. Eighteen miles away. Nobody lived there in the winter. Plywood was nailed over the cabins' windows. Boats lay belly-down on the beach. I was going to skate there. Show 'em...show 'em all. Eat my food, drink my tea, carve my name on the dock. Skate back. Write and tell Mum and Kennie.

"Sometimes I fell. Lost my mitt, found it. Thought about that guy Franklin we studied in school. Dead in the Beaufort Sea. Death was an idea: they'd all be sorry. But it wouldn't happen. I wouldn't die. I was the kid who jumped off the Lakeshore Hotel.

"I skated. One hour, two, who knows how long. Flat clouds jammed together. Grey, dull. Slabs of slate. Twice the lake groaned, deep goongs, ready to crack open. Like it did for the ice-road trucker. Sucked into the black water. Truck and all.

"As I skated, the blue line got pale, got closer, I was there. But it wasn't the Narrows. It was a wall of ice. Giant slabs all jumbled together. Bristling. The lake had reared up on itself. I skated back and forth, found two slabs pushed together like a ramp. Dug my skates in. Scrabbled up one side, slid down the other. The haversack flopped away from my shoulder, splashed into open water. I rolled away from the sound. Shaking.

"The light faded. I stood in the dusk, listened to my own breathing, the wind, the water slopping at the wall's base. The wet haversack froze against my leg. The cold found gaps in my clothes. My wrists, neck, lower back. My hands. My feet. I couldn't see the Narrows. Maybe it was there. Maybe it wasn't.

"I clambered back over the wall. It was dark now. Snow fell. Pellets stung my face. If I skated into the wind it'd lead me south. I bent towards home, numb, blind. Legs heavy, the sweat on my back going cold under my parka.

"Later, trees rose out of the storm. No dock, no street lights, no houses. The snow fell thick. The sky lightened. Like a dome. I followed the shoreline.

"At home Stephie cut my frozen skate laces, filled basins with cold water to soak my hands and feet. As they thawed, I cried. Because of the pain. The unfairness. Of the lake, of the weather, of Mum.

"And of me. Because that's the secret. Me. I'm not what I think I am. I'm a coward. And more. Even if I'd made it to the Narrows, Mum and Kennie weren't coming back. They just weren't.

39.

They lay in each other's arms, while outside the rain had stopped. Home from school, kids shouted in the street, and through her window a brassy light lit the curtains. Above them, Mister Green's slippers shuffled from his bed to the bathroom. The toilet flushed. The slippers shuffled to the kitchen.

She raised herself on one elbow, traced his face with her fingertips. Kissed him, then said that she was ready to finish the painting.

On her own.

She was sorry, she said, but she wouldn't be needing him anymore.

40.

Years before, during the middle of a team try-out, when he'd gone to practices, checked the list of hopefuls every morning and watched the names get whittled away, he'd discovered his name wasn't there. An assistant coach came by. Hendershot was standing at the bulletin board, feeling stupid. Equipment bag at his feet. The coach had told him the roster was full, his talents weren't needed, good luck, thanks for coming out.

Enough to have made him want to quit. But he didn't. As the singer once said, if it wasn't for bad luck, he'd have no luck at all. There were other teams.

As for Margaret, she was an artist. Not like other people. Maybe she needed help but didn't know it. Too proud. Maybe Connor Mack had warned her off him. Knew he was getting too close. Maybe her cutting Hendershot loose was his chance. To shine. Get even.

Which dovetailed with Arthur de Largo's plans the next time he visited. With his cosh, his big knuckles and his own pocket notebook. He'd been making enquiries, had tailed Connor to the Irishman's new digs. Had met with his policeman Constable Mayhew several times, given him descriptions of Connor's car, now Jimmy the joiner's, the licence plate, the van Hendershot had seen, the woman. De Largo had done his homework. And his legwork. Poor old guy had plantar fasciitis. Hobbled like a peg-leg. Twice he'd followed Connor Mack all the way from Bermondsey across the bridge to the Tower. From what he'd observed, Connor was up to something. But first he wanted Mister Green seen to.

"You look like death warmed up, George," he said.

"I'm as fit as ever I was," Mister Green boasted. "It's only the Green chest. My muvver had it. I've had it since I was a nipper." He sat in his armchair, buttoned up in his cardigan. Hot water bottle under his feet. Rum and hot lemon Hendershot had mixed to specifications.

De Largo said, "I saw the doc about my foot. I'll ring him up."

Dr. Wiseman made house calls. Short guy, tired face, balding. Open shirt, sweater. Soft spoken, but no nonsense. Listened to Mister Green's chest, tapped his back, took his blood pressure, looked down his throat. Bronchitis. Touch of asthma. He wrote a prescription. "Stay off your feet, George," he said. "Plenty of fluids. Consign all politics to the dustbin. Let your grandson take care of what needs doing. I'll see you in a week."

Seven days, Arthur de Largo pointed out. The time it took God to make heaven and earth. Also, the time Hendershot had left before he was to phone Steve Woz, though he said nothing. Because no sooner was Dr. Wiseman out the door than de Largo opened his notebook and the two old men put their heads together, one-hundred and sixty-three years between them to Hendershot's twenty-three. Hockey was hockey but it was only a game. With rules. And if people died while playing it, their deaths were accidental. But this game that obsessed these two old geezers was in a different league. Real life. Real death. Maybe Hendershot hadn't bought into it completely when he'd started, but he wanted to be there when it ended. He was vaguely aware he had the choice of whether to go or stay. But he didn't dwell on it. He got a chair from the kitchen and sat between them. Their knees almost touching. Age and experience meeting youth and innocence. Striking a blow for freedom.

"Do you still do your training runs?" de Largo asked.

"Every morning."

"Good. Then all this calls for is a few minor adjustments."

What followed Hendershot saw as a pre-game chalk talk. If-he-goes-there, you-go-here. If-he-does-this, you-do-that. When to improvise, when to use a set play. Attack. Defend. Bail. De Largo had maps, Hendershot had routes, Mister Green suggestions. Connor lived on the south side of the river. Walked to work every morning for an 8 a.m. start at the Tower of London. De Largo's big finger pointed out Hendershot's possible observation post overlooking the bridge, the Tower and points in between. Athlete-in-training his cover. Hooded Mr. Anonymous in a grey sweatsuit. Swooping his *modus operandy*, Mister Green said.

"Swooping?"

"He won't expect you ter swoop," Mister Green said. "Element of surprise, like."

"Now then, George," de Largo cautioned.

"I don't plan on arresting him," Hendershot said.

Mister Green nodded. "Still and all," he said. "If he makes his move, you'll have ter get a wiggle on, won't you?"

So away he went. Dog-trotted in reverse order the roads he'd galloped to escape Sasquatch and Pogo. Streets signs important now, he learned to tick them off as if he owned them: Chicksand, Brick Lane, Whitechapel High, Commercial, Alie, St. Mark's, Tenter, Portsoken, Minories. Muffled footsteps through morning fog. Jock-friendly waves to the nightshift dustmen and charwomen who wished him good morning. All of them early-birding the worm.

De Largo guessed the run to be 4.5 miles round trip, 5.3 if Hendershot nipped across Tower Bridge. "Should it be necessary." Which Hendershot took as a warning. But the truth was he enjoyed the exercise. Streets mostly deserted until he reached the grassy corner overlooking the bridge and the

Tower. Lonesome lorries scattering pigeons in the road. River fog like a snake of rolled cotton. If the tide was out, mud larks like ghosts in rubber boots sweeping the river banks with metal detectors, like sappers looking for landmines. Made him feel clandestine. Secret agent.

As the mist lifted, commuters streamed out of the tube station, pushing stale air, to see him doing peppy calisthenics on the grass. Loopy fitness freak. The Tower below them, a chain-link fence around the dried-up moat. Beyond that, stone walls and the main gate farther along. Beefeaters in red and black uniforms.

It took him two days to get his timing right. When the sun rose, traffic thickened. Buses spit out passengers, swallowed others. People clustered at curbs. On the third day, from the south, a crowd crossed the bridge coming towards him and crossed the street opposite him. They were going to work. Clerks, ticket sellers, workers in dusty coats. Among them Connor Mack, his head above the rest. Walking with his mates, arms swinging, head thrown back to laugh. Clubbing a mate playfully on the shoulder, nudging another in the ribs. Ahead of him two young women giggled.

Hendershot ducked behind a lamppost. Then jogged parallel to the Irishman, keeping the commuters and the road between them. At a walk light he crossed, slipped in behind Connor and followed the crowd along the cobbles towards the Tower's entrance. Two constables chatted at the guardhouse. A beefeater stood to attention, posing for a camera. In his effort to be unseen, Hendershot hunched behind a man and a woman, heard their scrap of conversation: "He scrubs away for ten minutes and then he says, 'Wait a minute, this isn't my car...'"

When he looked again, Connor was passing through an opening marked STAFF. At the same moment, a hand clamped his hood from behind, tightened the cloth around his throat. "Well, well," Sasquatch said in his ear. "It's the cunt, come ter pay a visit."

"Fancy that." Pogo appeared to one side. "Thought you'd have another go, didjer?"

"Not a chance."

Pogo peered into Hendershot's face: "That's a nasty mark you got on yer clock."

"Hazards of the job." He shrugged out of Sasquatch's grip. "Do you want us all to go to the police together?"

"Not bleedin' likely."

"Would it make you guys happy to know you really pissed me off?"

Pogo thought. "Yeh, I fink it would. What about you, Reg?"

Sasquatch frowned. Complicated calculation. "If it was up to me, I'd ravver have another go at him. But on the whole, I feel quite at peace wiv meself."

"So, we're even?"

Above them in the square, a tour bus wheeled into the parking lot. Sasquatch stopped to pick up the tin trunk that sat beside him. Pogo offered Hendershot advice. "I fink it's best if you fuck off."

"Right." He watched them go, both limping. Pogo from the leg, Sasquatch from the trunk bumping his thigh. When they'd gone a few yards, Hendershot yelled, "Hey. Break a leg!" Without turning, Pogo stabbed two fingers in the air.

Made Hendershot nervous. In England, two fingers were double what one was in Canada.

41.

Connor's routine was the same every morning, but Hendershot had to get there early enough to see it. The stonemason crossed the bridge from the south, always on the side farthest from the Tower. Walked alone to the middle of the bridge, stopped to light a cigarette, leaned over the railing to gaze at the water. Waited until the barges loaded with garbage passed underneath on their way out to sea. And always – at the moment their bows disappeared under the bridge – leaned out and spat. Sometimes twice, sometimes more.

"Why do you think that is?" Mister Green said.

"I'm not sure. But you're going to tell me."

Mister Green consulted his notes. "He's got the Guinness World Record for spitting on garbage scows," he said. "Six times at one go, you say. What's he after, you ask yerself? He's timing it, see. How long it takes for his spittle ter drop from the bridge to the barge. Mind you, a bag of explosives would drop a shorter distance, wouldn't it? Wouldn't get blown about by the wind. Not like spittle. He could spit and miss the barge altogevver. But explosives? Drop like a stone."

"Why would he want to blow up a barge?"

"Not the barge, mate. Not the Tower, neivver. It's a bridge. Not that one – he's standing on it, in't he then? But there's ovver bridges all the way along the Thames. London, Southwark, Blackfriars, Waterloo. I expect he's after Westminster – that'd be the one. Put the bomb on the clock, wrap it up like rubbish, drop it on the barge, go off ter work as usual. If he was careful, who'd notice?"

"Me," Hendershot said.

Mister Green smiled. Rare occasion. "That's the ticket." He jotted something in his notebook. Nothing too trivial for Mister Green. Connor's boot size (10½), scars (right hand, base of thumb), dominant hand (left; southpaw). "Course," Mister Green went on, "he's got ter have someone at the ovver end. Someone who can clock how long it takes the barge ter get to Westminster." Hendershot thought of the woman, the driver of the van, Connor's brother-in-law Jimmy the joiner.

Margaret.

Her name punched a hole in him. Couldn't be. Not Margaret. Whatever else she was, she wasn't destructive. Was she?

He found himself pacing the little flat. Kitchen to front door to living room window. Out of which he saw, as if she'd planned it, Margaret. Standing in the street in front of her flat. Looking up at him. The wind against her cardigan. Her tangled hair. As if she'd spent a sleepless night on a park bench. Or under a bridge.

She beckoned to him.

"I've got to go out," he told Mister Green.

"I'm expecting Arthur," he said. "Can't it wait?"

"I'll be back in an hour. Tell de Largo your barge theory. He'll like it."

"But you don't."

"An hour, Mister Green." At the door he turned. "And I love the barge theory."

42.

The sandwich bar was decorated early proletarian. Long zinc-topped tables, bare walls, wooden chairs. Two biddies sat by a bare window, between them a newspaper, an ash tray and an empty cigarette package. The only other customers were a woman with two kids and a workman wearing a white dressing over one eye. Long John Silver squinting at a newspaper. At the far end of the room, under a blackboard listing prices, a girl in a smock racked mugs on a metal drainboard. Margaret said the place would fill up once the surgery across the lane opened. Two wooden doors on a converted warehouse sported a doctor's shingle – green with faded gold lettering – listing office hours.

"I didn't know this place existed," Hendershot said. "I could've used a place like this."

She stirred her cup. "Tea and a bun for less than a bob. I used to come here every day when I returned to London. Some days it was the only meal I had."

"Returned from where?" He imagined an Irish crofter's cottage in a bog where Connor Mack cut peat and waved tara to his one true love.

"Paris," Margaret said. Where she'd spent a year studying print-making and etching with Andre La Roche. Did he know La Roche? No? A kindly man, who in 1942 lost his Jewish wife and children to the camps. When Margaret met him, he was alone and over sixty. "He loved still-lifes," she said. "The intensity of things." She pointed at the mug and bun in front of her. "This would've been epic enough for him. He didn't require narrative, you understand?" Her liquid eyes fastened on his, willing him to comprehend. Which he almost did. "For La Roche, the objects were large enough in themselves."

"And for you?"

"I had bigger ambitions. I was about the age you are now."

"What's that supposed to mean?"

"Time passes," she said. "Youth fades."

"Wow," he said. "Big news."

She pulled her coat around her. While he'd been playing road hockey with his friends, she'd been flirting with communism. Because there were a lot of old socialists in London then, left over from the 1930's. "Middle-aged men mostly," she said, "moving their furniture out of Stalingrad and into the Labour party. They appreciated a short Jewish girl from Golder's Green with artistic pretensions – and a bosom, of course." She stuck out her chest. "We mustn't forget the bosom." She glanced out the window. A woman with three kids tried the surgery door: locked, so she moved on. "It amazes me," Margaret said, "the distances a woman can travel on the size of her breasts."

He must've blushed. She laughed. "Liberation of the working class. In between jumping from bed to bed, I made pictures of tractors and big-shouldered factory workers. But I couldn't manage it. La Roche had done the unthinkable, you see. He'd instilled in me a reverence for the classical. It wasn't until I saw the Pollocks and Warhols and Pop Art that I realized I was out of date. Modern art wanted to shatter the past. I wanted to *paint* it. But no one wanted my sort of picture. Or my rather forced amorality. I was cold and hungry. A bad time. Places like this made it bearable."

"What'd you finally do?"

"Connor saved me. One day he simply turned up. Got a job as a builder's mate. He made enquiries and found me a position at a picture framer's. I stretched canvases and gilded frames."

"Connor told me and Mister Green that at one time he wanted to be a sculptor."

"Did he?" She laughed, eyes shining. "Well," she said, "he's an artist in his own way. Stonemasons serve a seven-year apprenticeship."

"Is that how long he spent working on his politics?"

She shook her head. "He's not what you think."

"Is he what Mister Green thinks?"

"George has never forgiven himself for surviving the Great War. He wants all the Irish to be like his friend Paddy Cahoon. Ready to die for king and country."

Hendershot thought of his father, tipsy in his Legion blazer and medals. "To you from failing hands," he said.

"Pardon?"

"War poem we learned at school. 'To you from failing hands we throw the torch, be yours to hold it high.' Montreal Canadiens have it over their dressing room door."

"Ice hockey," she said.

"Closest thing to war without being fatal."

"You believe that?"

"Beats planting bombs and killing people."

Her eyes unfocussed as they did when she'd painted him. As if he were nothing but line and light. She said, "So it's a competition, is it?"

"If you want it to be."

"Did I mention my formative years as a communist? It involved taking several lovers." Then, cruelly to her, "Many." She sipped her tea. "I've no interest in resuming the practice."

"You've got a husband."

"Ex-husband. A bourgeois lapse. Trevor fell in love with my art. He confused the art with its maker."

"There's a difference?"

"Sometimes an abyss separates the two. I didn't know that when I was younger. Now I do. Artists are mean, petty little beasts. But if they're lucky, their work outstrips them. On the whole, artists are miniscule in relation to their work." She spread her arms. "I offer myself as a humble example."

"But you still need Connor Mack." He tore into the bun. Stale. Set it back on the plate.

"Connor has been my friend all my life," she said.

"Oh yeah? What do you mean by 'friend'?"

She leaned forward, her voice low. "Someone who believes in you, who takes your work seriously, who goes without a meal to buy you paints and brushes and canvas, who smuggles you up the stairs past the landlord and risks being chucked out so you have a place to sleep, who'll pose nude when there's no heat. Oh yes," she added, "and who knows that making love isn't only passion and lust, but an offering of comfort and renewal."

While she was speaking, he broke pieces off the bun, crumbled them between his fingers. Death to all things stale. When she finished, he said that maybe Connor did all that so nobody would suspect what he was really up to. He thought she'd explode, but she didn't. "Oh dear," she said, "I've hurt your pride."

"A lot."

"I've been through this before."

"I haven't."

"It would do neither of us any good."

"Speak for yourself."

"I'd have to take responsibility."

"I've got shoulders."

"For ice hockey. For being young."

"You make it sound like a disease."

She sat for a moment. Quiet. Then: "There's a gap between the model and the art as well, you know. I needed to *paint* an epic hero, not manufacture one." She folded her arms. "And I don't need to be saved."

"Is that what Connor says?"

"He doesn't have to. He already knows."

"Connor, Connor, Connor." She pushed her empty mug and plate to the middle of the table. "Sometimes he has to wait for you."

"Pardon?"

"In the morning. On the bridge."

He must've gasped. But the two biddies at the window, the eyepatch workman, and the woman with the kids didn't seem to notice that the bottom had dropped out of the room.

"Jesus." He stood. "I gotta go."

"Don't be like this." She held his sleeve. Now they all looked. Even the tea girl. "Sit down. Please."

"No thanks."

"I have something for you." She handed him an envelope. Fifty pounds.

"No," he said.

"Take it. You'll need it."

"Big payoff? For services rendered?"

"It's what I owe you."

"No, it isn't. I worked 9 1/2 hours last week. That's nine pounds fifty."

"At least take ten."

"There's only tens here."

"Take ten."

He took a ten-pound note, reached in his pocket and gave her change.

In the end, they left together. Outside, the air was cold. A wind had got up. Facing her, he stuffed his hands in his pockets. "You're a lovely talented woman, Margaret," he said. "But he's got you fooled."

"And you're young, Robbie. Remember that."

They parted at the corner. Down the high street, the wind blew straight at his back. Old newspapers chased him. A plastic bag wrapped itself around his leg, and as he bent to peel it off, he expected the ligament behind his knee to shoot a warning flare.

He wasn't disappointed.

When he got back to the flat, Mister Green told him he'd just had a visit from Constable Mayhew. Arthur de Largo, he said, was dead.

43.

"Mayhew thinks it was a robbery," Mister Green mourned. "'A smash and grab?' I says to him, 'In Boreham Wood? A smash and grab? Not bloody likely. Arthur de Largo knew a villain when he seen one. There's not a villain alive could've put one over on Arthur.'"

"But how?"

"Broke his skull. Neighbour woman found him at the bottom of the stairs leading to his flat. Thought he'd had a fall. But his skull had been broke. I reckon they done it wiv his own bloody cosh. Whoever done it had been waiting for him. Took his wallet ter make it look like a robbery. Cunning they are. It's like I said. They get stuck in, see? And people dunno what they're after till it's too late. Somefink's got ter be done, mate. I'll not have Arthur de Largo end on such a note. He was a good bloke. You see that, don't you?" He shuffled into the kitchen to gaze at the picture frame that held his medals. Ran his fingers over the fractured glass before he lifted the frame off its hook.

"Aw, don't do that," Hendershot said, meaning medals about to be thrown in the garbage. The old man's grief and frustration.

But this time Mister Green was gentle. "I want ter show you somefink." He placed the frame face down on the table and pried off the back. Withdrew a loop of string from which dangled two disks the size of bottle caps. One olive drab, the other red. "The Yanks called 'em dog tags. We had our own name for these." He held up the green disk. "This

one stayed on the body. The red one went to Army Records."
From a finger he swung the disks. "Dead meat ticket, mate.
That's what we called 'em. Dead meat ticket." He fixed
Hendershot with bright cataract'd eyes. "Notice somefink
odd about 'em? No? Well I'll tell you, mate. Poor old Arthur
may not have his, but I still got mine, see. I still got mine."
He re-fitted the picture frame and hung it on the wall.

44.

It was the final sprint that nearly did him in. A hundred and fifty yards. Bridge crowded with people because he was late. Car exhaust burning his lungs. Pavement sending messages to his knee. Ahead of him, Connor at his railing, as usual, smoking, spitting, Mister Relaxation. Hendershot ran harder. Halfway there he saw it, felt his heart jump at his tonsils. A sack – no, a suitcase. Between Connor's feet. And down on the river, a barge heaped with garbage, chugging upstream. Perfect rendezvous, everything Mister Green said it would be. So when Hendershot got there, and Connor said, "Boyo, I was wondering when you'd get round to it," he didn't stop. Body-checked the fucker into the railing.

The suitcase was cardboard, painted black, plastic handle and a tag marked C. Mack, Dublin. The handle came off in his hand like a pin in a grenade. Connor's fist slammed into his nose and away they went, wrestling over the suitcase like a divorced couple over a baby. A crowd gathered and Hendershot yelled, "Get back! Bomb!" but nobody seemed to hear him. Connor roaring by then, "What the feck are yis on about?", raking the edge of his boot down Hendershot's shin. Noise and scuffle, an elbow to an eye, a thumb to a neck. Hendershot kicked at Connor's feet and when the Irishman went down, threw the suitcase over the railing.

Where it spun in the air, opened and scattered everything in it. Socks, underwear, shirts, pants, a pair of dress shoes tied together. A suit jacket and a wool sweater that spread-eagled like a man being crucified. "Yeh feckin' eejit," Connor said, watching. "Them shoes was just now paid for."

The clothes fluttered down, floated an instant before the current swept them under the bridge. The suitcase lasted the longest, as open as butterfly wings until it filled with water and sank. There was no bomb. Three seagulls wheeled under the bridge. Shrieking, because there was no food, either.

Connor leaned over the railing and spat. "Yeh feckin' gob-shite. Yer mad. That's the whole of me wardrobe gone under."

Hendershot leaned on the rail to look. "Sorry," he said.

45.

The failure was physical. Couldn't have been anything else. Physical was what he did, how he proved to the world he was in it. Other people had their paintbrushes, pocket notebooks, stone-carving tools, bombs, lead-filled nightsticks. He had his body. Muscles. Sinews.

Mister Green sat at the window. "Could it have been strapped ter the inside of his bag?"

"It sank empty."

He closed his eyes, rubbed his forehead. "I've let him down. Arthur, I mean. Like I let Paddy down. And Maeve."

"You didn't let them down. You did your best. But Connor wasn't what you thought he was, that's all. He wasn't what I thought he was. Maybe none of us are what we think we are," Hendershot added, though what he meant by this, exactly, he wasn't sure.

Mister Green brooded. "You think this is all a lark," he said. "That old George is having a fantasy. Is your ice hockey a fantasy? Is Arthur de Largo a fantasy? Connor Mack? Don't think I dunno about fantasies, mate. I've seen more fantasies than you've had hot breakfasts. During the Blitz, my Maeve seen God climb out a dustbin at the bottom of Leather Lane. At Ypres, before we went over the top, Paddy heard his mum tell him ter fill the coal scuttle."

"But there's no evidence, Mister Green."

He waved his notebook. "What's this, Scotch mist?"

"That's just...scraps of information."

But the old man wouldn't back down. "Connor wanted a

reliable witness."

"To what?"

"That empty suitcase. He wanted ter establish his credentials. That he's an ordinary bloke wiv a suitcase that don't have a bomb in it."

"He *is* an ordinary bloke with a suitcase that doesn't have a bomb in it."

"Arthur de Largo." Mister Green grieved. "If Arthur was here, he'd know what ter do."

Hendershot said, "Even Arthur wouldn't know. He *didn't* know. Look," he said, "you gotta let this go. It's not good for your health. Remember what Dr. Wiseman said. Lay off the politics. Put your feet up. I've dug the garden. I'll rake it. You figure out what to plant and where. I'll help you. But I'm through playing detective. I'm a hockey player, for chrissake."

Mister Green clenched his jaw, stuck out his chin. We shall fight them on the beaches. Never surrender. Reminded Hendershot of his father. Who saw eighteen months of action when he was twenty-three years old and then tried to use those months to shape the rest of his life. And whether he knew it or not, surrendered. The bottle had seen to that. And yet here was Mister Green, ready to work Hendershot over.

"What about that woman wiv the glass in her eye?" he said.

"Don't do this, Mister Green."

"There'll be ovvers, you know. Bombs everywhere you look."

"Jesus Christ."

"We can't just wash our hands of it. Carry on regardless."

Hendershot sat on the window seat. Faced him eye to eye. His collapsed old cheeks, wispy hair, stubbled chin. Thought of his father, his mother, Kennie. He said, "Goddammit, Mister Green. After all these years, you'd think your war was still going on."

"It lasts longer than you think, mate."

"Yeah? How long?"

"All yer bleedin' life," Mister Green said.

46.

Within two days, Hendershot phoned Steve Wozniak, who wired some money, names and a phone number. In Swindon, Stuart Biddiscombe was the CEO and Bobby Walker the general manager. "Remember Bobby?" Woz asked. "Sault Ste. Marie. Mister Hip-check." A power company had signed on as a sponsor, in addition to a grant from the Sports Council. "But you gotta get in there, Hen. Player-coach, hockey development manager – it's ground-floor stuff, man."

When Hendershot phoned, Biddiscombe said they'd seen him play when he was in Brighton and they'd been impressed. How was the knee getting on? Good, good. Yes, they'd heard about the changes in Dunfermline, but Dunfermline's loss could be Swindon's gain. "It's not just a team we're building here," Biddiscombe said. "It's a complete program."

They wanted him to be in Swindon on Tuesday. Would four o'clock suit him?

Out of the phone box he was seized with a sudden energy. Seeing him, an old couple stopped to watch. "What is it, love?" the old woman asked as his legs twitched and his arms wind-milled. "What's wrong?"

"I'm dancing," he said.

47.

Waving to Mister Green that morning, he stepped into sunlight. Stood by the doors on the tube with a new knapsack between his feet, while hanging onto the pole with one hand. Read in the overhead ads that Leonardo da Vinci was coming to the Tate Gallery. Wondered if Margaret would go.

The train took on passengers at every stop, before hurtling through the dark. Pale workaday faces. He felt sorry for them. Him with money in his wallet and the name of a man he had an appointment to see. Hope and possibility. Golden light of destiny. On impulse, he beamed at his fellow passengers: two workmen slumped in their seats, a girl in a short skirt across the aisle, a man whispering to his crossword puzzle, a woman reading her novel. He'd remember them all. Wondered if they could guess where he was headed. Wondered if they'd remember *him*.

But why would they? At the station, as they hurried toward their trains, what did they have on their minds besides a cup of tea, a newspaper, the right platform, an empty compartment, smoking or non-smoking? Like him, they wouldn't so much hear the blast as feel it. Noise and force. Bottom blown out of ordinary sound. Bits of glass metal coffee cup wood plastic dirt smoke his face arms chest legs his knapsack – where? What? Lifting him off his feet, slamming him with a fierce and solid weight so that he fell and fell until there was nothing but heaviness and roaring and finally not even that.

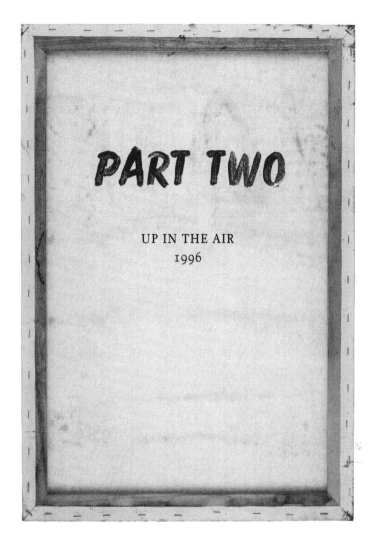

PART TWO

UP IN THE AIR
1996

1.

Clayton was thirteen, old enough to know when things were falling apart, young enough to hope they wouldn't. At first Louise said he couldn't go. She had to check with the school, the doctor and, possibly, the police. Hendershot tried to be easy, one way or the other. Even took a shot at being eager: "It'll be an adventure!" Though he wasn't sure if *adventure* was exactly what awaited them.

The call itself had unsettled him. Yanked him out of sleep at five in the morning, a week after he and Louise had declared a truce and he had returned to the house to move his few remaining belongings out of the basement. Junk that'd sat down there for a year, since the separation. Now it littered his one-bedroom apartment above the store. He'd had to hop around boxes in the dark to get to the telephone. Go through the annoyance of overseas operators talking to domestic ones, as if he wasn't there. And finally, a voice he hadn't heard for years, their usual channel of communication having been limited to exchanging cards at Christmas.

"Hennie? Hey, man. Had a hard time getting your number."

"Woz?" Hendershot not so much startled as bewildered.

"Sorry, man. Did I wake you up?"

"Doesn't matter, Woz. What's up?"

"Elsie's been after me to phone. She's been following it on the news. She figured it out. She said, 'That's Hennie's guy.'"

"What guy?"

"*Your* guy. The Irish guy." Woz's voice edged upwards. "What, Hen? You mean you don't know? He's been on trial over here. Couple of weeks now."

"I'm not over there, Woz. I'm here."

"Yeah. Okay." Woz, thinking. Long administrative pause, perfected over nearly two decades behind a desk, dealing with players. Or their agents. Steve Wozniak, Director of Hockey Operations, Swindon, Wilts. "His name is...hang on...Connor Mack. That was the guy, wasn't it?"

Hendershot's mouth dried up.

"Hen?"

"Yeah. That's him. But he must be an old man by now."

"Go figure."

"How did they *get* him?"

"Some kind of double-cross. IRA guy dying of cancer came clean. Catholic thing, I guess. He named names. Your guy was one in a list. Jeez, Hen, I thought you knew. Just wondered how you were holding up."

"What was his sentence, Woz? How long'd he get?"

"Nothing yet, man. Trial's not quite over. They'll know pretty soon, though. You want me to call you when the verdict comes in?"

Hendershot had leaned naked against the kitchenette counter. First his son Clayton, and now this. He had held the receiver to his ear as Woz talked. Something about expert witnesses, cold case investigators, legal delays. Hendershot half listened. Mostly what he heard was himself, twenty-two years ago, asking Mister Green how long a war lasts. And Mister Green's answer.

All yer bleedin' life.

2.

Louise finally agreed, following protracted negotiations and caveats: The trip could only last for the two weeks of Clayton's Easter break from school. Back in time for his transfer to the new school. Supervision at *all* times. In addition, Louise tacked on an addendum that Hendershot guessed was inspired by prejudice and paranoia: that Hendershot practise tolerance, patience and close observation. That he "feel out" what had happened to Clayton. *Feel out* rattled Hendershot. He asked Louise if he should take along diapers and a bottle.

"Oh God," Louise said. "You always do this. You always have to reduce things to some...literal meaning."

"I've got a Y chromosome."

"Oh please. Spare me." Louise sighed. "Look. I don't want him spending all his time in a courtroom. You've always wanted to find the painting. Do that. Take him places. Show him things. Try to get his mind off this...," she struggled for the word, "...complication at school. Try being," she played her trump card, "a dad."

3.

They left on the day before Good Friday, on a flight that took them over Baffin Island and Greenland, where Clayton sat glued to the window. No Land of the Midnight Sun down there, more like Land of the Midnight Murk. Descending through the clouds over London's Heathrow, the boy peeked out of his shell to infect the air with anticipation. "We're really here, Dad!" For him, escape. For Hendershot, revenge. "I bet we find it," Clayton said, as if Hendershot's ramblings about explosions, the portrait, and Margaret Lowenstein had been a complex and intertwined briefing for a treasure hunt. "I bet we find *her.* Plus we already know where the bomber guy is, right? You'll see, Dad. It'll be a win-win-win."

The boy's enthusiasm reminding him of the old pre-game jitters.

4.

The manager of the bed-and-breakfast was a stately old Italian. Cropped white hair, pencil mustache, snowy white shirt, old-world charm. The hotel had seen better days. Creaky stairs and crooked corridors honeycombed each floor like mineshaft galleries. But everything else – from newel posts to bathroom tiles – shone. They dumped their bags, went out for fish and chips, walked all the way to Trafalgar to feed the pigeons. Caught the tube back, went to bed. In booking their flight, Louise had managed to have them land with the prospect of an Easter bank holiday ahead of them. The same days during which the trial of Connor Mack would be on hiatus. Hendershot tended to view such serendipity as fate. Or failing fate, dumb luck. Whereas Louise credited their free time to careful planning. "You'll have four free days before the trial," she'd said. "Make use of them." Hendershot saw her point. Time enough to acclimatize, fight off jet lag, sightsee, enquire about the painting. *And*, he thought, *gather my scattered wits*.

Clayton, however, appeared calm. From his bed across the room he said, "We start tomorrow, Dad."

Hendershot answered, "Aye, aye, Cap'n," secretly wondering, *start on who, son? You or me?*

5.

Bright and early, they were on the street overlooking the river, the Tower, the past. Clayton squinted at the street map. Traced with his finger the route Hendershot had drawn in pencil. As if for twenty-two years a path had been carved through the cartography of his heart. Or brain, liver, whatever. "So, you ran along here, Dad, all the way up to... what's that street up there...Minories?"

"I think so, yeah."

"How come you didn't take the underground?"

"Didn't think of it."

"I mean, there's the red circle with the blue bar. See? All the underground stations..."

"I knew about the stations, son."

"Then why didn't you..."

"I was busy okay? Running. Hell, panicking. You know all about panicking, don't you, son?"

Wrong word. Poor kid. Tucked his chin for protection. Bowed his head in such a way that Hendershot could see right down to the scalp where the stitches used to be. Still puckered and raw. Hendershot didn't want to look at his son's head. He shifted his gaze to the people shouldering by them on the pavement, and found he didn't want to look at them either.

"You don't have to get mad, Dad."

"I'm not mad, son."

"Mum said you'd probably get mad at first. She said you'd probably get nostalgically depressed."

"Pardon?"

"Nostalgically..."

"Christ. Is that the language your mum uses now? Nostalgically depressed? Where's she get this stuff? From Julius?"

"Julian."

"Sure, Julian. What's he *do* in his spare time, play Scrabble?"

"No. Maybe. I don't know." Clayton muttered some secret to his feet. Hendershot moved them off the sidewalk onto the grass. Away from the crowd who seemed to be staring. Clayton said, "She gets it from the counsellor. Not the school one, Mrs. Stemholtz, she's the librarian. Mum talks to the district one, Dr. Witherspoon. I'm supposed to call him Dave."

"But you don't."

"Not yet."

"Well, when we get back home you can tell your mum – you can tell *Dave* – that I'm *not* nostalgically depressed."

"What are you then?"

"Worried."

"You don't have to be, Dad." Clayton looked thinner than he used to. Or maybe not – maybe he was just taller. Hendershot wanted him taller. Huskier, smarter. In the universal genetic crapshoot, bigger and better than his father.

"What's it like being nostalgically depressed, Dad?"

"No idea. That's your mother's term, not mine." Seeing him frown, Hendershot relented. "I suppose it means I'm sad because I can't live my life all over again. Your mum thinks that when you get paunchy and bald and pee a lot at night, you want to start over."

Clayton fell silent. Watched an open-topped double-decker bus go by, bristling with soccer fans. Hooray for their team. "I don't ever want to live my life over again," he said.

Louise had warned Hendershot not to push it, but here he was, first day of the trip, harassing the kid. *Old hockey players never die,* he thought, *they just skate away. Or fall down.* He moved in close. "Clayton, they don't have you on pills, do they?"

"No."

"You'd tell me if they had you on pills."

"I guess so."

He put his arm around the boy's shoulders but Clayton shrugged it off. "Not here, Dad. People will think we're gay."

Hendershot shoved his hands deep into his pockets. "Look, maybe this isn't such a great idea. Kind of morbid, really. I don't even know if she's still alive. Maybe we should just do the tourist thing until the trial. We could go up in the dome at St. Paul's. There's the Tate, Madame Tussaud's. I've got a list. All the places I never got to see when I was here."

"I don't mind doing this, Dad. I like it. It's more fun than..." He took off his glasses and cleaned them on his shirt. Hendershot couldn't remember when the kid got glasses. Before the stitches? After?

"More fun than what?"

"...being at home." Settled, Clayton's glasses rode his broken nose off-kilter.

"What exactly is wrong with being at home, son? Besides the school thing?" Because everything was a thing. Marriage, separation, love, violence. A thing. Things.

Clayton bit his lip. A *new* thing. When had he become a lip-biter? "Is Julian going to move in with Mum and me when we get back?"

Something went wrong with Hendershot's hands. They escaped his pockets and flew around like a magician's, fumbling a card trick. "Is that what that whole thing was about, Clayton? Your mum and me?"

"Not all of it."

"What part?"

The boy aimed his face up the street. People scurried past. He said, "We could do the tourist thing in the mornings, and the nostalgically depressed thing in the afternoons."

"Clayton."

"I don't want to talk about it, Dad." In profile he looked like his mother. Except for the lumpy nose. Otherwise, high forehead, strong chin. Classical. But face to face, he was enough Hendershot's son to make the father grateful. Not a bad-looking boy. Hendershot knew what others claimed to see, but what looked back at him was a regular kid. A little thin, maybe, wide in the beak, but the eyes were honest. Uncertain, that's all. Guards at the gate. Let you in if you knew the password. "I know what I said on the plane," Clayton said, "but I don't want to talk about it. Some people are made to talk about things and some people aren't. Can't we just *not* talk about them? Can't we just *be* here?"

"We are here, son."

Clayton pointed at the map. "Right here, Dad. This is us. That was you. And then you ran up Minories Street." His logic was unflinching.

A woman stepped out of the stream of pedestrians. Fuzzy blue housecoat, shower cap, carpet slippers. Plastic cup in her hand. "Spare change?" She was grinning into a loopy, uncertain future. Clayton dropped a handful of coins into her cup. "Fank you very much," she whispered.

The boy's generosity shamed the man. "Okay," Hendershot said. "Let's walk."

On the way, Clayton asked, "When you were running with the money, did you *feel* like a thief?"

"Wow, son." Hendershot had to think about that. "Yeah. Half a thief anyway."

"What did the other half feel like?"

"Stupid," Hendershot said.

People passed them. A man in a muscle shirt pushed a baby carriage, triceps like bridge cables. Wrist straps studded with rivets. *Another dad and his kid on a trip*, Hendershot thought. But then saw there was no baby. The carriage was full of magazines.

"Did you ever steal anything else?" Clayton asked.

Hendershot told him about the jackknife, buried but not forgotten. And a time before that when his older brother Lyle led him into a hardware store where Hendershot kept Mr. Ferguson talking about fishing rods while Lyle skulked the aisles, pocketing a box of chalk, a carpenter's plumb bob, a pair of pliers and a baseball. Which Mr. Ferguson saw and reported to their father who believed in honesty, honour and the RCAF motto *Per Ardua ad Astra* – *Through Adversity to the Stars*. Both boys were put to work sorting lumber for Mr. Ferguson. For free, because their father didn't want to raise any Al goddamn Capones.

"I've never stolen anything," Clayton said.

"Whoa. There's a heartbreak."

"Be serious Dad."

"I try to be."

"No, you don't. Mum says you're never serious. She says you're flippant."

"Nostalgically flippant?"

"And angry. You're always angry. You're always mad."

"Am I?"

Was he? Walking beside Clayton brought back the feeling of being in a foreign country, the place where everything had changed. What they were doing here, actually *doing*, suddenly struck him. Starting at his knee. Which for reasons of its own was throbbing. They came to a pub, green sign, gold lettering, *The Lion's Mane*. Of course. That's what the name had been. *The Lion's Mane*.

Hendershot felt a beer coming on. Looked in through the window. Empty tables, TV above the bar. And on the screen, a face. Took his breath away.

Connor Mack. Bearded, older, bald. But Connor Mack, all the same.

He turned away, shaken. Looked again. The picture had

changed into a newscaster. Blonde woman behind a glass-topped desk. The scene shifted to mud slides. People searching through rubble and broken palm trees.

"Here's the alley, Dad," Clayton called. Hendershot stumbled toward the opening between the two buildings. Graffiti gone now, new bricks – or the old ones scrubbed clean. He felt disoriented. But it had been Connor, all right. Adrenalin set his limbs on fire. *Welcome to Old Ghost Tours*, he told himself. At the same time, he felt strangely fearful. Ahead of him, Clayton stopped. "Are you okay, Dad?"

"Just short of dandy."

"Mum says sometimes you're like Uncle Lyle." Cut off from the traffic, Clayton's voice echoed off the walls.

In his pockets, Hendershot's fists clenched. "Uncle Lyle was a heroin addict, son. He once pimped for a hermaphrodite stripper. Went to prison. Owes me seven thousand dollars. When we were kids, he stuffed a syrup can with mice and shot it full of holes with his twenty-two. How am I like Uncle Lyle?"

"You were a thief, Dad."

"*Were*, Clayton. Key word. *Were, was*. Everybody's a *were* or a *was* at some time."

"Even Uncle Lyle, Dad." Clayton's voice dropped. "Even me."

Hendershot's hands got loose, galloped around in the air. Clayton backed off. In his eyes, fear. The thought that his own son might be afraid of him made Hendershot afraid. "Clayton, have I ever hurt you?"

"No." The boy studied the ground. "But you *could*, Dad."

Hendershot's knee was singing now. Blast from the past. Where the gap between the buildings opened into the lane, he saw a little park. A couple of trees behind a fence, a few shrubs, two benches. They followed the path inside, sat down. "We are experiencing minor turbulence," Hendershot said. A new gag, but Clayton didn't laugh. Hendershot rolled up his pantleg to adjust the straps. As he did, three pubescent girls paraded by; one eyed Clayton and whispered to her friends. Clayton stood in front, as a screen. Three heads swiveled as they passed, giggling. Got a good look at Hendershot's leg architecture: skeletal minimalism, metal rod diminishing from the severed tibia like a kabob skewer sticking out of a sausage. Skinny beyond fleshlessness. Naked as a tent pole. And ending in a sporty running shoe.

"Dad," Clayton said. "Do you want to go back to the hotel?"

"Not yet."

"Put your feet – foot – up?"

"In a while." And then, fishing for sympathy, forgiveness, whatever: "You know, Clayton, sometimes I blame other people for things that were my own fault."

"Everybody does that, Dad."

"Good to know."

The alley led them to streets whose names he remembered, warehouses he thought he recognized. But they took a wrong turn at the corner of St. Mark's and North Tenter, where two workmen in fluorescent vests were laying paving stones around a fire hydrant. Sand, shovels, rakes, a wooden mallet the size of a bucket. One guy telling the other that the man responsible for the ruination of the country was Lord Fucking Fansley. "Same bloke what paid the Americans three million pounds to buy back a British company." Seeing them, the workman paused. Hendershot asked him what had happened to the old bank building across the road. "Wrecking ball," the workman said.

And then they were at the end of the street where Pogo and Sasquatch had re-arranged his life. Gone was the import/export company, gone the corrugated steel doors. Now the place was a multi-level concrete car-park. In a kiosk a man in a turban eyed them suspiciously.

They stood side by side, taking the place in. Hendershot

surveyed the dead-end alley, tried to re-create for Clayton what it had looked like twenty-two years ago. Couldn't. Looked down at the puckered scar on the boy's head. "Clayton," he said gently, "can you tell me what you had in mind when you took that knife to school?"

The boy didn't look at him. "Not yet," he said, his father's son. "In a while, maybe. Right now, we go that way." Pointing.

The pedestrian subway was a dank tunnel seeping water. At the bottom of the steps a stained mattress. Bottles, bags, newspapers. Up and out landed them on the High Street, a wall of lorries, cars, scooters. Crowds pushed along the sidewalk. The mad or homeless stood in doorways or curbside: a blind man torturing bagpipes, a woman in red waving a cross, a man in army fatigues standing to attention. Hendershot walked in a daze. Thought he'd seen these people before. Thought he might've been one of them.

A short walk and Clayton tugged his sleeve. "We turn here, Dad." Off the broad thoroughfare, roaming narrow streets. Sooty bricks, crooked chimneys. Rusted wrought-iron fences, row houses, streets tipping away into a jagged grin under a sun smudged by rain. Horizon like the backdrop for a black-and-white movie about the monster that toppled London. Clayton walked close, his shoulder touching Hendershot's arm. Tall flat blocks watched them pass. Balconies cluttered with clotheslines and bicycles. Graffiti on the walls, swollen lettering, THE NEUTRAL ZONE WUZ HERE. FUNKY NATION. And names. Indecipherable. On the corner the sign on a cinderblock bunker: HOPETOWN SALVATION ARMY CENTRE. Hendershot didn't remember it being there.

In fact, parts of his memory were shot. In Brick Lane, men in Muslim caps and Sikhs in turbans pushed racks of clothing, carried boxes, bags, carpets, tarps, rolls of cloth. *Importers-Exporters. Cash and Carry. Sami and Samil Pty, Ltd.*

Horns beeped. Scarcely room for one vehicle to pass. Hendershot recalled a different bustle from twenty-two years ago. Or maybe he didn't. On side streets, covered head to ankles, Muslim mothers stood like Madonnas outside their flat blocks, watching their English sons dribble footballs in a vacant lot. Farther along a low brick building, blue glass over the entrance, METROPOLITAN POLICE. With a door in the alley for packing in the prisoners.

Hendershot caught himself sweating.

"Dad? This is it."

The street. Shabby, familiar, the two-storey brick flats rose in front of him. Or crumbled. Apartments abandoned, broken-windowed, plywood-boarded. Roof tiles lay shattered, window sashes sagged. Doors once loud and primary red, yellow and blue now hung flaked like old skin. Lepers. Painted lips over toothless holes.

Margaret's door was nailed shut. The brass *Uncle Tom's Cobbler and All* door-knocker gone, doorknob missing. He led Clayton around the side where the studio used to be. Down steps made from railroad ties, into the close where Margaret had grown roses, now a home for weeds and a rusty baby carriage. Hendershot felt like a stranger not only to the place but to the young man he used to be. Asked himself if he really shot a tennis ball against that wall.

Somehow, he'd miscalculated. Years separated him and his past – and the people who'd been there with him. What had made him think that the time and gravity that'd worked him over, hadn't worked them over, too? Yet here he was outside Margaret's flat expecting that it would've stayed the same. That the marigolds would be in the window box. The little clay face of Kilroy.

"There used to be..." he told Clayton, then stopped himself. *There used to be* was in danger of becoming his current mantra. Middle-aged guy always looking back over his shoulder and running into – what? He supposed he'd find out. He led Clayton back around to the front, where one of the panes in the upstairs window hadn't been broken. And despite himself said, "That's where Mister Green used to sit."

"Let's look, Dad." Already Clayton was picking his way through the weeds and broken glass, into the alcove where the stairs led up to Mister Green's landing.

The door to the flat was gone, replaced by boards nailed criss-cross over the entrance. Hendershot and Clayton stood with their toes at the doorsill's edge. The floorboards and joists of Mister Green's sitting room had heeled and sunk, leaving the room an empty well. Down below, Margaret's claw-foot bath tub lay in pieces. Broken porcelain legs like the bones of an extinct animal. Mister Green's window pane was the only thing intact. Dusty, cob-webbed.

"That's where they found him, right Dad?"

"Yeah." But it wasn't a memory. He'd been in hospital when Constable Mayhew had given him the news. Hendershot didn't believe it at first. Didn't believe Constable Mayhew was real, at first. But he was. Clean-shaven young copper, all spit and polish but genuinely upset at finding the dead old man leaning back in his armchair, facing the window, binoculars in hand. Like an astronaut waiting for lift-off. Now, looking at that window, Hendershot wondered what corner of the universe his friend Mister Green was investigating. What notes was he scribbling in his notebook? The one Mayhew claimed they never found.

In the rubble he looked for ghosts. But the only one he managed to conjure up was Margaret. The way she'd been the first time he met her. Cardigan, baggy sweatpants, corkscrew hair, energy. And those eyes. Where are you, Margaret? he wondered.

Clayton scuffed his foot, sent a nail spinning into the hole. Tinkle of glass, puff of dust.

"Let's get out of here," Hendershot said.

6.

They indulged in distractions. A film crew shooting a Dickens scene in Trafalgar Square. Buckingham Palace changing the guard, hundreds watching and one fan in jogging shorts waving a flag, cooing "Oooo, aren't they marvelous!" British Museum, where Egyptian mummies curled up behind glass. Anglo-Saxon battle helmets. Statues, crockery, carvings and clothing, history's lost-and-found.

Back at the hotel, an ancient man in tarnished black knelt at the fireplace, sifting through a bag of curled papers. Lit the fire in the grate, moving with antiquarian deliberation. The same old man had emerged that morning from a room marked PRIVATE and spoken Italian to a woman in a cook's apron and the teenaged girl who waited tables in the dining room. Hendershot thought of all three as generational, related to the white-haired manager. He imagined they'd traded a sunny Tuscan paradise for this dilapidated English hotel. What had brought them here? Family loyalty? Whatever it had been, Hendershot admired them for it.

"Look, Dad." From the rack of tourist pamphlets Clayton plucked a theatre brochure. H.G. Wells' *The Invisible Man.*

"You sure you want to see this one? We saw it on video when you came to stay over...when was it...Thanksgiving?"

"I read the book," Clayton said. "Julian gave it to me for my birthday."

"I guess Julian doesn't know they've filmed a few versions." Hendershot was embarrassed to resort to pitiable one-upmanship, but he couldn't stop. "Three, if I'm not mistaken."

Clayton studied the brochure. "This is a live play, Dad. How will they make him invisible in a live play? Can we go and see? Or not see, as the case may be."

A boy of modest requests. Irony a new feature in his conversation. Normally the kid suffered from too much civility. Something the school counsellors, principals, and psychiatrists seemed to overlook. Trotting out their labels and syndromes which Hendershot only vaguely understood. In Hendershot's view, Clayton was polite. Civilized. And like the meek (*who would NEVER inherit the earth*, Hendershot thought), the boy expected others to be polite too. And was disappointed when they weren't.

Hendershot phoned. He had to turn sideways in the hallway to let a family squeeze by. Parents, teenage daughter, all of them large. The daughter's hair was purple, a wire brush permanently startled. She was chewing gum. The mother and father talked. "You got the camera?"

"I got the camera."

"You got the tickets?"

"I got the tickets."

The daughter snapped her gum. "Melony, how many times?" The girl sulked. Eye makeup applied with a boot brush, though the eyes themselves were hazel, streaked with light. *God*, those eyes asked, *will this never end?*

Hendershot shrugged: *Hang in there.*

He reserved tickets. Clayton said they could walk. "It's not far, Dad. One and a half kilometres."

"How do you know how far it is?"

"I measured it." The boy pointed to a map pinned under glass beside the brochure rack. The city's streets fanned out in bright colours. "Down Southampton, then Kingsway, along Aldwych."

"Son, where were you twenty-two years ago?"

They stepped into the darkened street. "I like walking with you, Dad."

"Yeah? How come?"

"You go just fast enough."

"It's the leg."

"And you notice stuff."

"Like what?"

"People, cars, buildings, trees. You even read the posters people stick up on walls. You notice everything, Dad."

"Except maps, son. And not everything. Sometimes I'm plain stunned."

Clayton spoke with precocious wisdom. "It sure *seems* like you notice everything. And that's what counts."

"What do you mean, *counts?*"

"If you seem like you're paying attention, then people think you're *aware*. But if you're not *aware*, they think you're weird. And if you're weird, they pick on you."

"Do people think you're weird, son?"

"Most of the time."

"Do they pick on you?"

"Most of the time."

They passed a take-away and bought chips in cones of white paper. "They used to wrap them in newspapers," Hendershot said. "Health issue now, I suppose. Everything's an issue now."

"Julian says carcinogens are all around us."

"He must be a great comfort, that Julius."

"Julian."

"Right."

Now the streets teemed with people. Watching them from shadowy doorways, the homeless crouched or lay on pieces of foam, coffined in cardboard, their pleas seeping knee high out of the dark: "Spare change?" Skeletal people, their scrawniness swathed in sweaters and anoraks, age and sex swaddled to irrelevancy. Stretching out hands, hats, plastic cups at the river of people flowing by.

Clayton handed out coins until he had no more.

"You can't give to everybody, son."

"Did you ever beg for money, Dad?"

"Once. I didn't like it. I'd been told there'd be jobs." At a crossing, they waited for a line of taxis. "Hey, here's one. *Casablanca.* When Claude Raines tells Humphrey Bogart there are no waters in the desert. Do it, son."

"Here?" In the crush of people and the traffic's rush.

"Sure."

Clayton worked up saliva and delivered in perfect Bogie, "I was mish-informed."

"Exactly." Hendershot clapped his son on the shoulder. "I was mish-informed."

7.

Second row seats, a short leap to the stage and the worn threads on the curtain's edge. Magic's tattered hem. He hoped his son wasn't disappointed. At home in his video store, Hendershot rented out fantasy and dreams on tape or DVD. The grand old Hollywood classics and B-movie favourites, subtitled foreign gems and obscure cult hits. Six dollars apiece, two for ten bucks. Weekend specials. Black and white, colour, Panavision, Vista Vision, Cinemascope. Reformatted or letter-boxed. Academy award winners, festival jewels, runners-up, also-ran's. He had them all, floor to ceiling in the tiny shop. *Rewinds*, he called the place.

The play worked.

Black light and makeup dissolved Griffin, the mad scientist. The actor took off his hat and gloves, unwound his mummy wrappings from his too solid head to reveal: nothing. Even Hendershot, the old-movie buff, was startled. Next to him, Clayton searched for the flaw in the effect, found none. The invisible man was not; the invisible man was.

On the way home, Clayton said he wanted to be invisible.

"What would you do then, son?"

"Disappear."

"Goes without saying."

"No, I mean I'd disappear. People wouldn't find me, I'd find them. When I wanted to. You. Mum. Granddad. Only the people I wanted to see would see me. All other times I'd disappear."

"What about Jul – Julian?"

"He's not so bad, I guess. Kind of anal. Like when he stays over, he puts stuff away when you haven't finished using it, peanut butter and stuff. But he's okay. He's not a perv or anything."

"He stays over?"

"Sometimes."

"What's he talk about?"

"Baseball."

"*Baseball?*"

"Not all the time. Sometimes he talks about his patients. Like about gall bladders and ruptured spleens and that. But not much. Him and Mum talk about politics and music. But mostly he talks about baseball."

"Jesus."

"You used to talk about hockey, Dad."

"In a generalized way."

"You used to say that when the NHL had only six teams –"

"Okay, okay. But baseball? Statistics, I bet. RBI's, batting averages – your mum puts up with that?"

"He knows when she wants him to stop."

"What'd he say about that business at school?"

"He says it's good to talk about these things."

"And is it?" Jealousy constricted Hendershot's voice. This boy, his flesh-and-blood, telling a stranger, a miner of people's innards, what he wouldn't tell his own dad?

"I don't want to talk to anybody about it, Dad."

"I'm here, you know."

"I know."

Night dropped over the city. Near the British Museum, a young woman beside a brazier sold them roasted chestnuts. They strolled, cracked hot chestnuts with scalded fingers. A block away from the hotel, Clayton said, "Can I run once around the park by myself?"

"Now?"

"Yeah."

"Jeez, Clayton. There are muggers, pickpockets, perverts, who knows? What would I tell your mother?"

"Just around the perimeter, outside the fence."

"I thought I was the perfect walking partner."

"A run, Dad. By myself. There's nobody around."

"Ten million people in this city, Clayton. It only takes one."

"Around the park, Dad."

"And meantime what do I do?"

"Go back to the hotel."

"Or wait here."

"You could watch me from the window."

"Or from right here."

"I don't want you to follow me, Dad."

"And I don't want to wake your mother up at five a.m. to have a long-distance shouting match about abduction and murder."

"I can run, Dad. I'll be all right."

"Oh yeah. Nobody's ever said that before."

Clayton kicked the pavement. "Shit."

"Watch your language."

"You're just like Mum."

"Not quite. I don't want to marry a knife jockey."

"She's always watching me."

"She wants to protect you."

"Out of the corner of her eye. Even when I'm watching TV. She won't let me do anything."

"That's not true. She let you come on this trip."

"Yeah, only because I promised."

"Promised what?"

"That I'd phone her if you started acting like your usual self."

"What usual self?"

"You know, Dad. Like if you try to pick up women and

that. And then leave me by myself."

The kid thinks he knows, Hendershot thought. As if Clayton had been there at all the negotiations when he and Louise met on neutral ground. Not only hammering out divorce proceedings, a peace treaty signed in blood and recriminations, but also considering the fate of their son. The shy, kindly boy apparently turned monster. Who deserved some kind of explanation.

"I'm not going to pick up women, son. Your mother's got this idea I run around impersonating a randy goat. I don't. Too old, for one thing. But I don't want to watch you all the time either. The question is, what do *you* want?"

"I want to run around the park, Dad."

"Then do it. But I'm going to wait for you over there by that tree." The boy started to move. "Clayton?"

"Yeah."

"Can you still whistle with your fingers? Like I showed you?"

"Yeah."

"You get in trouble, you whistle."

"Okay."

Hendershot watched the boy jog away under the shadows of trees. Shadow of a shadow. Then the kid was gone.

The noise just under Hendershot's ears was his heart pounding.

8.

That night, lying in their narrow beds, a scratching in the dark. A bedraggled mouse in the metal waste basket. Clayton turned on the light, set it free, watched it scamper to its hole in the wainscotting. Back in his bed, he said, "If she's an artist, Dad, she must be on a list somewhere. Even if she's hiding. Even if she's invisible."

"I wouldn't bet on that, son."

"At school Mrs. Lipinski says artists who have exhibitions get listed somewhere. Like by the government or an academy or something."

"Is that a fact?"

"Mrs. Lipinski's had two exhibitions. One was in Ottawa."

"Tell you what, Clayton. If I do my best to find her, you do your best to tell me what happened at school."

Clayton breathed for a while on his side of the room: "*If* you find her, I'll tell you."

"What are we son, rug traders?"

"Pretty much," Clayton said.

9.

Inside the phone booth, Clayton opened his hand. "Only two left and that man's back again."

Older guy, nose like a light bulb. Head-to-toe tweed. Rapping sharply on the glass with his umbrella handle. Shouting. Hendershot cupped an ear. The man's spit showered the glass. "I've lodged a complaint! Thirty-seven minutes! Bloody outrageous!" Held up his wristwatch inches from Hendershot's face so they could both see the second hand ratchet down "...three, two, one! Thirty-eight minutes!" Cratered nose ready to explode.

Hendershot flashed him a thumb's up, checked his list. Catalogue of diminishing returns. "Just one more," he grinned. Cheery. Punched in the numbers, signaled Clayton to drop in the coins. But the woman at the other end said the West Kensington Society of Neo-Impressionists for Single Women over Forty-Five didn't know the current whereabouts of Margaret Lowenstein or the location of her painting *Victory*. Which made her the twenty-seventh artist's society, association, academy or council to give Hendershot that information.

As they left the phone box, Mister Nose said, "Common bloody courtesy."

"Absolutely," Hendershot said. "Sorry. It's all yours."

10.

They went for lunch. Café tricked out to resemble a 1950's American diner. Elvis Presley, Marilyn Monroe, James Dean etched into the mirrors. Service counter the front end of a '57 Chev. Burgers, shakes, fries.

Between bites Hendershot confessed, "There's no end to this, son. You gotta wonder what I was thinking."

"You didn't know, Dad."

"Good words for a tombstone: *He Didn't Know*."

"We've got to keep looking, that's all."

His son. Narrow-shouldered, curly-haired, eyes burning. Happy to be on the trail of something, *anything*, even a needle-in-a-haystack treasure hunt five thousand miles from home.

"You seem pretty confident, Clayton."

"I think Ms Lowenstein will be happy to see you."

"Oh yeah? Why's that."

"She put you in her painting."

"She put all kinds of stuff in her paintings. Trees, fire hydrants, a dead rat. She might not remember me." Hendershot said this calmly, but a north wind blew through his innards.

Clayton fiddled with his napkin and asked if she'd been his father's girlfriend.

"No." The feeling of regret taking him by surprise. "She was a lot older than me. She said that made all the difference. Turns out she was right. Hey," Hendershot said. "Here's one. Marlon Brando, *On the Waterfront*. Back seat of a cab with his brother."

Clayton tilted his eyebrows. Lifted the chin, nasal delivery: " 'I coulda bin a contender'."

"That's it, man. Coulda bin a contender."

"Maybe you still are, Dad."

"Yeah? Tell your mum that and see what she says."

The kid bit his hamburger, chewed, swallowed. "I'm not trying to be amusingly cynical, Dad."

"What?"

"A tendency towards verbal irony. That's what Mum says. I have that tendency."

"Jesus Christ." He imagined Julius, Julian, handing Louise a book. *Child Care for Dummies.*

"I'm serious, Dad."

"So am I."

"So tell me something serious," Clayton said, serious himself.

Warning horn in Hendershot's head. Alarm in a submarine, *wa-oogah, dive! Dive!* Serious? Serious made you think, thinking led to decisions and decisions – well – trouble, uncertainty. The trial of Connor Mack. But the boy wanted something and all Hendershot could offer him was the truth.

"The real reason I got cut from that team in Scotland wasn't because I hurt my knee. They cut me because I wasn't good enough. Replaced me with a guy who was better. Each team was allowed three imports, non-British. Gervais looked like a hit-man for the mob. Skated like a dream. Scored goals. So it was hello Gervais, good-bye Hendershot." He gulped his tea. "Margaret Lowenstein saved my bacon."

Clayton sat very still. "What do you look like in her painting, Dad?"

"No idea. I was in hospital when she finished it. On painkillers most of the time." He remembered the hospital bed, barred on the side like a baby's crib. Margaret in the chair beside it. Chin on the top railing. Hand covering his.

"Mum said you were her best patient. She said of all the people on her ward, you were the one who never complained."

"Pills. Permanent buzz. For a week I didn't even know my leg was gone."

"She said," Clayton spoke shyly, "that when you found the envelope under your pillow you cried."

"It was a lot of money. A fortune in those days. Enough for a plane ticket home."

"Did Ms Lowenstein ever visit you again?"

"No. By the time I was in rehab, she was long gone. Went to India, I think. And anyway, I was with your mum and there was all that confusion about Mister Green so..."

"You didn't bother."

"I'm as lazy and selfish as the next guy, son."

Clayton took this in. For him, a big deal. Shouldn't have been, he was too young. But big-dealness was part of his birthright. Of Louise's three pregnancies, he was the only one who came to term. Popped out squalling into the delivery room, where Hendershot clumsily cradled him. Wonder-struck. The little gaffer's eyes: *What a kid*, he'd thought. *Knows something already.* Didn't want to let him go, but laid him on Louise's breast anyway. "Oh, Rob," she'd whispered. "He's lovely."

That same kid. Across from him now in this restaurant. Grown-up, almost. Hair, face, those eyes. Other people thought there was something wrong with him. There wasn't. He was thin-skinned, that's all. Intense, that's all.

And he was talking. "...she'd remember doing that painting, wouldn't she, Dad? She'd remember *you*." Because it was important to him. His old man couldn't be a nobody. Could he? "I mean if she finished the painting and did it right, she wouldn't rip it up or change it."

"Not Margaret. If she did it right, she wouldn't change

anything. Not even for money."

Clayton nodded. Looked out the café window where traffic sat bumper to bumper in the rain. A woman collapsed an umbrella and stepped into a cab. "That's the thing," he said to the window. "When you do something right you don't have to change it. You don't have to do it again." His eyes swung to Hendershot's. "Have you ever done something that right, Dad?"

"I married your mum. We had you."

"I don't mean like birthdays or Father's Day, Dad. I mean like a painting or something."

"I'm not an artist, son."

"I mean something you're good at." Waiting. Pulling his father into unknown country. Looking for a guide, when Hendershot wasn't sure he was one. Life of mediocrity, perpetual fourth-liner. Flunked hockey, low marks in the marriage/fatherhood biz, fabulous career as Mister Average. He was about to tell his son nothing was perfect when he remembered.

Hockey game. Killing a penalty, tried for a breakaway. Raced to the opposition blue line where a defenseman hip-checked him just above the knees. Flew over the defenseman's back, puck drifting below. Landed belly first, laid the stick's shaft flat, tapped the puck into the net. Not, he realized, the stuff of legend. But at the time, magical. "Call it luck," he told Clayton, "but while it was happening my body knew what to do. I didn't have to think. Probably nobody remembers that play but me. But it's like the pathway's still there, you know? Like an electric circuit. If you hip-checked me today, my body would know what to do. I don't know if *I* could do it, but my body would still know what to do." Embarrassment shut him up. Still, Clayton waited. "What about you, son? Ever do something like that?"

Clayton licked his lips. "Yeah. What I did at school."

Hendershot's throat tightened. "What at school?"

"Franklin Burroughs and that."

"The knife."

"Yeah."

"You think what you did was right?"

"Yeah."

He had to be cautious. "A lot of people say what you did was wrong, son."

"I know that. But they weren't there, Dad. They don't know."

Hendershot didn't know either. He wanted to hear his son's version. Details. Who held the knife and how, which way the blade was turned, what its intention was. But Clayton's face was closing. The boy frowned, tightened his lips.

"This other kid," Hendershot said, "this...Whatsisname."

"Franklin Burroughs."

"What's he like?"

"Fat. And tall. Taller than you, Dad. He's only fifteen years old and he's taller than you. He weighs two hundred and eighty-three pounds."

"Lotta meat."

"He looks like a Sumo wrestler. Even his eyelids are fat. He's got a gang."

"He needs a gang?"

"He calls them his posse."

"Oh yeah? What do they do, this posse?"

"Sometimes they sell dope, stereo speakers, you know. Stuff they steal."

"And what does the principal say about all this?"

"Mr. Pritchard doesn't know, Dad. He sits in his office all day."

"And the other teachers?"

Clayton shrugged. "Teachers go home after school. What are they going to do, follow Fat Frank all over the place?"

Fat Frank was promising. "Is that what you call him? Fat Frank?"

"That's what everybody calls him. Not to his face though."

As a kid, when his father was out of work and dragged the family from one dead-end job to another, Hendershot had attended five different schools in two years. Always the new kid on the playground. House rules: fight or go under. Bullies pushed him to terror. At first, he spat out obscenities, but when *cock-walloping dick-licking sonofabitch* didn't work, he tried kicking and gouging. Usually lost the fight but gained a reputation: Scrappy Little Bugger. As a way of life, Scrappy Little Bugger wasn't all that reliable, but he couldn't think of anything else. What Clayton needed was a crash course in How to Kick Ass. As taught by a guy with one leg.

"There are ways to deal with guys who pick on you."

"He doesn't pick *on* you, Dad, he *picks* you."

"I get it, son."

"No, you don't." In his chair, Clayton transformed himself into a two-hundred-and-eighty-three-pound machine. Sitting very still. Eyes like stones. Jaw clenched. Whispering lovingly, "Hennn-derr-shawwwt!" Finger pointed, then curled into a fist and laid with terrible tenderness against his other palm.

"Okay. Creepy."

"That's the thing, Dad. And you won't know when or where. Washroom, upper hall, change room downstairs. Mezzanine, if there's nobody lifting weights in there. Somewhere nobody sees. His posse pins you against a wall so he can hit you. In the stomach, ribs, balls...someplace it won't show. If you pay him, he stops."

"He did these things to you?"

"Lots of times."

"Why didn't you tell me?"

"You'd already moved out."

"What about your mum... Julian, for god's sake."

"I couldn't."

"Why not?"

"Because if I did, Fat Frank would kill me."

The kid was serious. Made Hendershot feel like a parent. Practically grown-up. "Son, why would he want to kill you?"

"Because I can run."

"Good reason. *He can run, I think I'll kill him.* Come on, Clayton."

Clayton cupped his hot chocolate in both hands. "In Phys.Ed. we had to do this run. The length of the gym, pick up a bean bag, run back. I got the best time. So Mr. Kuznetsov made me do it again and he told everybody I had good form and to watch me. Then we all ran again, except Fat Frank, because he *can't* run, Dad."

"And for that he wants to kill you?"

"He said he would."

"Everybody says that. *I'm gonna kill ya.* Doesn't mean they'll do it."

"But he does, Dad."

"Come on, Clayton."

"He makes them dead. Same thing."

"I'm losing you here, son."

Clayton took a breath. "This kid at school, Rajinder Singh? He used to wear this cloth on top of his head because he wasn't old enough for a turban. Like it's his religion or something. Fat Frank picked him, like I showed you. Said Raj was a fag, said he had a Kotex on his head. That's how Fat Frank does it. He finds that one thing. Then his posse knows it, and then the whole school knows it. They called Raj Fag Boy. Or the Kotex Kid. Raj told Fat Frank to leave him alone. He told him he wasn't a fag. So one day they found a used tampon in the girls' washroom and after school, behind the backstop in the upper field, they made him eat a tampon hot-dog. Then on Monday Raj didn't come to school and his uncle found his brand new leather jacket folded up on the sidewalk in the middle of the 9th Street bridge."

Clayton's hands were shaking. He pinned his cup of hot chocolate to the table. Hendershot imagined his son's jacket neatly folded on a traffic bridge over dark and oily water. And couldn't tell if what instantly constricted his chest was sorrow or rage. Something complicated and ancient. Paleolithic.

"I know what you're gonna say," Clayton said. "Why don't we fight back or why don't we get a bunch of friends and beat the shit out of him or tell the principal –"

"All possibilities, son." Hendershot felt battle-worn, scarred, fatherly. "Why don't you?"

"Because that's old school, Dad. That might've worked back in the day but it doesn't work now."

"Who says?"

"I can't fight him. He's huge, he's got a posse. And I don't have a bunch of friends. All I've got is Hubert Belinski and he's a bigger wuss than I am. And if I told the principal all that would happen is Fat Frank and I would get stuck in the counsellor's office with a peer mediator and Mrs. Stemholtz and we'd discuss our *issues* for a hundred hours and then we'd *devise an action plan* and *outcomes* and sign a *mediation contract* and when it was all over Fat Frank would bust my ass anyway. And if I told you, you'd get mad and grab a baseball bat and do something stupid and get arrested. And then Mum would get mad and say 'See, violence doesn't solve anything' and Julian would tell me I can talk to him about my problems." The boy's lip quivered but he didn't cry. "I don't want problems, Dad. I just want to be left alone."

Hendershot didn't say anything. Against his better judgement. Or maybe because of it. The kid had a solid grievance and Hendershot wasn't sure what to do about it. So they sat.

Outside, the rain had stopped. A brassy light from the sky. "Hey," Hendershot said, "today's Sunday."

"So?"

"Time for a tourist thing."

"We don't have to, Dad."

"Sure we do. Come on." He was slow getting up. "I know a place," he said.

Because, he told himself, *the kid deserves a reward for being honest. For being brave enough to be honest. There are things we can set aside for a while – Fat Frank, Julian, Margaret, painting, knife, trial, leg.*

11.

Petticoat Lane. Open air market, world in miniature. Booths like carnival stalls lining both sides of the streets and adjacent alleys. The bustle of crowds, the beggars and buyers, holiday cheer. Vendors crying their wares. "Crazy, cray-zee prices!" "Wool skirts! Five pound straight off the rack!" Plus the IRA seemed to leave it alone. Nigel and Tony would've been pleased. Partial peace in their time.

"There's everything here," Clayton said. At a stall he bargained for a T-shirt, a key chain, a Union Jack tea towel and a ceramic beer mug etched with hounds and horses. "Tally-ho," he said, and calculated that by Westminster Book Store prices he'd saved three pounds. The woman who sold him the souvenirs glanced at his open wallet and when she said, "You'll want ter be careful round 'ere, luv. Keep an eye out for pock-pickets," they laughed conspiratorially.

They prowled the place. Saw a man with two plastic milk crates set up a pitch in the middle of the crowd. One crate to sit on, one to display the jewellery. "You got yer necklace, yer spangler, yer bracelet, fourteen karat gold, ten pound for the lot." Three sales in less than a minute, till the lookout behind him hissed, "Pack it in" as two constables rounded a corner. Farther along, a bearded man with a megaphone preached Jesus while next to him a bratwurst vendor lobbed wads of greasy paper at his head.

"Jesus loves you."

"Does he? Then he must be a poof."

Under an awning, a crockery salesman juggled bone

china off his forearms and elbows. Where the booths petered out, bobbies in helmets ringed the rear entrance to a chicken processing plant against demonstrators who shouted, "Evil bastards! Don't you know how wicked them cages is?"

Two swarthy men in a warehouse doorway offered RAF sheepskin flight jackets left over from WWII. Another stall contained a pitchman demonstrating why the Veggie Matic Slicer was even better than the knife he waved around like a pirate's cutlass. "Dangerous, this is. Lop yer finger off, spurt blood all over the shop. Why take the risk when Veggie Matic can do the job?" And diced onions, tomatoes, apples and cucumbers with the simple turn of a crank.

Clayton watching, suddenly solemn. "I should get one of those."

"Your mum's already got something like it, son. Never uses it. It's probably still in the cupboard above the fridge."

"Not for her, Dad. For Fat Frank."

Hendershot was blind-sided. Former penalty killer whose job it'd been to steal the puck and keep it away from the other team. The old dipsy-doodle buttonhook faker, out-deked by his own kid. "What are you talking about, son?"

"That knife the Veggie Matic guy has..."

"...okay..."

"...is something like the one I took to school."

"Christ. You couldn't find a bazooka?"

"They're too big, Dad. Plus they're illegal."

"And a knife isn't? What was your plan, son?"

"I didn't really have one."

Like father, like son. Neither of them big on blueprints. Hendershot wasn't sure what he'd hoped for from the market visit. Or from the whole trip, for that matter. Answers, maybe. Questions, for sure. But as they climbed the cement steps and looked back down to the market, it seemed they'd lost track of something. As if they'd burst out into the world just long enough to make a grab at fun, before they ducked back inside themselves. He hoped Clayton had a place inside himself. A warm corner, shady tree, sunlit clearing – something. As a kid, Hendershot'd had the hockey rink. Where he practised alone and listened to the play-by-play in his head. Shots echoing off the boards, skates rasping the ice. The sounds of freedom.

He leaned against a wall to adjust his knee straps. "Your knife," he said. "Was it one of those black-handled German jobs from the woodblock in the kitchen?"

"Yeah."

"Good steel, but how good an idea was that, son?"

"Six outa ten, I guess." He started along the sidewalk. "It worked, though."

A wind tumbled old newspapers. A busker on a blues harp blew a lonesome train whistle at the passing cars. The rush of the city. People moving, bundled in coats, cocooned in vehicles. Meeting appointments, keeping promises. While Hendershot hobbled behind his son, *number twenty-three on your...* Trying to keep up.

Ahead of him, Clayton was stopped by a scarecrow. Tall guy in a poncho, rasta dreadlocks like felted wool, hemp bag over one shoulder, face like a saint. Handed Clayton a pamphlet.

It was a folded piece of paper creased into thirds like a home-made party invitation. Black lettering on white. The blurred photograph of the building's façade took Hendershot right back to Connor Mack's bullet head leaning out of the scaffolding: *"What're yeh doin' here? Have yeh lost yourself?"*

Clayton flattened the paper against the wind so they could both read it:

WHITECHAPEL ART GALLERY INVITES YOU

Well of course, Hendershot thought. *After all these years it would, wouldn't it.*

12.

"Margaret Lowenstein."

"And when did you say she had an exhibition here?"

"1974. March or April, I think it was."

"Oh dear. That *was* a long time ago, wasn't it?" Because for that young woman, the past was water under the bridge. Under the bridge and out to sea. But that didn't mean she wouldn't be helpful. Behind her computer screen, she adjusted glasses as thick as swim goggles. She had a calm, underwater look about her. Pale skin, black hair jelled and spiky. Goth, Hendershot, decided. Or punk. Whatever they called it. Black lipstick, black eye shadow, black fingernail polish, rings on both thumbs, a dinky barbell dangling from her lower lip. On their side of the counter, Clayton seemed naively scrubbed. Unhiply simple.

"Does your computer have access to any records?"

"Well, we've only just set up." Her fingers rattled the keyboard. "But let's just see, shall we?"

What old age was going to be, what Hendershot could look forward to: the indulgence of the young. Clayton was thumbing through a gallery brochure. A planned expansion of the premises. He was either engrossed, embarrassed or bored. Held the brochure close to his face.

"Here we are," the girl said. "March 29 to April 15. Daniel Adams, Norman Greaves, Margaret Lowenstein." Sighting Hendershot through scuba diver lenses. Blue eyes, maybe green. "We have archival material on all three artists."

Hendershot rested his elbows on the counter and spread

his hands: supplicant throwing himself on the mercy of the court. "The thing is, we're only here for a couple of weeks. Ms Lowenstein is an old friend of mine. I haven't seen her since before the exhibition. Is there an address there for her?"

The girl's face softened. Understanding bordering on pity. "We don't actually have that information. And even if we did, we probably couldn't divulge it. Privacy laws, you see." She spoke primly, as if Hendershot had wandered out of some hillbilly'd wilderness and into the big city. "You might try the Arts Council or one of the artists' associations."

Hendershot told her about the twenty-seven organizations that had no listing for Margaret Lowenstein. "She wasn't a member of any special school of painting or anything like that. She was...a free agent, I guess you'd call her."

The girl's hands hovered over the keyboard. "I'm sorry I can't be of more assistance."

And then, somewhere near Hendershot's right shoulder, Clayton's voice: "My dad's in one of her pictures."

"Pardon?" The girl smiled. Flash of kindness. Spectacular beauty. "What picture?"

Clayton told her about *Victory*. "Beowulf, you know, after he killed Grendel. My dad was the model...for Beowulf, I mean." He tipped his head at his father. Apologetic. "He was a lot younger then." He and the girl smiled at each other. Youth in cahoots against the elderly.

"That," the girl said, "is so cool." She turned to Hendershot. "Look," she said, "we have quite an archival collection here. Saturday and Sunday are the only days of the week it's open. The reading room is very small – only enough space for two researchers at a time. Normally you'd have to make an appointment a week in advance. But I saw Mr. Houghton-Browne go out and he hasn't returned. I'll just go and ask Patricia if you can pop in." She disappeared through a side door.

Hendershot leaned on the counter. "I have always," he drawled, "relied on the kindness of strangers."

"Stell-aaa!" Clayton whispered.

"Course, you're not a stranger, son." Hoping this was true.

"You gotta brag sometimes, Dad."

"I guess so. Do you brag?"

"Not much."

"At all?"

"Not really."

"Why is that?"

"Not much to brag about."

"You get good marks at school."

"Good marks don't mean squat, Dad. Everybody thinks you're a suck."

"Your mum told me you won the Milk Run."

"In my age group."

"That's pretty good. You get a ribbon?"

"I got a T-shirt."

"Better than nothing."

"Everybody says that. Mum said that."

"Well, isn't it?"

He looked at the floor. "It's got a dairy company's name on the front and a picture of a cow wearing running shoes."

"It's meant to be funny, son."

"And on the back, it says *Quiters Never Win and Winners Never Quit.*"

"You mean, quitters."

"No. They spelled it wrong. Q-u-i-t-e-r-s."

"Jesus Christ."

"You see? At school, basketball players get trophies, football players get trophies, volleyball, rugby – they all get trophies. Runners get a T-shirt with a cow on it. We don't even have a track team. We were supposed to, but then Mr.

Jocelyn went and had a heart attack and died and now nobody wants to coach. And if you wear a T-shirt with a cow on it, people moo at you in the hallway."

"Who moos at you?"

"You know who, Dad."

"You spend a lot of time worrying about that guy, Clayton."

"He's a lot to worry *about*, Dad."

"I can see that." He wondered how long they'd have to carry Fat Frank around. Now and then fatherly outrage boiled through his chest on its way to his brain. Fat Frank. That butterball bastard. Fucking squint-eyed sea mammal. Whose mother, if he had one, lay awake at night staring at the ceiling and asking *why me?* Where'd that miserable blubber butt come from? Who dropped that goddamn beluga on *Hendershot's* doorstep? He thought: *time to harpoon the prick, torpedo the sonofabitch, Das Boot the cunt to the bottom of whatever oily sea he climbed out of.*

Then he caught himself. Louise had always accused him of being overly protective. He saw now she was wrong. He was overly psychotic. His fists were clenched. He was worked up enough to climb a clock tower with a .306 tucked under his arm. When the girl came back, he took a deep breath. Noticed she wore a name tag: Miranda. The name calmed him. A little.

Miranda smiled. "If you'll just follow me?"

13.

Lowenstein, Margaret
English, 1933 -)

Brick Lane (1969)   Street scene with road workers
Oil on canvas
30 cm x 18 cm
GF Wheeldon Collection, 1969

Nigel and Tony (1973)   Heads of two young males
Pen and ink, watercolour
and gouache on laid paper
26 cm x 20 cm
P&D Galliazzo & Co Ltd, London, 1974

Goodbye Sir Walter (1974)   High-heeled shoe, lower female
Oil on canvas   leg, puddle
62 cm x 49 cm
Mrs. Faisal-Phipps collection (1975)

Lily Tarn (1974)   Supine female nude floating in
Oil on canvas   tarn viewed from above
30 cm x 30 cm
Tate Gallery, Permanent Collection (1976)

Victory (1974)   Beowulf, seated, contemplating
Oil on canvas   Grendel's arm and shoulder
78 cm x 102 cm
London City College, 1974
Midland Bank, 1975
Ridgely Collection, 1984
Estate of Trevor Tayleur-Stocking, 1989
(1)Ibrahim Yousef al Rashid, 1992

At first, he couldn't speak. The photos of the paintings were the size of matchbooks. At a distance, they were dabs of colour; close up they were chaos. He bent over the catalogue, tried to find Margaret in those pipsqueak reproductions. Margaret at the easel, weight on one leg. Rifling through tubes of paint. Rattling a can – looking for a brush. Fuzzing her eyes, staring. Lifting the needle on the record player. Pachelbel's *Gigue*. The smell of paint, turpentine, pots of tea. His rump numb on the bench. Goosebumps down his back. Bucket under the leaky skylight catching drips. Margaret's eyes.

He moved down the page from *Brick Lane* to *Victory* and back again. Only when their heads touched did he realize Clayton was studying them too. And in the chair next to them, a mop of hair and a scribbling pen.

"Brick Lane still looks the same, Dad."

"Yeah."

"But those two kids look tougher than you said. This guy's got a scar."

"That's Tony. Had a harelip."

"The other guy looks mad."

"He usually was."

"Boy," Clayton pointed, "look at the muscles in her leg. Is that Ms Lowenstein?"

"Could be."

"She could have been a sprinter."

"She never wore shoes like that."

"And that's her naked in the lake, huh?"

"Nothing on but the radio."

"I don't see a radio."

"Old joke."

"Ms Lowenstein sure had big boobs."

"Okay, son."

"I mean they're huge."

"It's art, Clayton."

Clayton stood back. "In art, Mrs. Lipinski says it's not just the figures in the painting that're important. It's the total composition. Like this one. The total composition's a circle, see? The lake and the trees on the horizon and the sky – it's all a big circle. Like the lake and trees and sky are the whole world. And there she is in the middle of it, floating on her back. Like her arms and legs are spread out, X marks the spot. She's the centre of everything." Clayton was getting excited. "Hey, that's why she doesn't care if anybody sees her boobs, Dad. She doesn't even care if they see the hair around her thing. Because she's the centre and that's all that matters." He took off his glasses and did something Hendershot hadn't seen him do since he was little: fluttered his nose with his fingers as if he were a mad saxophone player improvising a riff. "She's the centre," he said. "Think of that, Dad."

The mop of hair in the next chair raised itself. A whip-like woman, sharp chin and enormous purple-framed glasses. Eyes like an owl's. "Hate to intrude," she said.

"Sorry. We're being noisy."

"Absolutely." Common sense her strong suit. "Very disruptive." She rested the tip of her pen on her notebook and leaned toward Clayton standing behind Hendershot's chair. "Young man's comments rather perceptive."

Clayton ducked his head.

"Must be an art critic."

"No, I'm...I'm in grade nine."

"No idea what that means. Middle school, I suppose. Do you paint?"

"No. Well, just at school. I'm not very good though. But I like art. It's fun."

The woman nodded. Curt enough to be a declaration of war. "Excellent. Good show."

Clayton flushed. "My dad's in one of these paintings."

"Really." The woman laid down her pen, folded her hands. Short nails, no rings, no nail polish. "Which?"

Clayton showed her.

"*Victory*," the woman said. "Lowenstein. Engaging piece. In its way, controversial. Fell out of favour during the Falklands War. Main condemnation? Not enough jingoism. No uplifting Anglo-Saxon fervour. Offended the Tories. May I?" She pulled the catalogue to her and with it, Clayton. Hendershot watched from the fringe. Pride in his boy. Close to sappy. The kid seemed to know what the woman was talking about. Hendershot went along for the ride.

"You see?" She aimed her oversized glasses. "Ambivalence here. Ambiguity. Beowulf obviously a warrior. Note muscularity of chest through rent in tunic. Bruises and lacerations on face. Hands and forearms scratched and battered. Fingers like a labourer's, square, powerful, practical. Rather good, that. And see here. Scrapes along the knuckles of the right hand. Devastating blows have been delivered. Now grips Grendel's arm just above the elbow. Almost reverential. Act of determined if reluctant possession. Now. Grendel's arm and shoulder. Ripped from socket. Rended. You can hear the cartilage crack. Why? Ligaments here and here. Coiled like white worms. Against red of shredded muscle. Grey scaly skin. Lesser artist would make grotesque, blood and guts, Hollywood horror. Not she. Few meaty strands. Nice touch. Horror of it. Pain. Been torn away, you see. Death in small details. Impressions. No to slavish realism. Brush work decisive, however. Paint laid on. Texture."

"Now look here." She produced a magnifying glass. "Beowulf's face." Hendershot leaned in. Stifled a gasp. The resemblance was uncanny. She glanced at Hendershot. Accusingly. "Daddy has changed. This is beyond Daddy. But look." She handed Clayton the magnifying glass. "Around the eyes. One swollen, but even so. Look. Triumph and weariness of course. But also regret. For what? Battle over, challenge won? Or regret for promise unfulfilled – Grendel maimed, not dead. Or deeper regret – assault on moral sensibility – maiming and killing need to be repented." She watched Clayton as he studied the face through the magnifying glass. "This painting," she said, "is a good one and I'll tell you why. Raises questions. Has a touch of Mona Lisa – you know Mona? Of course, you do. Enigmatic smile. Mystery. Paradox. Smile or tarted-up smirk? We'll never know. Our ignorance allows unending fascination. Now: not suggesting this is Mona Lisa. Good god. A matter of greatness. But Beowulf *engages*. *Victory* engages. You see. Victory. And its corollary. Defeat."

Holding the magnifying glass steady, Clayton said, "He's proud and ashamed at the same time. He's happy and he's sad."

"Absolutely."

Clayton set down the glass. "Have you ever seen the real painting?"

"Many times."

"My dad hasn't."

She swiveled to face Hendershot. Her hair like cotton candy. "Incomprehensible."

"I stopped sitting for her before she finished it."

"Reason?"

"A question of time and money." He opted for the short version.

"Unacceptable." The woman frowned. "Must see it." She bent to the catalogue. "What provenance? Hm, Al Rashid. Not familiar. But here: Tayleur-Stocking. Lowenstein his second wife, I believe. He is dead. The son runs the shop." She scribbled an address on a clean sheet of paper. "Not far. Across from Spitalfields Market. TTS Gallery. Tiny place. Converted shoemaker's shop. Ask for Peter. Say Charlotte sent you."

Hendershot said, "There must be a way to thank you."

She picked up her pen. "Have to think. Perhaps one favour."

"Yes?"

"Get out." She started to write. "Sorry. Terribly pressed, you see."

14.

On the street, Clayton said how strange it was for him to see his father painted. As if the painting had made Hendershot 900 years old. "All those cuts and bruises, Dad. I could hardly recognize you."

"Neither could I." And considered not telling the boy. Why ruin it for the kid? Clayton was enjoying himself, thinking, maybe, they were in a movie. One of those old black-and-white gumshoe flicks, detectives who wore fedoras, smoked and talked tough out of the side of their mouths. *Mysteries and Murders* Hendershot called that section in his store. *Whodunits.* Except now, he knew whodunit. And clumped along the street, exaggerating his limp. Helped him generate self-pity.

Beside him, Clayton caught his mood. "What's up, Dad?" Teasing. "Nostalgically depressed?"

"Sure, why not."

"It was a long time ago. You were in shape. You've changed, that's all. You still look pretty good for..."

"...for a guy my age?"

"Well, *yeah.*"

Hendershot stopped in the middle of the sidewalk. Let the crowds and the city wash over him. "Clayton," he said, "Dat ain't it."

The kid dropped right into it – tough-guy Brooklyn: "Whaddya mean, dat ain't it?"

"I don't think that was me."

When he was surprised, Clayton's mouth didn't gape. It

shut. When Louise and Hendershot had told their son they wouldn't be a family under the same roof anymore, his mouth had slammed closed. Like a car trunk. *I got that*, his look had said. *What's next?*

"But the cuts and bruises, Dad," he said.

"Those are mine. But the face is another guy's." Grief was the last thing he expected, but there it was.

"What guy's?"

"An Irish guy's," Hendershot said.

Clayton thought for a moment. Put his hand on his father's shoulder. As if Hendershot was the kid. Or a cripple. "That was just a photograph, Dad. You can't really tell from a photograph." He paused, shy, then decisive. "We gotta see the original."

15.

Peter Tayleur-Stocking welcomed them to his shop, and said that his father had never mentioned Hendershot. Big surprise: over the years, Hendershot hadn't mentioned Tayleur-Stocking's father, either. "My father's interest centered around the artists' work and to a lesser extent around the artists themselves. Models...if you don't mind my saying so...were necessary furniture, like easels, paints, that sort of thing. A means to an end."

"My end was to make a little money. And do the artist a favour. I didn't go into the job expecting to come out a big-time headliner."

"No. Quite." Long, lean, this Tayleur-Stocking had dignity. Three-piece suit, light grey wool interwoven with fine red threads. Gave off warmth and formality. Like his father, he owned poached-egg eyes, made larger by his glasses. Face round, pale, smooth. Coppery hair clung to his skull. A comfortable Tayleur-Stocking. A *tailored-stocking'd Tayleur-Stocking*, Hendershot thought, *ha, ha.* But said, "To tell the truth, I only met your father once. I knew your mother quite well, though."

"My mother?"

"Step-mother. Margaret Lowenstein."

Peter Tayleur-Stocking laughed.

Hendershot turned to Clayton for support, but the kid had wandered into the main showroom. Crammed with more bric-a-brac than a Victorian parlour. Wall-to-wall art. Facing Clayton, a sleek figure in black stone lounged like something between human and harbour seal. A few steps away, a cast iron *Man Walking*, skull, ribs and limbs Auschwitz'd to a skeleton, though he still strode, head high, toward the wall.

"Margaret was the second of my father's four wives," Peter T.S. said. "My mother was the first. I am an only child, the lone issue of my father's loins and heir to the Tayleur-Stocking empire." He spread his arms, laughed again. Hendershot found he liked the guy. "The marriage to Margaret was an interlude, less than a year. I was only seven at the time. It happened while I was away at school. *Everything* happened while I was away at school." Tayleur-Stocking's grimace reminded Hendershot of old-movie montages, the ones that flipped through squabbles, divorce, alcoholism, abuse at school. His heart went out to the guy, but the guy himself was cheerful. "Every school holiday, my father took me with him to buy art. Expeditions, he called them. We went to Paris, Provence, Italy. The Netherlands, Germany, Poland. Once to Yugoslavia. Hungary. We tried the USSR but the paperwork defeated him. One year, we went to America."

"Sounds like fun."

"Smashing," Tayleur-Stocking said without a trace of sarcasm. "Gear. Fab. Absolutely ripping." His gaze, which had overlooked his father's romantic bungles, settled on Clayton. "Your son is a very intense young man."

"This is our first big trip together," Hendershot said, suddenly realizing he wanted others. Short, long, far afield. The pyramids. Norwegian fiords. The Taj Mahal.

Feeling himself watched, Clayton moved towards them.

"See anything you like?" Tayleur-Stocking asked.

"The *Nude Reclining*," Clayton said. "Is it black marble?"

"Chlorite." Tayleur-Stocking smiled. "The sculptor is Henry Hobbes. He works in other media as well. His smaller pieces are quite striking. Abstracts, primarily. He uses serpentine, alabaster, soapstone and various woods."

Clayton nodded. "Our art teacher showed us slides of different kinds of stone. Wood too. This year, a native carver came to our school and blocked out a totem pole. Yellow cedar. When you're in grade twelve you get to work on it. They had to build a huge tent to put the log in. It's behind the woodwork shop."

They talked about carving tools, chainsaws, West Coast Haida art, Emily Carr. Left Hendershot dumbfounded. Who were these strangers that his son could talk to so freely? The kid volunteered information without stint or stammer. Honest, earnest, no secrets here. The totem pole would be raised in front of the school. The carver would be present at the dedication. The sports teams were called the Thunderbirds. All news to Hendershot. Louise and he had parted ways before Clayton entered high school, but where'd Hendershot been, on the moon? How had he missed all this stuff?

"Dad?" He heard Clayton's voice from a distance. "Mr. Tayleur-Stocking says he thinks *Victory* is going to be sold."

"Sold?" He shook himself. Dozy sometimes. Residuals from old concussions.

"At auction." Tayleur-Stocking seemed to know. "For reasons not entirely artistic, I suspect. This global penchant for terrorism has given rise to patriotic feeling. Nationalism is cyclical in this country. Comes and goes, like the weather. A resurgence in all things Anglo-Saxon...Lowenstein's *Beowulf* being one. The present owner is a well-known speculator."

"How much do you think it'll go for?"

"Difficult to say. The owner will have high hopes."

"A million?"

Tayleur-Stocking smiled to himself. "Oh, a bit lower than that, I should think." The judgement discouraging. Hendershot wanted Margaret up there with the Big Guns. The Kahlos, the Turners, the Van Goughs, the Whoever-else's there were.

Tayleur-Stocking seemed to sense the disappointment. Took pity, saying, "But likely the tens of thousands. It's a remarkable piece." His soft face turning sharp. Keen nose of the entrepreneur. Hendershot had worn that look himself on occasion. "Interested in bidding?" Tayleur-Stocking asked. Perhaps giving Hendershot and son – his only two customers at the moment – the benefit of the doubt. Secret collectors perhaps, their jeans, sneakers and windbreakers a camouflage, the maybe-badges of the possibly rich.

"I own a video store," Hendershot confessed. "Old movies. Modest, I guess you'd call it. We flew over here economy class."

"Ah. Pity."

"I was a hockey player when I knew Margaret Lowenstein. Ice hockey – Canadian version of a 'great ape on a football field.'"

Tayleur-Stocking looked puzzled. "Sorry?"

Clayton jumped in. "It's from an old movie. Richard Harris. *This Sporting Life.*"

T.S. gazed as if Clayton had levitated. "But that was a British film."

"My dad's into old movies," Clayton said. "So am I. In our store (*our store?*), we like to cover all the bases."

That kid. Good P.R. Won points with Tayleur-Stocking and why not? *His* gallery covered all the bases too. Sculptures, watercolours, oils, blown glass, found objects. All the realistic, surrealistic, junk-istic, pop-istic, abstract, you-name-it of the Tayleur-Stocking empire. Varied as ethnic backgrounds. Diverse as souvenirs. Hendershot liked the place. Didn't understand it, but liked it. It had presence. Something for everyone. He was wondering what it had for them, when Clayton said, "We'd like to see *Victory*, wouldn't we Dad?"

Catching Hendershot off balance. "Yeah," he managed.

Then: "Even more, I'd like to see the artist. Have you any idea where she lives?"

T.S. straightened. Stuck between kindness and killing time. *Probably wondering how deep he should get into this,* Hendershot thought. Giving them an art dealer's assessment: paunchy gimp-legged ex-hockey player and his polite if edgy son. Reminded Hendershot of himself in front of Nigel and Tony. *That's it, mister, that's the ticket. Upright and breaving.*

"If you'll excuse me for just a moment." T.S. left, not quite bowing. Signaled his shop assistant, whom Hendershot had peripherally noticed – a young woman in a black dress who gave him a look, *Yes, I'll keep my eye on these two.* As did the high-mounted security cameras in the corners. Which made him feel instant guilt. Not the guilt of the guilty, but the guilt of the innocent suspected of being guilty.

"Are you okay, Dad?"

"Sure, fine. Christ, it's hot in here."

"He'll be back in a minute, Dad. Look at the paintings."

They'd worked their way through a dozen abstracts called *Genus fontinalis* when Tayleur-Stocking came back. "She has an answering service." Handing Hendershot a card. "Enquiries directed to this number. And these are the addresses of some of the smaller auction houses. It's possible one may have admitted the painting as a late addition."

"Thank you." Hendershot offered his hand. "I hope we haven't been too much trouble."

"Not at all. If you do see Ms Lowenstein, give her my regards."

"I will."

"And you, young man. Best of luck with the totem pole."

"Thank you very much," Clayton said.

Back on the street, Hendershot remembered how the neighbourhood used to be. The old brick buildings, patchwork windows, uneven paving stones, faulty drains. The sprawling, dirty, clanging marketplace. Vegetable stalls, used clothes, books, pots and pans, antiques, boots. Shabby crowds, dreary weather. Mobs of kids in hand-me-downs and snotty noses. Skinheads in paratrooper boots and stove-pipe jeans. Old women in cardigans and flowered skirts, elastic stockings and dark leather shoes.

Now he scarcely recognized the place. Renovated shops and refurbished flagstones. Broad clean pedestrian thoroughfares. Crowds in cheerful colours, as if they'd stepped off a cruise ship. Business was good, capstans glistened, shop signs gleamed. He had to regroup. Took his son to a café for tea and donairs. "Let's relax for a while." He stretched his leg. "After that we'll phone." Trying to sound confident. But now that she was only a dial away, he understood that all those years waited with her. All that'd happened – or would happen – and the thought made him cautious. Afraid. What could he demand of her? His face in a picture? His leg back? Or worse: what might she demand of *him*?

They sat at a table, their backs to the wall. Like linemates on a players' bench waiting for a signal from an on-ice teammate so they could vault over the boards, take their shift, get into the game. He confessed to his son that back then he'd stayed in this city longer than he should have. "I got fooled by the routine," he said. "Training, working for Margaret, Mister Green. Steve Woz was going to call. The painting was going to be finished. And I was going to be ready. For anything."

"Except the bomb," Clayton said.

"Life is full of surprises."

He recalled that in Harrod's a woman had had two fingers blown off. Later, a kid outside Victoria station had suffered third-degree burns to his face. Another time, a pub in Shepherd's Bush had gone up. "You got used to hearing about disaster." Garbage piled up in the streets because the litter barrels were locked. Trains rerouted. "Even so, people went about their daily business. What about you, son? You got a routine?"

"Yeah. I run in the mornings. Before breakfast. It's not like hockey or anything. I just run."

"But you like it."

"Yeah."

"Why?"

"Because it's something I can do myself. Nobody bothers me. When I run I get to be alone." Clayton frowned. "Does that make me weird?"

"No weirder than I am."

"When I get old, will I be nostalgically depressed?"

Hendershot laughed: too long, too loud. Ended in a coughing fit. *Hysteria*, he thought.

"Dad," Clayton said, "if you pee your pants, I'm outta here."

"Get me a bucket then." Hendershot wiped his eyes. "That's the thing about this bladder. Unpredictable. I wish I could figure out *its* routine." He chuckled, but didn't put much into it. The boy's face had settled into a stoney cast. Almost, Hendershot was alarmed to see, a mask.

"At school," Clayton said, "I tried to avoid him. I tried going in at different entrances. Like, one day I'd go in the main doors. And the next day, the upstairs hall door. Or the one by the art room. Or the gym. But he'd always find me. I don't know how he did it. It was like he had radar or some-thing."

The air between son and father thinned. Hendershot heard the boy's breathing. "Son." His mouth was dry. "What did you do to Fat Frank with that knife?"

Clayton's eyes were clear and steady. "I messed up *his* routine."

16.

"That's really fascinating Mr. Hendershot, and a testament to your determination." Over the phone the woman's voice rang with the bouncy conviviality of an aerobics instructor. "But as I say, she's not in."

"Do you know when she'll be back?" At his end, Hendershot sounded wheedling. Squeezed against him in the booth, Clayton held the coins. Like alms for the poor. Hendershot had the urge to talk fast, thought better of it, offered diplomacy. He suggested that he'd call again if the woman could give him an idea when Ms Lowenstein would be at home.

No answer. Where there'd been energetic breathing, now was silence. Auditory void. He half-expected the plaintive *bweep* of a lone satellite. He imagined the woman's hand over the mouthpiece, her whisper: *He wants to know when you'll be back.*

"Hello?" he said.

Then she was on again. "Sorry. Bit of an eventful day. As I was about to say, I don't expect her in until late tomorrow afternoon. If you leave your number, I'll see that she gets it."

Though he suspected a brush-off, he gave her the hotel's number, his room number and, redundantly, his name.

She said, "That's in connection with the Beowulf portrait."

"Yes. Could you tell her it's Rob the hockey player? I'm sure she'll remember." Certain of no such thing.

The woman's voice pitched to athletic brightness. "Oh,

absolutely."

"Thanks. Tomorrow afternoon then."

"I did mention *late* afternoon, didn't I?"

"You did."

As they left the phone box, Hendershot said, "Crackpots. Cranks."

"Who, Dad?"

"The people who phone her. Fruitcakes, groupies. Her secretary thinks I'm a nutbar. It's probably that auction. Like everything else: one whiff of money and all the wackos crawl out of the woodwork."

"Flakes," Clayton said. "Freakoids."

"You got it."

"But we're not in that category, are we Dad?"

"No, we aren't."

"How do we know that?"

"Because we've got vision. Purpose. We've got...hey. Where are we going?"

"I don't know."

"Tayleur-Stocking said the picture might be a last-minute item at an auction." Even to himself, Hendershot sounded mildly unhinged. Edging toward giddy gratification. Or total disappointment. He was riding a high of some kind. Energized. Anticipatory. His reluctant leg ate up the pavement and he felt a sudden recklessness, as though after a long, confined voyage he and Clayton had finally landed and were striding the exotic, wide world.

He told his son to name something he wanted to do. "We're on a roll, Clayton. We've got the rest of today and all day tomorrow. The trial's not until Tuesday. Pick anything, and we'll get 'er done."

"Tourist things?"

"Absolutely." The word the secretary had used. *Two can play at that game, aerobics lady,* he thought.

17.

Dressed in red, the pavement artist rolled across the flagstones weeping for all the lost beauty of the world. Howled that philistines had pissed on his chalk-drawn *Crucifixion of Christ*. Bearded and bony, he twitched like a penitent in the throes of ecstasy. The crowd looked on, bemused and embarrassed until they could safely drift away. Leaving the artist gasping.

Clayton's face showed worry for the man. The eyes that'd rolled back in the head, the face that dripped with sweat. As the street artist struggled to a sitting position, Clayton stepped forward to drop a one-pound coin on the black cloth. Then, to Hendershot's astonishment, leaned over and spoke to the man, who nodded and replied. The two talked for several seconds.

When the boy returned, Hendershot said, "What was that all about?"

"I asked him if he was tired."

"And?"

"He said he was. I told him I hoped he could get some rest."

"And?"

"He said he would."

"He said all that in English, did he?"

"Dad."

"Not in fluent werewolf or whatever that was?"

"Come on, Dad."

"It's a schtick, son."

"Maybe. But he works hard at it."

They walked on. Traffic rushed alongside them. Ahead, Big Ben chimed. A young mother wheeled her pram to a bench under a tree where she watched a barge dredging the river while her baby slept. Hendershot glanced at his son as they passed her. The politicians' catch-phrase creeping into his mind: *We're moving forward...aren't we?*

The entrance to the London Dungeon was cavernous; cold stone and dim light. "Are you sure about this?" he asked his son, already hearing Louise's *You took him where?* And Dave the counsellor spouting psychobabble which, translated, might make sense. The dungeon was a museum of human misery. Torture, execution, murder and mayhem. "I mean," Hendershot tried levity, "kind of a bummer. You're bringing me down, man."

"Dad," Clayton was gentle, "nobody says bummer any more."

Yet we still manage to torture each other, Hendershot wanted to say. But instead, dug out his wallet.

They stood in a queue, blocked into sections like cattle at an auction. The cadaver in charge of ticket stubs wore an undertaker's coat and stovepipe hat. A voice at Hendershot's elbow whined, "It doesn't last forever, you know." A shaven-headed figure in a stained nightshirt. Sinewy neck, her eyes wild. Barefoot. "Not forever." Hendershot wondered if she was part of the performance or an actual mental patient who'd wandered in. "Forever is impossible, don't you see?"

They moved along a cobbled corridor of prisoner's cells, each an exhibit of horrific cruelty. Waxwork figures manacled, flogged, branded. Until Hendershot, his revulsion surfeited, suggested he and Clayton leave.

But Clayton said, "Let's finish it, Dad."

"What for? I think I've caught the drift, son. People catch people, people hurt people, people die. Did I leave anything out?"

"It's history, Dad. Something that happened. You can't make it go away."

The last exhibit, the Algerian Hook. A bound man impaled on a meat hook and suspended from a pulley.

"Jesus Christ," Hendershot said.

When they emerged into the late afternoon, Hendershot sighed, "Well!" but Clayton said nothing. From the boy's intense stillness Hendershot sensed the kid was ruminating about everything he'd seen. Head angled to one side, as if listening to something far away. Retreating into a meditative quietude that Hendershot, not given to abstractions, found disconcerting. Once, when he was eight, Clayton, being driven around to look at the Christmas lights, had told them, "Time is like those lights. It looks like it's moving, but it's not. Time just shines where it is. We're the ones that're moving." Hendershot and Louise had looked at each other: philosophical kid. The possibility made them proud, nervous, inadequate.

Now Clayton stopped on the bridge.

"What's up, son?"

"That dungeon."

"Yeah, well, we knew it wouldn't be a funhouse."

The boy stared down at the water. "When your leg... when it happened...did you suffer?"

"Not at the time. At the time, I fainted."

"But later?"

"Later I was too pissed off to suffer. Anger's a good anaesthetic."

"Mum says you're still angry."

"I'd say irritable. You get older, you tone it down."

Below on the river a tugboat chugged its snout against the current, waddled upstream.

"Did you think you were going to die, Dad?"

"I'm as morbid as the next guy, son."

"I'm serious."

"I thought I'd have to whittle a peg-leg, wear an eye patch and buy a parrot to perch on my shoulder."

"Dad."

"I don't know, son. I guess I figured if losing a leg was going to kill me, it would've done it already. The doctor said I was lucky, so I took his word for it."

Clayton considered this information. "Do you remember Angie, Dad?"

"Of course I do." Hendershot shifted uncomfortably, not sure he was up to a foray into ghoul country. He supposed Doctor Dave encouraged this sort of thing, but he himself had always considered psychology a subtle, educated form of claptrap. Upbringing gave him a straightforward view of human action: either you did a thing or you didn't. What his father had called a shit-or-get-off-the-pot philosophy, an approach eminently practical and shamelessly simplistic.

Angie had changed all that. A border collie of sweet temper and great intelligence, she'd come into their lives when they were renting a frame house on the outskirts of the city, where farmland was being carved into suburbs. Gravel trucks shook the ground from dawn to dusk, cement mixers and carpenters' saws tore the silence. Clayton was five, Louise was training as an OR nurse at the university hospital, and Hendershot was working part-time as a one-legged skate and running shoe salesman. Angie lived for Clayton; sought comfort at the foot of his bed, woke in the morning with her head next to his on the pillow, followed the boy everywhere. Until, on a drive home from work, Hendershot found the dog dead on the side of the road.

Still warm, she lay as if sleeping. Hendershot wrapped her in a black plastic garbage bag, placed her in the trunk of his car and drove, grief giving way to rage, through the maze of suburban cul-de-sacs until, on a naked expanse of scarified ground, he reached the construction company's office, a portable tin shack he entered without knocking. "There's been a killing," he told the foreman behind the desk.

At the car with the trunk open, the man said, "I'm sorry for your loss," and shot a surreptitious glance as a gust of wind plastered Hendershot's pant-leg against his skinny prosthesis.

Hendershot had touched Angie's muzzle. "Somebody hit her, stopped, dragged her to the edge of the road. You know your drivers?"

"I know them. Accidents happen."

"Accidents are caused."

The man studied him for a moment, said he'd look into it. "Best I can do," he said.

Which was nothing. Leaving Hendershot to take his son's dog home and prepare to explain death. Vengeance, justice, explanation, apology – Hendershot had wanted all these and more. He'd wanted the kid's experience of death to be incremental, starting with a goldfish, say, and ending in the inevitable future, with Hendershot himself. Death's ascent by degrees, so Clayton could ease into its democratic finality. But this? Oh, he knew. Everywhere on the globe kids like Clayton faced more horrific devastations – war, famine, earthquakes. But what five-year-old, whoever or wherever – was ready for death's sucker-punch? Even one delivered to a dog?

When Hendershot explained to Clayton what had happened, the boy listened intently, but the expected rush of grief did not come. "Really, Dad?" he'd said. "Is Angie really dead?" As if impressed that his dog had reached this improbable height.

"I'm going up the hill now to dig a grave for her," Hendershot had said. "You can come with me if you want."

Clayton followed Hendershot and Louise with his sandpail and shovel, but sometime during the clearing of rocks and tree roots, Hendershot looked up to find the boy gone.

Clayton was in the woodshed. Had freed Angie from the garbage bag and sat on the floor, her head cradled in his lap. Weeping silently. "Aw come on, Angie," rocking back and forth, "wake up. Wake up, Angie."

So what could Hendershot do but wrap the dog in the blanket Clayton pulled from his bed, lower Angie into eternity, and fill the grave with dirt and stones to discourage other animals from disturbing the dead. Hendershot had watched as his son and Louise, with a can of white house paint, printed on the stone marker *Here lies Angie she was my friend.* Time and weather would peel the paint away, the grave would be plowed under by the contractor's machines. Anonymity the ultimate price of death. Even Angie's killer remained unknown.

And yet. Now on the bridge as dusk was falling, street lamps winked on. Farther upriver, Tower Bridge was garlanded in strands of light. Clayton stopped, leaned his elbows on the railing and began pensively, "Do you think everybody has a soul, Dad?"

"I don't know. I'd like to think so, but I've never been big fan of God. Is this a religious question?"

"I don't think you need God to have a soul, Dad. And I don't think anybody can prove whether God exists or not. In Socials we took India and Mr. Jamieson said they've got hundreds of gods there."

"Hey. Whatever works."

"Do you think Angie had a soul?"

The boy's seriousness sobered Hendershot. Scared him. As if the kid were wading into deep water. As a toddler at the beach, Clayton faced waves head on, got knocked down, rose up sputtering. Souls, gods – where was the kid going with this?

"Angie had a soul." Hendershot believed this.

Clayton said, "I think souls are like stars. They die out, but we can still see their light." He pushed himself away from the railing, rocked forward again. Back and forth, as if deciding the difference between *near* and *far*. "When I took that knife to school I..."

Hendershot's breath caught: he waited, played the odds. Finally, unable to keep his mouth shut: "You what, son?"

But Clayton seemed to have changed his mind. "I thought a lot about souls." He turned perfunctorily and started to walk.

Hendershot was limping. Fatigue freighted his limbs. Traffic over the bridge thickened, a stream of headlights and exhaust. The air was heavy. As they neared the end of the bridge, he was forced to the parapet, where he leaned. A heron seeking stiller waters.

Clayton led him to the Cannon Street tube station where they dropped into seats across from two builders with tool bags between their feet. Backs as wide as moving vans. Discussing a fellow worker.

"The trouble wiv him was, he wasn't in sympafy."

"He weren't a wally, though."

"They should've put him on that ovver job wiv old Bert. You don't have to be in sympafy wiv old Bert. He dunno you from Adam's off-ox."

"Not to mention deaf as a post."

"Yer, well – every situation has its advantages."

18.

As his kidneys processed three pints of beer, Hendershot lay in bed and debated whether to strap on his leg to dignify his trip to the bathroom down the hall or simply hop the distance like a circus clown on a pogo stick. *Who's Pogo now?* he was asking himself when Clayton spoke into the dark. "Dad?"

"I thought you were asleep, son."

"I think you were grinding your teeth."

"That's possible." At the foot of Hendershot's bed, the window curtains fluttered, light splashed over the coverlet. "I should've brought a pee-bottle."

"Do you need help, Dad?"

"If you could convince my bladder to go to sleep, I'd appreciate it."

"You should've eaten something."

"You sound like your mother."

The boy fell silent. Hendershot linked his fingers behind his head, to con his body into relaxing. Attempt to fool his bladder. Convince Clayton that there was no tension here, that they were all *in sympafy* here.

"Any minute now," he told his son, "my back teeth are gonna float."

Clayton was interested. "Why do you pee so much, Dad?"

"Beer. Beer and a prostate the size of a softball."

"It's not...not cancer, is it?"

"No."

"How do you know?"

"I go to the doctor once a year and he checks it out."

"Is that where he –"

"Yeah. He wears a rubber glove."

Clayton absorbed this information. "Isn't it embarrassing?"

"You bet."

"Does it hurt?"

"Doc Senghara's got hands the size of Easter hams."

"What does the doctor say? I mean, how does he act? Is he embarrassed too?"

"I guess so. When he's finished, he always turns his back and makes a big deal out of throwing the gloves in the garbage. Then he says everything's normal. A little enlarged, but okay."

'And what do you say?"

"Well, the last time I said, 'Is this just a summer thing, Doc, or will you call me in the city?'"

"Jesus, Dad."

"Watch your language, son."

"You say Jesus all the time."

"That's true."

"What did the doctor say when you told him that?"

"He said he was sorry, but his calendar was full."

Clayton laughed. "Do people think you're a funny guy, Dad?"

"People think I'm a one-legged guy."

"Mum thinks you're a funny guy."

"Does she."

"Except she says you're too full of gallows humour."

"Right now, I'm too full of beer. I gotta go, son." He swung out of bed. "I'm going to have to put the light on to strap my leg. Close your eyes."

"I've seen your leg before, Dad."

"That sounds like hangman material to me, Clayton."

"I can go with you. You don't have to put on the leg. I gotta pee too."

All the way down the hall Hendershot leaned on the boy's shoulders. The kid didn't complain. The kid, Hendershot noticed, hung in there.

At the door to the W.C. Clayton said, "I'll be right out here, Dad."

Hendershot grabbed the door jamb and hopped inside. "'Louie'," he rasped, "'I think this is the beginning of a beautiful friendship.'"

"Just pee," Clayton said.

19.

The man on Speaker's Corner was talking about God, with whom he had a personal relationship. Tall and stringy, the speaker stretched tiptoe on his box and roostered his message over the heads of doubters. "Infinite! Not the constrained infinitude as perpetrated by your Steven Hawkings and Darth Vaders! For if, as the poet says, the mind has mountains no man fathomed, what then is the mind of God? Infinitude, yes, but more than that! Infinitude infinitized! Exponent exponentialized! God is omniscient, omnipotent, omni..."

"Codswallop, mate! Rubbish!" a harsh voice shouted. The crowd tittered, guffawed, argued.

"Isn't this great?" Clayton said. He swung his knapsack to the ground and dug his camera out of the side pocket. "Just a couple of shots, Dad."

"Okay." Thinking, *Maybe the kid's headed for journalism. TV reporter, foreign correspondent. National Geographic. Something beyond Rewinds Video, that's for sure.*

To get a preview of Clayton's news-hound future, Hendershot chose a bench away from the crowd. "You go ahead, son. I'll be over there."

He sat and watched his son patrol the crowd's periphery, camera at the ready. Rapid fire. *Machine gun photos*, Hendershot was thinking, when he noticed the tabloid newspaper at the end of the bench. The headline:

VERDICT EXPECTED IN ACCUSED IRA MAN'S TRIAL

The banner of words spread above the full-page photograph. A telephoto longshot taken, he guessed, through a chain-link fence. The prisoner facing the camera. Balding, bearded, herded by two policemen towards the back door of some public building. Still heavy in the back and shoulders, the man had grown fat and slightly stooped. Head still like a bullet, but softened around the edges. A faint halo of fuzz.

Connor Mack. The name seemed suddenly hollow. The echo of someone Hendershot used to know. As if the Irishman had been reduced by time and his alleged villainies, shrunk to the size of a newspaper column. Hendershot stared at the photo. Having loomed so large for so many years, Connor disappointed. Hendershot reached down to touch the point where his leg joined his prosthesis. The point of retribution.

Clayton appeared at his shoulder. Immersed in the news report, Hendershot was barely conscious of the boy until the kid said, "God, Dad. That guy's face looks like the one in Ms Lowenstein's painting."

"I know. That's what I thought, too. But now I'm not so sure." *Because I'm afraid*, he thought. *Afraid that it's only jealousy that's kept me going all these years. She used his face and not mine.* "Listen to this," as Clayton sat beside him: "'Mack is charged with engaging in conduct in preparation for terrorist acts.' What do you suppose *that* means? Why not 'engaging in conduct in preparation to become a heartless asshole'?"

"Dad," Clayton reprimanded him.

"Maybe that's why...*Ms Lowenstein*...doesn't answer my phone calls. Too embarrassed. Too ashamed."

"But Dad," Clayton was irritatingly reasonable, "she didn't have anything to do with it, did she? Why should she be ashamed?"

"Because...," Hendershot began, then stopped. *Because I have to believe there's such a thing as justice*, he wanted to say.

Or at least revenge. Because somebody stole my leg. Because, he knew he'd come back to it, *she used his face and not mine.* He looked up, escaped into the trees whose leaves, he noticed, had begun to bud into a faint green tinge. *Spring,* he thought, as if a season could offer comfort.

Clayton sat beside him. Hendershot was aware of the boy as a permanent presence, though he knew this couldn't be so. Clayton tucked his camera into his back-pack, zipped the pocket closed. Waited. Then: "That religious guy who was giving a speech said the universe is in a constant state of balance."

"And that's supposed to help us out, is it?"

"He said good balances out evil. Time's beginning balances time's end."

"Son, I don't even know what that means." Remembering: *So, it's you, boyo. I wondered when you'd get round to it.* Hendershot leaned back. "I've got to think this over for a while."

Clayton sat with his pack on his knees. Ready to move. "Tomorrow we have to go to that trial, Dad."

"I know."

"And tonight, you were supposed to phone Ms Lowenstein – or she was going to phone you?"

"What's this, Clayton, countdown to blast-off?"

The boy fiddled with his pack's shoulder straps. "What I mean is, we've got the whole afternoon, Dad. I've always wanted to see Greenwich. That's sort of where time begins."

"But I don't know how to get there, Clayton."

"I do."

Hendershot felt tired. Also, relieved. Even grateful. He bundled the newspaper into a trash can. "Lead on," he said.

20.

The train rattled through rowhouses and smokestacks. The park was green, soggy, treed. They hiked up the slope towards the observatory that squatted like a football helmet next to the gingerbread museum. Hendershot hobbled behind Clayton's buoyant step with all the enthusiasm of a condemned man. Twenty-two years. Time might balance its beginning and end, but in between it merely limped.

Grey clouds overhead. In front of them, on a graveled path, uniformed school kids bleated behind their teacher, a young woman who, to Hendershot, looked barely old enough to be out of school herself. Kids as raucous as crows.

"But I can't remember what it was called," Clayton was saying.

"What?"

"The *movie*, Dad." Clayton waited for his father to catch up. "The one I've been telling you about. The guy who tries to blow up the Greenwich Observatory. Amanda ordered it for the store."

Amanda, Hendershot's assistant manager. Middle-aged woman of sturdy girth and infallible instincts. Lived with her partner Doris and their three cats, Forster, Galsworthy and Conrad.

"It was a book," Clayton said. "This terrorist gets a mental guy to carry the bomb."

"Smart move," Hendershot said.

"The mental guy doesn't really know what he's doing."

"Who does?" Hendershot said.

"The Secret Agent." Clayton's delight at remembering the title lengthened his stride, and again Hendershot was forced to keep up.

The observatory was closed but Flamsteed House was open. Designed by Wren. Opened by Charles II, 1675. Clayton read these historical details aloud from strategically placed plaques. They washed over Hendershot like muzak as he imagined Connor Mack facing vague charges. *Conduct in preparation for terrorist acts* sounded dubious. Subjective. And while Clayton pointed to the original clocks and contraptions used to establish Greenwich Mean Time, reassuringly precise, impossibly complicated, Hendershot thought, *Is anything ever really exact?* And a slower, calmer, *At least the bastard has been brought to trial.*

Clayton tugged his arm. "It's through here, Dad."

Outside, a cobbled patio bisected by a red line set between two metal strips and edged with flagstones. "The Prime Meridian." Clayton's voice was hushed.

Hendershot thought the Prime Meridian looked like a single railroad track to nowhere.

"It goes right from the North Pole to the South Pole," Clayton said. "Each new day starts here." He walked the line, balanced between the earth's two hemispheres. Straddled them, one leg in the East, the other in the West. Bounded from one hemisphere to the other, marched their length, paced their distance. The meridian led him to the patio's far end, where misty trees fell away into valley fog. There he stopped, glanced about him, straddled the meridian. Flung his arms wide and shouted words Hendershot couldn't decipher.

Seconds passed. From behind, Hendershot studied his son: narrow back, outstretched arms, neat round head. The kid, he realized, was surrendering himself to something. Hendershot's heart stirred.

Later, as the train chuffed back to the city, Hendershot asked, "What'd you yell when you were standing at the end of the meridian? Secret agent stuff?"

"No."

"It's all right, son. You don't have to tell me."

Clayton frowned. "No, it's okay." He stared out the window. "Franklin Burroughs sucks," he said.

"Goes without saying."

"No, I mean that's what I yelled. . . Franklin Burroughs sucks."

The train talked *abricabrac, abricabrac.* "Did it feel good?"

"Yeah."

"You stood there for a long time."

"Yeah."

"What were you thinking about?"

The boy turned. His eyes clear. "I wasn't thinking about anything, Dad. I was standing on both sides of the world and I wasn't thinking anything. It was great." He paused. "Is that stupid?"

"It's what a lot of people would like to do."

"Would you?"

"Sure." Hendershot didn't know this until he said it.

"You should've tried it. I should've told you."

"It's a kick, huh?"

"Nobody says kick anymore, Dad."

"A rush, then."

The kid grinned. "Sure, Dad. It's a rush."

They were on the tube train when they heard the announcement. In a dark tunnel a woman's calm uninflected voice came over the speakers and told them that due to security reasons, the train would not stop at Leicester Square.

The other passengers sighed or sat impassively.

"What do you think it is, Dad, a bomb?"

"I don't know, son."

"But it couldn't be that guy, could it. He's in jail."

"No, it wouldn't be him."

"Somebody else, then." Clayton was confident.

21.

"Am I getting the run-around here?"

"I beg your pardon?"

"Are you stonewalling me? Are you," Hendershot enunciated clearly into the phone, "giving me the gears?"

"I'm afraid I don't know what you mean."

"Yesterday, you told me to call back in the late afternoon. I've phoned five times. Nobody answered. Not even a machine."

"Ah. And the name again was?"

"Rob Hendershot. The Beowulf guy."

"Of course. Mr. Hendershot. I passed your message along to Ms Lowenstein."

"And what did Margaret say?"

"Well – I passed your message along."

"Look, Ms ... ?"

"Miss Wiens."

"Look, Miss Wiens. I'm trying not to be rude and for me that's not easy. I've been told the *Beowulf* painting's going to be sold, probably at an auction house. I've phoned around, but I can't find out which one. Or when. Is that where Margaret is? Is that why she can't call back?"

"I'm sorry, Mr. Hendershot. I'm not permitted to divulge that information."

"Call me Rob, Miss Wiens. The whole time I posed for Margaret, the whole time we shared pots of tea and ate kippers out of the same frying pan, she called me Rob. I don't think we'd go too far wrong if you called me Rob, too."

"All right – Rob."

"And your first name is?"

"Miss Weins."

"Miss Weins. I like it. Tell me, Miss Weins, where is the painting to be sold?"

"I'm not permitted to divulge..."

"...that sort of information. Okay. But somewhere in London, right?"

"That would be an accurate assumption."

"If I go to all the auction houses, is there a chance I'll see her?"

"I can't say."

"A chance that she'll see me?"

"I shouldn't think so."

"Why?" Hendershot was bewildered. "Have they got her in a back room somewhere?" He imagined helmeted policemen, shields, rubber truncheons. "What's so important about this painting? Do they have to protect it?"

Miss Weins sighed. "I can't say."

"Okay. All right. Just one more thing. Bear with me here. Would you know if the painting has been sold already?"

"That would be an accurate..."

"...assumption. Yeah. So, has it?"

"No."

"Great. It is to be sold, but we don't know where. Maybe in London, but we don't know at what auction house. And if we knew the auction house, we'd find out when. Or would we? And all this secrecy is because...because...? Feel free to jump in here and enlighten me, Miss Weins." Through the phone box window, Hendershot saw his son aim his camera at a passing brewer's dray draped in advertising and pulled by four Clydesdales. He beckoned Clayton to him. *We've got to be careful*, he thought. *Due to security reasons, this train will not stop...*

"Tell me something, Miss Weins. Does Margaret ever talk

about the trial?"

A pause. "What trial would that be, Mr ... Rob?"

"Now we're getting coy, Miss Weins. The trial of Connor Mack. Suspected IRA guy. Margaret's old boyfriend."

Another pause, into which Hendershot tried to sneak in a head shot. "She's probably been to it every day, am I right? Ever since it started. Might even have testified. What do you think, Miss Weins? Am I in the ballpark here?"

"That I can't say."

Hendershot controlled his breathing. "I've got to hand it to you, Miss Weins. You're doing a great snow job here. Stellar. I hope she pays you enough."

"She's been very kind to me."

"She was kind to me, too. Most of the time, anyway. If I don't see her, tell her thanks."

"For what?"

"The painting, for one thing."

"I'll do that."

"And you're sure there's nothing more you can do for me?"

"Not a thing, I'm afraid."

"Well, you've been unhelpfully helpful."

"I'll take that as a compliment."

"And I'll mean it as one. So long, Miss Weins."

"Goodbye, Mr. ... Rob."

22.

A bove the main archway the words were chiseled in stone:

DEFEND · THE · CHILDREN · OF · THE
POOR · & · PUNISH · THE · WRONGDOER

A bailiff stood blocking the main entrance with his back to a pair of open wooden doors as he faced a large restive crowd. Helmeted London bobbies patrolled in pairs the roads adjacent to the courthouse. Two television vans were parked alongside the curb, their camera crews uncoiling cables and setting up reflectors.

"Christ," Hendershot told Clayton. "You'd think this was a rock concert."

Clayton hooked his thumbs in the shoulder straps on his pack. "Do you think they're all going to the trial, Dad?"

"I don't know. Must be more entertaining than we think."

They joined the long queue of people. Hendershot tried to distinguish those who, like him, were waiting for reconciliation, or what most fools called *closure*. As opposed to those who were merely curious, morbid, or bored. He couldn't tell the difference. One large group was led by a tour guide, whose informational pitch drifted back to him and Clayton: "The Old Bailey houses eighteen courtrooms in all." An older couple ahead of them remained sombre at this disclosure, while behind them, two young men talked festively. "In Victorian times," one said, "you used to be able to watch 'em hang."

"They knew how to have fun in those days," the other

observed.

The crowd shuffled towards the entrance which, from a distance, Hendershot saw opened into a central space. A soaring dome of light and marble.

"Wow. The majesty of the law, huh, Dad?" Clayton said, when he could see inside as they neared the threshold.

At which point the bailiff asked them to step out of the line.

"Problem?" Hendershot asked.

"You'll want to talk to my supervisor," the bailiff said, indicating an older man in a uniform. "This way." Extending a protective arm as a barrier to usher them aside.

The head bailiff settled his pale eyes on Clayton. "Is this young man your son, sir?"

"He is."

"And how old are you, young sir?"

Clayton flushed, stammered. "Thirteen...I'm...thirteen."

"Ah. Bit of a problem there, then. Only children fourteen and older are permitted as observers in the courtrooms. As well," glancing at Clayton's knapsack, "no bags, telephones or cameras are allowed inside, as there are no storage facilities for such items. Those who visit the building are advised to bring nothing with them." Already he was dismissing them. At first, he'd been standing at ease, now his hands came out from behind his back to hitch up his trousers.

"I don't suppose you're kidding," Hendershot suggested. Embarrassment dove-tailing nicely with annoyance at his own ineptitude, made clearer as the line of courtroom sightseers – those who'd *prepared* – filed into the building.

"Dad, I can stay out here," Clayton offered.

"No, you can't, son."

"I'll be all right."

"Not a wise idea, young sir." The head bailiff maintained professional courtesy. Turned to Hendershot. "Was there a particular litigation you were interested in observing, sir?"

"The IRA trial."

"*Alleged* IRA," the head bailiff reminded him. "People are already being turned away from that one, sir. Public gallery is full. Very popular this morning. Understandable, as a verdict is expected." Tipping his head, he indicated the board listing court times. "Several courts close at one p.m. and open again at two. Perhaps you'd like to return alone and observe a different court proceeding. Galleries are open to the public."

Hendershot glanced at his watch. "When do you expect the *alleged* IRA trial to finish?"

"I couldn't say for certain, sir." The head bailiff nodded at the camera crews. "The media are expecting statements. I expect they'll be here at least until one o'clock."

Hendershot looked to his son for an opinion. Tried to hold himself in the posture of the stoic. Undaunted. But harbouring excuses.

Clayton, seeming to sense this, asked solemnly, "Am I allowed to take pictures out here?"

"By all means," the head bailiff said.

"Thank you."

"No need to thank me, young sir. We live in a democracy."

Clayton led the way back across the street. Got out his camera, shot photographs of camera crews filming reporters who used words to describe other pictures. Gave the whole enterprise a Russian doll-inside-a-doll feel that put Hendershot on edge. He wasn't sure what he wanted from this experience, still less certain of what he'd get. What if Connor was guilty? What if innocent? Hendershot tried on clichés and other forms of wisdom. *You can't change the past. What's done is done. Vengeance is mine, sayeth the leg.*

Clayton ran out of camera angles. And subjects. He packed his camera away and joined Hendershot, who apologized. "I'm sorry, Clayton. Maybe it's this one-legged thing, but I always seem to be a step behind."

"Not too funny, Dad," Clayton cleaned his glasses. "But it doesn't matter. There's a coffee shop on the corner. We could wait in there."

"We've got a couple of hours yet, son. Besides, that place is full."

"Okay. If you don't mind." The boy consulted his street guide. "There's St. Paul's Cathedral, Dad. We just go down here, and turn left on Ludgate Hill."

They started to walk. Hendershot said, "Your mum took me to St. Paul's once. After I got my prosthesis. She wanted me to practise with it."

"I know," Clayton said. "She told me."

23.

For a non-believer such as Hendershot, the great dome of St. Paul's was not the roof of heaven. But when he looked up at it from inside the cathedral, he admitted it was a magnificent approximation. A cavernous glory, expanded in all directions. As Clayton would have it, a fitting shelter for the bones of Wellington and Nelson. Because if warriors couldn't be blessed in death, when would they rest? In truth, the place had mostly faded from Hendershot's memory, except for the echoes of himself and Louise, whispering to each other around the curve of the dome. That they'd love each other. Be true to each other. Even if they both lost legs, and had to crawl through the world.

When it came to his turn with Clayton, Hendershot hesitated before he put his lips to the stone and whispered to his son that he loved him. Bad timing, maybe, Hendershot thought, but what the hell. The kid needs to know. On a gut level, Hendershot believed the statement would have more legs than the vow he and Louise had made to each to other. Marriage was a deal on a long-term plan, but not necessarily forever. In contrast, a son was a son was a son.

For his part, Clayton whispered that he had a secret he was ready to tell. But that he couldn't tell it now. When Hendershot whispered, "Why not?", the boy answered, "Uvver weep'll sanding affa all."

"What?" Hendershot said.

"Other...people...are...standing...at...the...wall."

"Maybe...later...then." Hendershot wasn't keen on exacting

promises. But held his breath for the response.

Which came, finally, when Clayton said later would be okay.

24.

The television crews had converged on the robed lawyers in front of the courthouse. A discussion behind microphones, which for Hendershot and Clayton was little more than sibilant hissing. In the end, it was a disgruntled tourist who filled them in.

"Looked like an open and shut case to me," said the man, who admitted to owning a window-cleaning business in Cleveland. "Witnesses done, arguments finished, jury instructed. Jury goes out and then we waited," he turned to his wife, "how long, honey?"

"Two hours and twelve minutes," she said.

The husband nodded. "We took a little tour around the lobby."

"What was the verdict?" Hendershot asked.

"Well, that was the other thing. They had to run through all the charges. Guilty on this charge, not guilty on that charge. Jeez, for a while there, I thought we'd have to come back tomorrow to hear the end of it."

"Only we won't be here," the wife said serenely.

"We got the Salisbury-Stonehenge tour tomorrow," the husband said. "Bus leaves at 6:30 a.m. Guy at the hotel says it's a long haul. We took one out to Hatfield House the other day. Elizabethan banquet. Beef so raw you could hear it moo."

"Rare," the wife said. "Ardon, time to say good-bye."

Hendershot was ready to give up. Went for one last appeal. "On what charge was he found guilty?"

"The long one," said the husband. "Preparing and conspiring to indulge in terrorism. Something like that. The other charges...building bombs, possessing bombs, setting 'em off...they didn't stick. Some other poor Mick got stuck with those."

"And the sentence?" Hendershot thought vaguely of ropes, firing squads. Prison riots, hunger strikes.

"That happens next week," the husband said. "The English. Takes 'em forever. They got lower standards."

"Ardon," the wife said.

"World War Two," Ardon called, being drawn away. "We saved their ass."

The couple picked their way through the thinning crowd. During their conversation, Hendershot had marked the faces that filed out of the courthouse, on the off-chance Margaret was among them. Her tiny stature might've hidden her in the crowd, but one glimpse was all he needed. Height didn't announce Margaret, energy did. But she wasn't there.

"Dad?" Clayton had pulled into himself. Not withdrawn, exactly, but hardened. Consolidated. Held himself brittle, as if his secret was in danger of shattering. Though nervous, the kid looked stubborn. Jaw tight, head rigid. Even if Hendershot hadn't seen him do it all those years ago, he could imagine this same boy kneeling over a rock, on which he painted that here lay the dog who'd been his friend. "Dad, the coffee shop looks empty now."

25.

The only other customer in the shop was a woman seated at a table near the door. Hendershot and Clayton chose a table in a far corner, a marble-topped toadstool flanked by two chrome chairs. Over Hendershot's cappuccino and Clayton's hot chocolate, Clayton retreated into contemplation. Pushed his napkin across the table and back again. Reminded Hendershot of the days when the boy had carried a dinky toy truck, which he trundled along car seats, fences. The napkin's trip was simpler. There and back. Now and then stopped: napkin idling.

"Are you sorry you didn't get to see the trial, Dad?"

"Not sorry. Little disappointed, maybe." The boy was onto something big. Understatement was the safe route. "Are you sorry, son?"

"No, not really. That Irish guy," Clayton said slowly, "he'll go to prison, right?"

"I would think so."

"Does that make you happy, Dad?"

The question Hendershot was asking himself. Happy being a relative term. He'd have liked to report news of Connor's guilty verdict to the one person who would've celebrated it: Mister Green. Who now appeared, in hindsight, prophetic. But who also appeared, in foresight, out of the picture. "Actually, son, I feel...relieved. And a bit sad. Too bad they didn't catch Connor earlier. Would've saved a lot of people a lot of pain."

Clayton pushed his napkin. "I wonder what that

courtroom looks like. That bailiff said children under fourteen aren't allowed in there."

"So?"

"So, what if a kid committed a crime and wasn't fourteen
yet? Where would they put him on trial?"

"Maybe they've got a juvenile court somewhere."

Clayton's index finger ground the napkin into the table's
surface. He spoke softly. "That's where they'd send me."

Inside Hendershot's chest something dropped. Dread. A
spectacular case of nerves. As if his thorax had been knifed
open and too much air allowed in. At the same time his
throat constricted, his pulse hammered his neck. *This is it,*
he thought. *Here it comes.*

He'd hoped it would happen sometime, had imagined
where and when. A quiet walk along a canal, a secluded
park bench, or better yet – he liked this one – in their hotel
room, each in his own bed and weary from a day's sightsee-
ing, in the anonymous confessional of the dark. But not
here, bumping shoulders at a tiny table, while behind a
counter baristas ground coffee beans and filled glass jars
with over-priced biscotti.

Hendershot wasn't sure how to phrase it, so simply
asked, "Did somebody say you have to go to court, son?"

Clayton, head down, took off his glasses, folded them
carefully and set them on the table.

"Son?"

When the boy lifted his head, his eyes were sad, his face
twisted in torment. "Dad, am I a bad person?"

"No," Hendershot said, "you're not."

"I feel like one."

"Why?" Hendershot grasped his son's shoulder. "Because
you stood up for yourself?"

"It's not that." The boy was shivering. He hitched his
chair even closer to Hendershot's, his voice low and urgent.
"When I took that knife to school, I didn't take it to kill Fat

Frank."

"Of course you didn't," Hendershot soothed the kid, "you're not the kind of guy that would..."

"I took it to kill myself."

A noise clawed at Hendershot's throat. The woman at the table near the door twisted sharply toward him, as if doubting the sound.

"Oh, Clayton," Hendershot moaned. And clung to his boy.

26.

A single light in the hotel room cast a shadow over Clayton's face. "It was pretty stupid," he said.

Shaving, Hendershot glimpsed his son in the mirror above the chipped washstand. The boy was sitting on his narrow bed, hands pressed between his knees. Hendershot held the razor over the sink and opened the tap. Just as the hotel patriarch had promised, no hot water. The soap on Hendershot's cheeks dissolving. The brush in the mug whipping up fresh foam.

"Julian uses an electric razor," Clayton said.

"My dad bought me an electric razor when I was sixteen," Hendershot said. "Gave me a rash." He scraped the bristle along his neck, rinsed the razor. Apparently shaving didn't keep his voice or his hand steady. "What do you mean 'stupid'?"

"Well," Clayton said.

Hendershot used the silence to drag the razor over cleared ground. Smoothed the stubble under his jaw. An artery pulsed there and the enormity of his son's intention caused his hand to falter. He ran the razor under the tap longer than necessary. When he looked into the mirror, he saw the boy lower his head.

"For one thing, the knife wasn't big enough."

"Oh yeah?" Hendershot gulped. Considered washing his face, drying it, sitting next to his son, draping an arm over the boy's thin shoulders. But he'd started this now. This not-quite banter of one man interested in another man's plan –

and he wasn't sure how to stop it. "How big does a knife have to be?"

"Longer than the one I had. I took the one we use to cut up carrots. The stumpy one."

"I thought it was bigger than that."

"I wanted one small enough to hide in my knapsack."

"That'd be the one, then." Hendershot resumed shaving, as horror clawed up the back of his neck. In the mirror, his own eyes stared back at him: naked consternation. As he pulled the skin taut with his left hand, the razor rasped up his right cheek. There were blades everywhere in this life. If you wanted a blade, you could find one anyplace.

Finished, he packed away his shaving kit and sat on the bed opposite the boy's. "What was the plan, son?"

"You sound like that cop."

"You mean there was no plan?"

"You're supposed to ask me why, Dad. Everybody asks me why. Even Mum."

"I figure you must've had your reasons."

"Yeah. I did."

"And a plan."

"Yeah. I did. Sort of."

The boy told him. At first haltingly, then with growing confidence. How one night he slipped into the kitchen and sharpened the knife on the gizmo his mother kept in the serving spoon drawer. How, the next morning, he palmed the knife and hid it in the zippered pocket on his knapsack where he kept his geometry set. How he picked a spot in the school's upper hallway, a secluded alcove where the row of lockers ended. How he sat there with his back to the wall and his wrists in his lap. How they'd find him there with the knife and the note.

Hendershot sat very still. Under the window the radiator pinged. "That's some plan."

"Yeah."

"Of course, you realize I'm glad it didn't work out."

"Yeah."

"What changed your mind?"

"Bowels. I had to go to the toilet."

"Okay."

"I read somewhere that when you die you shit yourself. I thought if that happened and everybody found out – if Fat Frank found out – he'd laugh. Everybody would laugh."

"So, you went to the toilet."

"The one downstairs next to the gym. Hardly anybody uses that one in the morning."

"But he was in there?"

"No, he came in after."

"He followed you."

"No. If he follows you, he brings his posse with him. They guard the door while he does his gangsta shit."

"His gangsta shit?"

"You know, 'Yo muthafucka, you dissin' me?'...you know."

"All right. But this time he was alone. And he saw you."

"No, he didn't. I was in a cubicle."

"But he heard you."

"I heard *him.* He breathes funny...asthma. Plus his jeans scrape. I heard his legs rubbing together, and then they stopped. At the urinals."

"And you stayed in the cubicle?"

"Yeah. I waited until I heard him taking a leak, and then I wiped myself and pulled up my pants. I thought he'd finish peeing and leave. But he must've heard me. He walked down the line of cubicles and banged the doors open. He went down the line like that – bang, bang, bang. When he got to mine it was locked and he asked who was in there."

"And you told him."

"I didn't say anything. He asked again and I didn't answer so he bent down to look under the door. I could smell him,

Dad. I could smell his sweat. I hid my feet behind my knapsack, but he knew who I was because he said, 'Hendershot you little fuck, come out of there.'"

"Holy cow, son."

"I was sort of shaking."

"Yup."

"I told him to fuck off."

"Wow."

"Yeah. I told him to fuck off and melt himself down into cooking oil and fry chips with himself."

"That's pretty complicated, son."

"Yeah."

"Did he get it?"

"He kicked the door in."

Hendershot saw the screws pop off the latch, heard the door slap against the cubicle. The sound echoed off the floor tiles and the cinderblock walls.

"He just stood there," Clayton said. "I couldn't get past him. He was mad. He's got these piggy eyes that go all squinty. He told me I was dead."

"He said that. 'You're dead.'"

"Yeah."

"What'd you say?"

"Fuck you."

Hendershot's throat tightened. "It's an answer."

"I had the knife out, Dad. I don't remember taking it out of my knapsack, but I must've because it was in my hand pointing at him. When he saw it, he stopped and I told him if he didn't back off, I was going to slit his guts open. I didn't know if the knife was long enough to go into his guts or even get through his fat, but I didn't care. I was shaking." The boy's face twisted in anguished ferocity. "I was shaking, but I really wanted to hurt him. I think I wanted to kill him." Forlorn, the boy glanced away. "I wanted to kill him, Dad."

"Better him than you, son."

"You think so?"

"Yes."

Clayton breathed deeply. "When I told Dr. Witherspoon about it, he said I was probably having a panic attack. But I don't think so. I think I was having a hate attack. I was gritting my teeth and holding the knife in front of me and I said these awful things. I told him if he didn't leave me alone, I was going to cut off his balls and stuff them down his throat. And I wasn't yelling, Dad. I was calm. I was still shaking, but I was calm."

"Did it work?"

"Huh?"

"Did he back off?"

"Yeah. But I meant that stuff I was saying, Dad. Like... when I said it, I meant it."

"Well sure. You have to mean it. Otherwise they don't believe you."

"I guess."

"Sure. And then? What'd you do then?"

"Then I wasn't sure what to do. I just wanted to get out of there. Or get him out of there. I couldn't stop shaking. It got pretty bad. I backed him up to the urinals and told him to stay there but he saw me shaking and he said, 'Make me.' And then he came at me. I swiped at him with the knife but I missed and he hit me in the nose and broke it with his arm, and I banged my head on this tap thing on top of the urinals and there was blood all over the place. That's when I lost it, Dad. I went totally nuts. I was waving the knife and yelling stuff – I don't know. I don't remember all of it. It was like when I'm running. My arms and legs are moving and I know I'm running but my brain is someplace else. My brain goes someplace else."

"You were in the zone."

"I don't know. Yeah. Maybe. I was in the zone."

For a moment they considered the zone.

"And then what?"

"The next thing is I'm alone in there. I'm sitting on this cement step you stand on when you pee in the urinals and my hair's all sticky and so's my face and my hands and it's blood. And then Mr. Kuznetsov is putting a bandage on my head."

"Where was Fat Frank?"

"I didn't see him. He was gone. Mr. Kuznetsov picked up my knapsack and he took me upstairs to Mr. Robertson's office. Mr. Robertson phoned Mum and the ambulance and they came and we went to the hospital and I got twelve stitches." He grazed his head with his fingertips. "I think the hair's growing back."

"Your mum said the police came to talk to you."

"Yeah."

"What'd you tell them?"

"Not much."

"Did you tell them everything you've just told me?"

"No."

"Why not?"

"Because it's stupid."

"I don't think *stupid's* the right word, son. Your mum told me you seemed to be sorry about what happened."

The boy hunched his shoulders, tensed his fists. "That's just it, Dad. That's the thing."

"What is?"

"I'm not sorry. I'm not sorry at all." His face, to Hendershot, looked naked. "Am I a bad person, Dad?"

"No, you're not. You're an alive person."

"So's Fat Frank."

"That's true."

The boy looked around the room – the two beds, the window, the washstand in the corner, the rack that held their suitcases, their coats on hangers. Frowning, he licked his lips. "The thing about...about killing yourself...is you sort of think everybody's going to be sorry. Like, you think when they find you, they're all going to cry and they're all going to feel bad about the way they treated you and all that. Like when Rajinder left his jacket folded up on the bridge, a bunch of girls in our class cried and they read a poem they wrote for him over the p.a. system. But what if..." his eyes clouded, "...what if after you're gone you don't hear the poem? What if your soul...or whatever...doesn't wait around? Or maybe you don't even *have* a soul. What if after you die there's nothing, Dad? If everything's just...*nothing?*"

At a loss, Hendershot watched the kid shoulder this sad and ancient burden. There were fatherly words that needed to be recited, but he wasn't sure what they were. His own father, the taciturn ex-rear gunner who carried bits of shrapnel in his left arm, once told him that when he was wounded over Berlin, he knew for certain he was going to die, but that anger and dumb luck had changed his mind.

"When I lost my leg..." Hendershot began, but checked himself. Who was he to compete with this boy for a share of life's pain? The kid had enough of his own.

He changed tack. "Look," he said. "To be honest, I don't know what to tell you. You faced something I never had to, you dealt with it, and you're still here. And you did it honourably. That's good enough for me. And as far as the afterlife goes, it could be curlicues and hot fudge sundaes or it could be a mud bog, I don't know. Never been there. The point is, you're here and I'm here. That's us guys two, the afterlife nothing. We got a shut-out going."

The boy's smile was uncertain. "So, it's just a game?"

"I'm not saying that. But it's *like* a game."

"What if it's not?"

"Then it's something else."

The boy hunched in on himself. "Dad? Are you going to tell anybody? About what happened?"

"Not if you don't want me to."

"But isn't it illegal, Dad? What I did – isn't it against the law?"

"I'd call it self defense."

"But that's you, Dad. What about...the police and a judge and...I mean what about them?" The boy set his jaw. "Will I go to jail, Dad?"

"Not if I can help it. Look, son. The way I see it, you were attacked and you defended yourself."

Clayton lay back on the bed, his feet on the floor, his fingers locked over his chest. "Mum says you always simplify complicated issues."

"Oh, does she? Well, maybe she's right. That's what simpletons do."

"Are you a simpleton, Dad?"

"I'm working on it. There are guys out there peddling Twelve Steps to Nirvana. I'm trying to scrape up just one."

"Which is?"

Hendershot stood. "Right now, beer and a burger."

"That's two, Dad."

As they passed the desk downstairs, the manager handed them a message. When Hendershot phoned, Miss Weins told him that Margaret Lowenstein was back, and would like to see him. "Albert Memorial, Kensington Gardens, ten a.m. tomorrow," Miss Weins said. Adding, "If that suits, Mr. Rob."

Blunt, but consummately professional, in Hendershot's opinion.

27.

Which was more than he could say for himself. Because he was late. Too long in the bathroom, indecisive at breakfast, argumentative with Clayton about subway lines and stations. Out loud, he ranked these obstacles as simply more evidence of a fucked-up modern world; privately he acknowledged them as a delaying tactic. The prospect of MARGARET loomed somewhere between delight and terror. He seemed to want to rush headlong into avoidance. Even the walk to the rendezvous was too long and too short.

The memorial itself was at once a monument to love and loyalty while at the same time a glorified gazebo. The prince was either sitting on a throne or lounging in an armchair; Hendershot wasn't sure which. A few sightseers stood on the steps of the plinth, but his attention was drawn immediately to the figures on the path in front.

"Dad." Clayton pointed. "Is that her?"

Short and round, the woman was dressed in a long dark coat, stretched tightly over her humped shoulders and bulging back. A high storm collar obscured the back of her head, leaving frizzy white hair floating above like wisps of frosted grass. She was a dark egg. Seemingly armless, legless and headless. Swollen. Ovoid.

Hendershot's throat tightened. "That's her, all right."

"Whoa. She's fat."

"People get older, son." He approached the rotund figure with trepidation, suddenly afraid it might *not* be Margaret, or equally, that it was.

"Hello, Margaret."

She turned to face him. In one hand she carried a cane. The curly hair was white and thin, the smooth face mottled, the voluptuous figure bloated. But inside it all he sensed her old solidity. Looked for it in her eyes.

"Is it you?" she said, lifting her face slightly away from him. He saw from her opaque gaze that she was blind. "Albert?" she called over her shoulder. "Albert?"

A powerful-looking middle-aged man in a tweed jacket, who Hendershot had assumed was another sightseer, stepped near. Placed a protective hand on her arm. "I'm here, ma'am."

The hand not holding the cane clutched Albert's sleeve. "Who is it?" she asked the air.

"It's me, Margaret. Rob Hendershot. The hockey player, remember? I stayed with Mister Green." Embarrassment stifled him. He was willing to admit to being a nobody, but not here. Not with her. He wanted to tell her he remembered the fullness of her lips, the softness of her skin just above her collar bone, the glory of her breasts under his palms, her eyes. But he couldn't. Not in front of his son who stood one pace behind him. He took a breath, determined not to grovel. "I'm Beowulf," he said. "I'm Victory."

Her hand on Albert's rough sleeve stilled. "*Victory*," she said. She handed her cane to Albert, reached up to Hendershot with both hands. "Come closer."

Her touch was light and thorough. The pads of her fingers brushed his forehead, eye sockets, cheeks, nose, lips, jaw. Her hands slid down both sides of his neck, shaped his shoulders, squeezed his arms.

"It's you," she said softly.

"Yes."

"Not as fit."

"I got lazy."

"Rob." She fumbled for his hand. Held it in both of her

own. "It was your right leg, wasn't it?"

"Yes."

"May I?"

Wheezing heavily, and despite a grumbled protest from Albert, she stooped in front of Hendershot to cup between her palms, his thigh, his knee, the buckles of his prosthesis and finally the metal piping. Her hair was so sparse he could see her scalp. "So cold," she said. "So thin." She had trouble breathing. "Is it strong?"

"Titanium," he said. "Sports model. I have the old one at home. Flesh-coloured, more meat on it. For formal occasions." He reached for her hands to help her rise, while solicitous Albert, hovering, almost single-handedly set her on her feet.

"Thank you." Her face was florid. Sweat beaded her brow. Recovering her breath, she said, "As you can see, I am no longer svelte." Her laugh that of a much younger Margaret. "I have metamorphosed – from a toadstool into the toad itself."

"You were never a toadstool, Margaret."

Her smile was mischievous. "You were so young."

"At night I chewed my blankets."

"Oh dear. Does that mean I'm supposed to count you as another of my regrets?"

"I know I have."

She laughed delightedly. Behind Hendershot, Clayton grated his feet on the gravel path. Margaret lifted her face. Listened. "Is someone there with you?"

"My son. Clayton."

"Your son? How wonderful!" She was genuinely pleased. Took Clayton's hand and when he said he really liked her paintings, she glowed. "What a kind young man you are," she said, "and what an astute critic." To Hendershot's amazement, the boy allowed her to explore his face. "So handsome," she told the kid, who blushed. "Your nose is finer than your father's, but it's been broken, too. Are you an ice hockey player as well?"

"No. I'm a runner."

"Well, what a marvelous face. I should love to paint you, Clayton, but..." she shrugged. "Macular degeneration, you see. Runs in the family. My father had it. He was a furrier and needed his eyes, so he took his blindness as one of God's cruelties. If I were a believer, I would too." She turned her face to include Hendershot in her remarks. "A poet once wrote that art should not *mean*, but *be*. I used to disagree with that statement, but now I think it applies to life as well. It simply is, isn't it?"

Hendershot gazed at her. "So you don't...*work*, anymore?"

"Oh, of course I do. But of necessity, my work has changed. When I first found my eyesight failing, I threw myself into abstract painting – the shapes, you know. But once the sight was completely gone, I turned to other things. I made pictures out of found objects – bits of metal, plastic, wood and so on. The *texture* of things. Most people wince when I rattle on about it, but *touch* has always held a primary place in the world of the senses. Two years ago, I had a showing of my little pieces. The critics were unkind, but the viewers were moved. By viewers, I mean those who share my affliction. They 'saw' the whole exhibition through their fingertips."

"I've been telling Clayton about when you painted *Victory*," Hendershot dared.

"Ah," she said, "*Victory*. It caused quite a stir recently. What with Connor's trial." She lifted her face. "But of course, you know all about that. My secretary said you mentioned it on the phone."

"Yes," Hendershot managed. "Did you go to the trial?"

"Yes, at the beginning. But when details of my relationship with Connor came out, there was a flurry of publicity and the reporters got hold of me. Some assumed Connor was Beowulf, and the contradiction was too delicious for them to ignore. Beowulf the alleged bomber. Beowulf the fallen hero."

Hendershot felt himself on the edge of an important truth. Finally. His tongue felt thick. "What did you tell them?"

"What I'd always told them. The portrait was a composite. You, of course. Connor, certainly. But others as well. The Hungarian boy whose ears I used. One, anyway. It'd been nearly torn off by the secret police in an 'interrogation.'" She turned her milky eyes directly on Hendershot's face, as if she saw him there. "My Beowulf was meant to be vulnerable, you see. To carry his mortality with him everywhere."

But what else did you tell them about Connor, Hendershot wanted to shout, when suddenly Clayton cleared his throat. "My dad and I have been looking for it."

Margaret smiled quizzically. "I beg your pardon?"

Hendershot shook his head as a warning, but the kid ploughed on – proudly, defiantly. "*Victory.* We went to Whitechapel Art Gallery and saw it in a book and a lady there told us it was in another gallery, but the man there said it might be auctioned off. If it is, we're going to see it. My dad's never actually seen it." Clayton paused. "He's pretty excited."

To Hendershot, the look on Margaret's face was close to beatific. "My god," she said.

"It was just an idea," Hendershot offered.

Clayton said, "It's a great painting, Ms Lowenstein."

Margaret's chin lifted. Had she sight, she might've been studying the clouds. "Albert?" she said.

"Ma'am."

"Could you bring the car round?"

"I can."

"I think we should take these two gentlemen to lunch, don't you?"

"In all likelihood, ma'am."

They waited curbside while Albert fetched the vehicle. Not a long limousine, but a late-model Ford whose upholstery was worn on the driver's side. Margaret was seated regally in the back seat, while Hendershot squeezed in next to her. Metal leg jammed against the front passenger seat, into which Clayton belted himself like a co-pilot on a moon shot. Despite the car interior's shabbiness – nicks in the ceiling fabric, frayed nap on the floor mats – Hendershot felt as though in the presence of royalty. Margaret, a stand-in for Queen Victoria, had her Albert, though their precise relationship was ambiguous. *Maybe an aged nephew*, Hendershot thought, *family retainer, queen's ghillie*. Albert hunched forward in the driver's seat and strangled the steering wheel between meaty fists.

"Where to, ma'am?"

"I think dim sum, Albert."

28.

The restaurant was a two-storey walk-up, smorgasbord on the ground floor, gourmet menu on top. Albert parked the car, then he and Hendershot assisted Margaret up the stairs where an elderly Chinese waiter welcomed her.

"Ms Lowenstein. Good to see you."

"And you, Percy. These are my friends from Canada."

"Welcome," the waiter said.

The window table overlooked the quiet street, a series of whitewashed Georgians fronted by wrought-iron pickets and marble steps. Glistening black doors. Once the residences of the gentry, now bed-and-breakfasts, law offices and holistic medical clinics. Peaceful. And when the dim sum arrived, Hendershot was excessively pleased to see Clayton use chopsticks. Sensed his wife's influence. Possibly Julian's. The kid handled the chopsticks like a gourmet, whereas he, and Margaret and Albert used cutlery.

As they ate, Margaret chatted with Clayton. Where had he been, what had he seen, where would he like to go next? And Clayton answered happily. Trafalgar Square, performance of *The Invisible Man*, the palace, the street artist, Greenwich, the retracing of his father's run.

"Really?" Margaret said. "He showed you?" Turning her face to Hendershot. "He never showed me. Didn't even describe it – unless I've forgotten."

"You haven't forgotten," Hendershot said. "I don't think I ever told you." He thought for a moment. "Whatever happened to Nigel and Tony?"

"Ah. Nigel and Tony."

"Mister Green once called them the Spelman Street Irregulars."

"Oh god," she laughed. "I didn't know that." Her face brightened. "Such eager, nosy little beggars. They made me laugh. Little mercenaries, obsessed with money. Money, money, money."

"Do you see them at all?"

"No." Her face composed itself. "Nigel died not long after you left. Nineteen seventy-eight, I think. He'd got mixed up with a crowd of skinheads – real ones. Neo-fascists, swastikas, all that. Anti-Asian, anti-coloured, anti-everything, I expect. The National Front Squadron, they called themselves. Attempted a Kristallnacht in Brick Lane, and in the melée he was struck on the head. Death by misadventure was the official line."

Hendershot, who thought all death was by misadventure, said, "And Tony?"

"Ah. Well, Tony. You'll never believe this. Tony went off to agricultural college. Can you imagine? An uncle helped pay his way. Market gardener. Somewhere in Kent. I haven't seen Tony in fifteen years. He'd just married a very large woman. I expect they have several large children by now."

"And Connor?" Because he might as well get down to it. An interrogation, of sorts. Because what he'd been looking for from this trip, in addition to Margaret, the painting, the time with Clayton, was an explanation, apology, retribution. What other fools like him called closure. As if there was such a thing.

Margaret paused. Felt for her tiny cup. As he poured her request for more tea, his hand trembled, though he managed not to dribble from the teapot spout. And kept his voice even. "Clayton and I went to Connor's trial. Couldn't get in. Sold out performance."

She lifted her cup halfway to her lips, felt for a spot on

the table to set it down. Gazed at him with opaque eyes. A veil between him and her that he wished he could tear down. Whenever he had thought of her, it hadn't only been her short stature, her voluptuous body or her capable hands that lingered in his mind. It had been her eyes. Large, liquid, intelligent, accepting. He wanted them now. He missed them. If he could fall into them now, if only for a moment.

"Of course, I attended his trial," she said. "I was called upon to testify. As a kind of...character witness."

"What did you tell them? In court."

"I told them the truth, as I knew it."

"Which was?"

"That he was a stonemason. That he was my lover. That when I knew him at school, he was kind to me. As he was when he grew up. To me, Connor was always Connor Mack. His mother was Mrs. Mack. Kind, decent people. I never thought of them as otherwise."

"Mister Green did."

She raised her chin. "George Green *guessed*. He was always guessing. Grasping at straws. But after that day on the bridge, I don't think even George was sure what he knew or didn't know about Connor." Her voice softened. "I don't think you knew, either."

She must have thought she had him there. At the mention of the bridge, he remembered the cold wind coming up off the water. The pain in his ribs as he drove Connor into the railing. The cry of seagulls.

"I had no idea what he was up to," she finished.

"I don't buy that, Margaret. How could you not know, for chrissake?"

She reached for his hand, but Hendershot pushed hers away. Across the table, Clayton had gone very still. He had stopped chewing. The boy was nervous. Frightened. "Dad, may I be excused?"

"I don't think that'll be necessary, son." Hendershot felt

reckless. He was going to Beowulf his Grendel right now. In front of Clayton. So that the kid could see, so that the kid would know, so that the kid...

"I have to go to the bathroom," Clayton said.

"No, you don't."

"Dad."

Again, Margaret's hand sought Hendershot's on the table. She nearly knocked over the teapot. Pinned his hand under hers. "Let him go," she said. "Please."

Albert, quiet until then, pushed back his chair. "You'll want to be careful, sir." He stood. "I can show the lad where it is. He'll be safe with me." He waited, hulking. "I'll just be down the hall, ma'am. Should you need me."

Margaret nodded.

Hendershot waited until Clayton had disappeared down the narrow corridor, and Albert had stationed himself outside the men's room. "What's the deal here, Margaret?"

"I know how you must feel."

"That's the thing, though. I don't think you do. One day I could run, probably skate. The next day I couldn't. *Ever.*"

She said, "I came to the hospital as soon as I heard."

"Yeah. I found your little present under my pillow. I figured: Tooth Fairy. No, wait a minute: Leg Fairy."

"I know how it must have looked."

"Did Connor put up the money?"

"Don't be absurd."

"He helped you most of your life, Margaret. You testified for him in court." Promising himself he'd shut up, he kept talking. "That day on the bridge was a set-up, wasn't it? From start to finish. And you knew it."

"You're wrong."

"Am I?" He leaned back from the table. Albert down the hall, arms crossed over his chest. "Here's a question, Margaret. One I've wanted to ask you for years. Why did you let me make love to you?"

"You wanted to, so badly."

"You had Connor."

"No, I didn't. That's what no one understands. I never had Connor. Even when I had Connor, I didn't have him."

"And he told you to take me to bed to...what...distract me? Keep me from following him?"

"I think you overestimate the effect you had on him."

"I sure overestimated the effect I had on you."

"You were lovely. But I was older than you and..."

"...those May-December things never work out. Yeah, I know all that. I've seen all the movies. But at the time, that wasn't it, was it?"

She dipped her head. "No."

"What was it then? If you weren't bedding me to keep me away from Connor, what were you trying to do?"

"I was trying to finish a painting."

"What?"

"I needed to bed you so I could finish the painting."

"Jesus."

"The whole thing about Connor seemed so ridiculous, don't you see? All that spy business with George Green and Arthur de Largo."

Hendershot had a sudden flash of understanding, mostly because he'd always hoped it'd be inevitable. "So, Connor *did* know what those old guys were up to."

"Of course. He called them Holmes and Watson. It was just a bit of nonsense to him."

'Nonsense that cost me a leg. And them their lives."

"There was never any proof Connor had anything to do with their deaths. Or that the IRA did, either. George Green died of an aneurism. It was in the coroner's report."

"Yeah. Convenient. But they never found his notebook, did they? It was blue – what you'd call 'faded indigo.' I told one of the cops about it while I was in hospital. And I made a statement to another cop when I was in rehab. I told the cops everything. Did you know that whoever killed Arthur de Largo beat him to death with his own nightstick? And took his notebook..." Hendershot felt weary. Not tired – weary. His bones ached. Though he knew exactly where his tibia ended and the titanium began, he still had questions.

But Margaret had all the answers. "Arthur de Largo's killer was caught and convicted."

"Was he."

"You wouldn't have heard about it. You'd gone home by then. Off with your little nurse by then."

"That 'little nurse' is Clayton's mother."

"Ah."

Hendershot surrendered to exasperation. When it came to Connor Mack, he wanted to have been attacked as a worthy opponent. Not duped and peg-legged as a bumbling incompetent. "You're forgetting, Margaret, that Connor has been found guilty. I've seen it on TV, read it in the newspapers. 'Guilty of conduct in preparation for terrorist acts.'"

Margaret's face crumpled. "That is true. And it pains me. I confronted him, you know. After you and he fought on the bridge, and after the blast that hurt you. I asked him if he belonged to the IRA. He said no. I asked him if he'd ever built or planted a bomb, if he'd ever killed or maimed someone. He said he never had, and never would."

"And you believed him."

"Except for lying about his connection to the IRA, he was telling the truth. It was proven in court. Others were directly responsible for what happened to you." She folded her hands in her lap. In prayer. Or defeat. "But..."

"But what?"

"But what I didn't ask him, and what I should have, was *who* chose the targets."

Hendershot wasn't sure if he pitied or despised her. Pitied or despised himself. He'd asked her, she'd answered. Why then, did he feel unsatisfied? "I was young, Margaret. I just wanted to play hockey. Be in your painting. Love you, if you wanted."

Clayton came out of the washroom. Approached the table, Albert a respectful pace behind. Hendershot rose from his chair. "I think we'd better go now, son."

"Oh don't," Margaret said.

"No, I think we should." Hendershot signaled the waiter. "And don't worry about the bill. I've got it covered."

"Rob," she said.

"Hey." He herded a flustered Clayton ahead of him. "No problem. It's on me."

Later, Hendershot and Clayton spent the evening at a laundromat, eating pizza from a box under fluorescent lights, while clothes somersaulted in the dryer. Clayton packed the leftover slices into a plastic bag. On the way back to the hotel, they passed a piece of cardboard pinned to a wrought-iron fence that surrounded a defunct pump-house. Hungry, the sign said. *Need food.*

Clayton hung the bag of pizza from a fence spike. "Lucky we came this way," he said.

29.

"I wish," Louise's voice crackled through the line, "that you would've booked a hotel with phones in the rooms. Every time I've tried to get in touch with you, I've had to go through operators. And sometimes they haven't been able to connect. And even if they do, I have to leave a message at the front desk. It's like being trapped inside one of your old movies."

"They're not *my* old movies, Louise, they're..."

"Classics. I know. Look, I'm glad you called." Her voice dropped. "Is he there with you?"

"He's just outside the booth. I sent him to the corner to get a newspaper."

Her voice, aimed, he thought, at hysteria. "You *sent* him ..."

"It's okay." Hendershot craned his neck, caught sight of the curly hair in the crowd. "I can see him from here."

He heard her breathe in, blow out. "Has he told you anything?"

"Lots of things. We talk, if that's what you mean."

"About the attack at school."

"I wouldn't call it an attack. More like a skirmish."

Her breath again. In, out.

"Louise, are you smoking?"

"What did he tell you?"

"You are, aren't you? Julian smokes, you smoke. You guys *are* health professionals, aren't you?"

"Oh, for god's sake, Rob."

"Sure, he told me what happened."

"Which was?"

"Which was in the strictest confidence."

"Do you enjoy being *completely* obtuse?"

"I promised him, Louise. If he wants to tell you, he will."

"He's thirteen years old."

"Yeah, I know. I counted it up. Used all my fingers."

"Is it too much to ask that we be civil about this?"

"No, we can try civil. But it's up to him, Louise. I can put him on the phone if you want. Better yet, can't this wait? We'll be home in a few days. Then you can drag him into the interrogation room. You got the lights and the rubber hose?"

Louise inhaled, exhaled. As long and slow as contemplation. He tried to picture her smoking, the cigarette between her fingers, but couldn't. He'd never seen her with a cigarette, though it was the tobacco smell on her clothing that first alerted him. That time when he went to pick her up at the end of her hospital shift, and the sight of Julian lighting up a cigarillo in the parking lot set loose his insecurities.

When she finally spoke, her voice quavered. "I got a call three days ago. From the police. They're thinking of pressing charges against Clayton."

Hendershot's stomach soured. The taste filled his mouth. "Why would they do that?"

"Not the police, exactly. But the family of that..." She started again. "Franklin Burroughs's father. You know, the father of..."

"Fat Frank."

"Please, Rob."

"Fat Frank's father. Fat Frank Senior. Big Fat Frank. Fat Frank the First."

"He's been released from a halfway house or a rehab centre or something."

"Of course he has. Naturally he has. And he's got post-traumatic stress disorder or substance dependency or bi-polar disease or some other goddamn..."

"Will you *listen*, please? *Please?*" She waited. "He wants to press for assault with a weapon. I wasn't going to tell you but I..." She paused. "I haven't been able to sleep, Rob. At work I don't remember what I'm doing. Yesterday I took a patient's blood pressure, changed her IV bag, wrote it in her chart and five minutes later I started to do the whole process over again."

"That's just being efficient, Louise. That's just being over-the-top goddamned, unappreciated *efficient.*"

"I can't talk to you when you get like this."

"Sure, you can. Talk. Go ahead. Christ, he's a kid, a *minor.* And *he* was the one that got hurt. Who the hell are they to lay charges against *the kid that got hurt?* Do they know that blimp was bullying him? Threatening him? Do they know that? Do they know we can press charges, too?" Though in his rage, he couldn't see himself doing that. What he saw was himself, unstrapping his titanium leg and swinging it like a baseball bat. Home runs with the heads of Fat Frank, Fat Frank Senior and anyone else standing between him and his kid. He'd Beowulf them, the fuckers. Except that this one-legged Beowulf would probably fall down.

Suddenly, he was sweating. Leaned his forehead against the cool glass of the phone box. "Listen," he willed himself calm. "Listen. Have you seen a lawyer?"

"The charges haven't been laid yet. I think the detective was being kind. He said they'd have to investigate further."

"The *detective?*"

"Inspector, detective – whatever they're called. But yes, I've consulted a lawyer."

"Not the divorce guy."

"No, not him. Emma Whittaker. You remember Emma."

"Is she good?"

"She's good, but...it could be expensive, Rob. Julian's offered to help, but he has his child support payments, and I know the store isn't exactly..."

"Don't worry about the store. I can handle the store. The thing is," he breathed a couple of times, "are you okay?"

"I'm worried, that's all."

"But you're holding it together."

"Yes." She paused. "You know," she said hesitantly, "when that policeman phoned me, I remembered that policeman in London – the one that visited you. The one with the mustache."

"Constable Mayhew. But I don't remember a mustache."

"I felt like things had come full circle, somehow."

Clayton was panting outside the phone box, holding a rolled-up newspaper like a runner's baton. "Look," Hendershot said, "he's here. Want to talk to him?"

"For a minute."

"You won't tell him about the charges?"

"No."

"Because he's had a good time here, Louise. He's having a good time."

"I won't tell him. I promise." The cigarette must have gone out. "What about you, Rob? Did you have – are you having a good time?"

"Me?" He didn't know the truth until he said it. "I could be wrong, but I might be having a *great* time." Outside, Clayton was tapping on the glass. "He's here. I'll put him on."

The kid opened the door. Excited. "Dad."

Hendershot passed him the phone. "It's your mother."

Clayton handed him the newspaper.

30.

They were crunching along a gravel path towards the zoo when Clayton asked Hendershot if he was happy. An overcast sky wept cold mist. The park was almost deserted. Solitary benches slumped under dripping trees. A bearded jogger passed them, sleek in black spandex, tinny music leaking from his headphones.

"*Should* I be happy?" Hendershot asked.

"He's guilty. They're going to lock him up, Dad. For twenty years. He'll be ninety-one when he gets out."

"That's a long time."

"Then you should be glad."

"Tickled to death."

"I bet Ms Lowenstein isn't very happy, though."

Hendershot regarded his son. "What makes you say that?"

"I don't know." But from the way the boy spoke, Hendershot surmised the kid had recognized a tolerance in Margaret that Hendershot had chosen to overlook. "Maybe," the boy went on, "if she knew you were happy, she'd try to be happy, too."

Hendershot was tempted to discredit the boy's observation. Chalk it up to innocence and inexperience. However, he was reminded that this same boy had, if viewed through hockey lenses, won a face-off against Fat Frank, sometime-centreman for Team Death. In which case the kid deserved answers. "I wouldn't say she was happy, son. Resigned, maybe. Like everybody else." Hendershot himself felt unaccountably flat. Whatever joy or satisfaction he'd hoped to find in a Connor Mack conviction wasn't enough to bathe his entire personal existence in sunshine. Like some cartoon character from his childhood, he wondered if he carried a permanent cloud of gloom over his head. Seemed to follow him everywhere.

A notion that pushed him into thinking about wins and losses. He saw himself in a game somewhere, third period, clock ticking down to last chances. He was awarded a penalty shot. Took the puck from centre, stick-handled in, drew the goalie across, pivoted, the puck suddenly on his backhand, the old spinnerama. *Ting!*

Connor's conviction and sentence had hit the post.

"You know," he said, summing up something, not sure exactly what, "I've lived almost as long without this leg as I lived with it." He kicked the gravel, sprayed stones. "Maybe she could be happy."

"You should go and talk to her, Dad. In the restaurant, you were pretty rude."

"You didn't hear it all, son. I was trying to be honest."

"Sometimes, Dad, being honest is just...harsh. And you didn't even ask her where the painting is."

They followed the signs to the animal enclosures. Clayton's knowledge was eclectic and thorough. Asian elephants were smaller than African ones. The white rhino had a smaller head than the black. Australian crocodiles were the largest reptiles on the planet.

At the penguin pool, the attendant discoursed on his flightless charges. "They mate for life, you know." Pointed to a disheveled bird standing at the pool's edge. "Scruffy Arnold. Lives in that box." Arnold teetered on the tiles, a derelict in shabby white shirt and tails, hands behind his back. "His wife Moira's in the box at the moment. He wanted her to come out for a stroll, but she won't have it. But he's patient, is our Arnold. You'll see. She'll come 'round."

But she didn't. And when Hendershot and Clayton left, Arnold still waited on clawed feet, in grave and rumpled dignity. Hendershot couldn't help but look back at the bird in admiration. As they walked, Clayton wondered aloud if Louise had ever met Ms Lowenstein, and Hendershot recounted how the two women had stood over his hospital bed while, submerged under pain killer, he could only guess at their conversation. "I was on your mother's ward for six weeks. When they moved me to another hospital for rehab, your mum visited me every day. Brought me fresh fruit, books and magazines. Chocolate."

"Did Ms Lowenstein come to see you too?"

"No. She saw that your mum and I were becoming an item."

The boy absorbed this information. They were nearing the park's gate and the busy street beyond.

"But you're not an item anymore," Clayton decided.

"No," Hendershot said. "And I'm sorry about that, son."

Clayton stopped in the middle of the path. Turned his back to the noisy traffic, as if he didn't want to be overheard. "When we get home, Dad, do you think I could live with you?"

Hendershot pictured the apartment above the store. The kitchenette. The murphy bed folded up into the wall.

Anticipating objection, Clayton said, "I could bring the fold-up cot from home. And pillows and blankets and every-thing."

"What about your mum?"

"You could talk her into it."

"Oh yeah? You *do* know my record for talking your mum into anything."

"You *could*, Dad. For one thing, I'd be closer to my new school."

And the courthouse, Hendershot thought. *And the lawyer's office, and the police station.*

Clayton said, "I could work in the store on Saturdays. I could gain maturity and responsibility."

"You could write a mission statement."

"I'm serious, Dad."

"I can see that."

"So you'll let me?"

"I snore sometimes."

"I know. I pinch your nose until you stop."

"How come I don't know that?"

"You're sleeping, Dad." Clayton shifted his weight from one leg to the other. "Will you talk to Mum?"

"Soon as we get home."

They left the park through York Gate. Allowed the blustery weather to propel them towards Madame Tussaud's, where they bought tickets to get in out of the rain. Inside, the royal family stood unmoving on a dais, mop-haired rock musicians lounged on a couch, all seemingly frozen for eternity. Clayton wandered through them all in a state of meditation. "Wax," he said when he rejoined his father.

Hendershot laughed. "What tipped you off?"

"Nobody asked for spare change." Clayton surveyed the figures, as if he were a stranger at a cocktail party. "What happens to them when they're not famous any more?"

"Don't know. Melted down, I guess. Made into candles. Or maybe stored in a walk-in cooler in the basement."

"Whoa," Clayton said. "Think how that must feel."

"I'm losing you here, son."

"I mean when the real people see their own wax figures melted down, or whatever. They must feel like they've died or something."

"Maybe not. Not if what they're famous for is still around." Hendershot touched the kid's shoulder. Feared his son was leading them into ghoul territory. Prelude to despair. The All Flesh Is Grass Blues. "Why all the worry about fame, Clayton? Do you want to be famous?"

"Kind of." Looking at his feet. "Or at least really good at something."

"Like what?"

"I don't know yet."

"What? Thirteen years old and you still haven't got your whole life mapped out?"

"Not too funny, Dad."

"No, I don't suppose. Shot in the dark."

A troop of tourists marched single file downstairs to the Chamber of Horrors, but Clayton didn't want to follow them. "Could we just go now, Dad?"

Outside they bought samosas and stood under an awning to eat them. Traffic hissed along the rain-soaked street, the whisper of people going places. Hendershot asked, "Well, where to now?"

"You'll think it's stupid."

"Try me."

"Can we see the hospital?"

"The hospital."

"Where you met Mum."

Hendershot watched the rain. "It's a couple of miles from here."

"We can take the tube."

"It's just a big building."

"I want to see it."

"With lots of windows."

"We can find it though, can't we, Dad?"

31.

The hospital had been expanded. Extension wings, glass towers, residences, emergency entrances and exits had sprouted adjacent to the main building. A labyrinth of health services. Signs pointing in all directions. Standing on the pavement, dwarfed by progress, Hendershot saw his own tragedy miniaturized. His amputation one of thousands.

"Which room was yours?" Clayton asked.

"No idea." Then, seeing the boy's disappointment: "I think it was that window at the end there – second floor."

Clayton nodded, gazing. For him, Hendershot thought, this is history.

"And Mum worked here," Clayton said.

"Yes."

The boy remained staring at the building. "Was she a good nurse, Dad?"

"Your mother," Hendershot told the truth, "was a great nurse. Is a great nurse."

Clayton continued to stare, before facing his father. "You could've died, Dad."

"But I didn't."

"Me neither."

They stood together for an awkward moment, each considering the implications of *could've died*, one of which, Clayton pointed out, was that they wouldn't be standing there considering the implications of *could've died*. "So, if we're still alive," Clayton said, after slow deliberation, "we should celebrate."

"Hey," Hendershot said, "party on, man."

"I mean we *have* to find the painting, Dad. What if some-body just...melts it down?"

32.

Both the whereabouts of the painting and Clayton's insistence on seeing it pushed Hendershot toward a desperation that he put down to two things: a desire to show his son he wasn't a shmuck, and the knowledge that in a few days they'd be on the plane home. Where Louise waited. Not to mention Fat Frank, assorted lawyers, judges and shrinks. *Victory*, he decided, was what was needed. On several levels. To find it required planning, patience and time. *To hell with that*, he thought, swallowed his pride, filled his pockets with coins and strode to his favourite phone box.

"Ah, Mr. Hendershot."

"I thought we'd settled on Rob, Miss Weins."

"Of course. Mr. Rob."

"I'm going to come clean, Miss Weins. I'm using you as a short cut. No doubt you've heard of my disaster."

"The dim sum," Miss Weins said.

"It didn't go well."

"Really?" Miss Weins was genuinely surprised. Or genuinely faking surprise. Hendershot didn't care which. She said, "I was under the impression she found her visit with you stimulating."

"Not the word I'd use, Miss Weins."

"She said she found you and your son refreshing. Gave her inspiration. That, of course, is classified information."

"Safe with me," Hendershot said, fighting the urge to be flattered. "The thing is, my refreshing son and I have a problem." And laid out for her the rumoured auction, the plane ride home, the completed portrait he had never, in fact, seen completed.

"Never?"

"Well, in a book. About the size of a postage stamp. Can you tell me, Miss Weins, where and when I might find *Victory*? Or point me to someone who'd know?"

Silence. Not even yoga breathing. When her voice returned, it sounded stern. "I'm a personal secretary, Mr. Rob. I'm meant to be a professional."

"I think you're as professional as they come, Miss Weins."

"Thank you."

"But what I'm talking about here is compassion. Pity, even. You know – good guy stuff."

"And you think I'm a 'good guy'?"

"I'm hoping so, Miss Weins."

Huge sigh. "I'd like to say this is more than my job's worth. There is, however, no law in this country that says you can't view a work of art that is on public display."

Hendershot made an effort to sound casual. "And if a guy wanted to attend this viewing, where and when would you say he'd have to go?"

"Sotheby's in New Bond Street. Tomorrow at one p.m."

Hendershot fumbled for his pen and scribbled. Repeated the address and time out loud for Clayton, who crowded next to him. "You've been very generous, Miss Weins. Thank you. For everything."

"Surely not everything."

"For your help, then. Professionally speaking."

"Not at all."

"If the opportunity ever arises, maybe you could tell Margaret that there are no hard feelings."

A pause. "Are you sure about that, Mr. Rob?"

"Not really. But it sounds good, doesn't it?"

"It certainly does. In any case, I've given you the information. I expect something in return."

"And what would that be?"

"That once you've seen the portrait, you'll give me a ring and let me know how you got on."

"Will do, Miss Weins."

Hendershot hung up. Clayton consulted his street guide. Finger in the index. Flipping back to the maps. Saying in his best, clipped Double-Oh-Seven, "Bond. New Bond." Picked out the underground lines, tube stations, transfer points. Calculated travel times. "Is this," he said, looking up from his plotting, "a tourist thing? Or a nostalgically depressed thing?"

"Both," Hendershot said.

33.

Hendershot half-expected the security guard to turn them away from the door, though he wasn't sure why he thought this. Maybe he emitted a B-league aura which time and experience would never diminish. A wavelength that goalkeepers, gatekeepers, *maitre de's* and security guards could easily detect and dismiss. The people who'd already entered the auction house were better dressed than he and Clayton. Those buyers wore fashionable black, while this drizzly day he and his son were in jeans, oily shoes and the olive drab raincoats they usually wore when they went fishing. *Right out of the boonies*, Hendershot thought. As if the two of them had rattled south by train out of a great northern bush, only to run smack into civilization.

Once inside, he imagined the art buyers more cunning than he was. Wealthier, better informed, more sophisticated. People with capped teeth and weighty portfolios, employers of chauffeurs, members of a club. He suspected he was out of his depth until – after the guard stashed Clayton's knapsack on a rear table, handed them a claim check and waved them through to the public viewing gallery – Hendershot saw the painting.

It hung in a corner at the far end of the room. Past the Rothko, the Frida Kahlo and the da Vinci cartoons. Past the charcoal drawings of the Transvaal and the British watercolour landscapes. Past the Elsie Few and Claude Rogers. Past all the names he should've known, but didn't.

Lot 77. Lowenstein, Margaret. *Victory*. Oil on canvas,

1974.

It took his breath away.

As they stood in front of it, Clayton said, "It's smaller than I thought it'd be."

"Yeah. Good though, huh?"

"It's like we're spying on him," Clayton said. "Like he doesn't know anybody's watching."

"He doesn't."

"And Grendel's arm. Almost as if he's not sure what to do with it."

"Pig's leg," Hendershot said. Feeling the cold grease of it.

Clayton peered close, stood back, took it in. "It's you, Dad. And not you. At the same time. How did she do that?"

"You'd have to ask *her*."

"He knows he won," Clayton said, "but now he doesn't know if it was worth it."

'Yeah."

"It's good." Clayton folded his arms across his chest. Decisive. "I like it."

Hendershot entered the painting. Felt again the swelling under his right eye. The stiffness in his shoulders. Remembered Margaret plugging in the electric heater when he'd begun to shiver. Recalled the smell of paint, the noise of kids playing soccer in the street, Mister Green thumping upstairs.

He shook himself. "Doesn't seem that long ago. I never expected to see it."

Clayton nodded. "'Of all the gin joints in all the world', huh, Dad?"

"'Play it, Sam'," Hendershot agreed. "'You played it for her, you can play it for me.'"

But what tune? he wondered. And stepped back two paces to study with forced objectivity the figure in the painting. Saw now what he guessed was Margaret's deliberate balance between light and dark, colour and shadow, triumph and regret, youth and – he saw it now, *saw* it, not with his eyes but with some inner vision. Age. *What she saw*, he thought. *Connor and me.*

"Christ," he said. "What an artist." He placed his arm around Clayton's shoulders. Just the two of them. Hanging out with Beowulf. Who looked back at them. Protective, and needing protection. "Think what it would be like to own that picture," Hendershot said.

Clayton grunted. "Yeah. You'd have to have a lot of money."

"How much, though?"

"Tens of thousands of pounds," Clayton said. "That's what the man at the gallery figured." The boy had a look of earnestness, coupled with an anticipation of danger. Eyes bright, brow furrowed. "Whoa. What're you thinking, Dad?"

"We could hang it in the apartment," Hendershot said. "I mean, if we wanted. Hell, we could hang it anywhere."

"Seriously, Dad? Where are you going to get the money?"

"You forget, son. I own a store. I'm a business. Incorporated. I've got the store's credit card with me. Twenty-two thousand dollar limit."

"Mum says credit cards belong in the freezer. Frozen in a block of ice." Clayton sighed. With regret, it seemed to Hendershot. Like a referee forced to make an unpopular decision. "Besides, it's an auction, Dad. You have to bid."

"So, let's bid. At the store we sometimes bid on consignments of out-of-print films. A lot of stinkers, but sometimes we net a few gems. Come on, son. What's the worst that could happen?"

"We end up naked and we have to phone Mum for a ticket home." But the kid was grinning. At possibilities. At, Hendershot was pleased to see, impulsiveness.

Clayton said, "I think you have to register or something. There was a sign when we came in."

"A sign," Hendershot said. He hadn't seen it. *Why do I never*, he thought, *read the signs?* "We'd better go and register then."

Clayton was patient: "You can change your mind, Dad."

"I bet that's what they told Beowulf."

Hendershot wove through the crowd, excusing himself as he rocked on his metal leg, a sailor among landlubbers. At one point a woman, about his age, in a tweed skirt, matching sweater and colourful splash of silk scarf, met his eyes. "Pardon me," she said. "Leslie Braithwaite?"

"No. Sorry."

"The one who does the charcoals?"

"No."

"Oh. Which one are you?"

"I'm not any of them."

"Oh dear." The woman coloured and turned away.

34.

The black paddle was embossed with a white number 63. Armed with it, Hendershot felt like a table tennis hopeful who'd parachuted into a tournament at 100 to 1 odds.

For protection, he and Clayton slid into back row seats. Turned out a necessary ploy, since the auctioneer was playing to a packed house. Crowd humming at the subdued level of a theatre audience just before the houselights dim. Whatever items had struck their fancy, whatever their financial resources or bidding stratagems, they were sitting on them now, hushed and secretive. As were he and Clayton, whose knee jiggled nervously. As were the two men and three women who sat behind them at a long table, before a line of telephones. Professional bidders for anonymous buyers. Cool as secret agents. Impassive as poker players. Something clandestine about the whole business. Undercover, subterfuge. Now and then, Hendershot and Clayton glanced at each other covertly. Hugger-mugger. The credit card their ace in the hole.

Hendershot calculated that with the $22,000 card limit, he could go as high as £15,000, $21,450 Canadian. Be responsible and save the leftover $550 for emergencies. The Lowenstein would not be one of the big-ticket items. He'd heard it called *The Lowenstein* among the milling crowd in the viewing gallery, where some glanced disdainfully at Beowulf's far corner, commented on *the Lowenstein's quaintness, the Lowenstein's disingenuousness, the Lowenstein's* – as one man had it – *uncontemporarity. Victory* was to be eclipsed by the Rothkos, the da Vincis, and the South African char-coal drawings. Hendershot decided that, like cereal, art had a shelf life. He and his son sat unobtrusively. Biding their time. Clasping their paddle to wait for Lot 77.

He had an urge to go to the bathroom by the time *the Lowenstein* arrived. One of the Rothkos had gone for over eight hundred thousand pounds, the da Vinci fetched enough to feed a small nation, and the cost of a Frida Kahlo would've plunged his video store into a second mortgage for the next 227 years. As two assistants carried Margaret's *Victory* onto the stage, Hendershot's heart bumped his tonsils.

The bidding started at £8,000 and climbed by £500 increments. Hendershot waited. Pre-game skate. Scout out the competition. Down in front, a woman with orange hair. To his left, man in a tuxedo, grey pony tail. Behind, nobody at the telephone table. To his right, bald golden ager with blond trophy wife. As the auctioneer ratcheted the price skywards, Orange Hair pushed it to £10,000, Pony Tail to ten-five, Golden Ager to twelve-five. Hendershot's paddle went up at twelve-five, rallied again at thirteen. By fourteen he was sweating. At fifteen his paddle wavered. At fifteen-five a new bidder jumped in, Ms Buzz-Cut. The race was on. At seventeen thousand, Hendershot fought the urge to clamp his paddle between his knees. At thirty thousand he sat on it. Watched Orange Hair drop out, Golden Ager collapse. Buzz-Cut and Pony-Tail charged for the finish. Pony Tail closed for seventy-five thousand pounds. "Sold," said the auctioneer. At which point Hendershot led Clayton out of the sales room like a man pulling his child away from a house fire.

Back on the street, he inhaled the damp air. "Talk about being misinformed."

"It's okay, Dad."

"There are gaps in my education."

Clayton shouldered his knapsack. "Just think how much money we saved."

"Boggles the mind."

"Now we don't have to explain anything to Mum."

"True."

"We don't even have to tell her."

"Plus, we've robbed Julius of a funny story he can tell over the operating table."

"Julian."

"Julian, right."

"You do that on purpose, don't you, Dad."

"Is it obvious?"

"Kind of. It's okay, though."

"I like to throw it in once in a while."

They came to a corner and turned east. The rain had stopped and in its place the sky was burnished to a golden hue, so that people passing seemed dipped in sunlight. *Or jaundice*, Hendershot thought, feeling himself vaguely uncharitable, defeated, foolish. He had rushed out of the auction house without visiting the bathroom. Now the exigency of his bladder trumped everything.

Clayton was asking him a question. "Do you think Ms Lowenstein will be mad that we didn't buy her painting?"

"I doubt it."

"Maybe we could phone her again. You said Miss Weins..."

"Maybe we could find a bathroom."

"We could phone her and tell her we saw the painting. Tell her how much we like it."

"Later, son. Right now, my pee-pee's at centre ice, waiting for the face-off."

A fruitless search for public facilities along Oxford Street. *What's next*, Hendershot wondered, *diapers?* Eventually they were forced to order chips and hot chocolate in a fast food joint before Hendershot was presented with the keys to the john. When he came out, Clayton was at a table reading a newspaper. Someone in the royal family had swum nude in Italy. A bigamist in Clapham had been released on bail. A telephone company had billed a widow in Hertfordshire for long distance calls totalling £433,000. A bomb scare on the Piccadilly Line had set the train schedule back a full forty-five minutes during rush hour.

Hendershot stared at the bomb story without reading the words. There seemed no point. He thought he knew how that scene would play itself out. *No Arrests Made.* Or, *Arrests Made.* Or, *Bomb Scare Deemed Hoax.* The possibilities were various. And discouraging. He was sliding into a gloomy funk when Clayton's voice broke through.

"We've only got four days left, Dad."

"I know that."

"Easter break will be over. I'm supposed to start school on the seventeenth."

"I know that too."

"But I don't want to go."

Hendershot folded the newspaper. "Can't you feed me a different line here, son?"

Without hesitation the boy said, "Okay, here's one: we've still got four days left..."

"Clayton..."

"...*and*..."

"And *what*?"

"This is the best time I've ever had in my whole life."

35.

"So. Miss Weins."

　　"Mr. Rob."

"It was wonderful, Miss Weins. More than I thought it would be. I saw, I bid, I lost."

"What a shame. I told Ms Lowenstein that you'd probably try to buy it."

"Is she in?"

"She is."

"May I talk to her?"

"Not on the telephone."

"How then? Telepathy?"

"Ha, ha. No. If you could just hold on for a moment." Click of the phone being set down. Footsteps, rustling. Door. Then she was back. "She'd like to send Albert round with the car tomorrow morning. Very early. If I could just get the address of your hotel."

He recited it carefully. "Is she sure she wants to do this?"

"She thinks some discussion is in order."

"It's what I think, too. Would it help if I say I really appreciate this?"

'It would. And may I say, I think the feeling is reciprocated."

"Oh? And why is that?"

"I'll leave that for Ms Lowenstein. To elaborate further would be indiscreet."

"And we don't want to be indiscreet, do we, Miss Weins?"

"Absolutely not."

"I'll be bringing my son with me."
"Good. I look forward to meeting you both."

36.

The land appeared flat and unambitious from the motorway, the open grassland cloaked in morning mist. Black-faced sheep grazed in ghostly pastures, cattle stared numbly out of the fog. Once off the main road, the car crept through a stone-cottaged village and past a lone petrol station. Later, seemingly miles from nowhere, they glimpsed a solitary man holding a long staff as he stood motionless over a tree-shrouded pond. Then the car began to climb, the fog dissolved, and the vast rolling downs opened before them. To this point, Albert had hunched taciturn over the steering wheel, but now he cleared his throat and observed that the landscape was "proper Wiltshire."

To which Hendershot confessed he once had a job offer there. "Swindon."

"You didn't accept it, sir?"

"It went to someone more qualified. Friend of mine."

Albert nodded. "Isn't that always the way."

"We're going to visit him before we go home. Are you from Wiltshire, Albert?"

"Aye, sir," Albert said satirically. "That I be."

"How long have you worked for Margaret Lowenstein?"

"Twelve years this November."

"And before that?"

"I was driver to Colonel Oldham-Ramsell, retired. Until he passed on. Before that," Albert offered, "I was in Her Majesty's service, Belfast."

Hendershot glanced at the man's face. Mostly expressionless. Son of the soil, ferrying strangers. But, Belfast? "You must have thoughts about the Troubles then."

"I do, sir."

"What are they?"

"I prefer to keep such opinions private, sir."

"But Belfast." For Hendershot, same war, different battle. "Must've been pretty ... eventful."

"There were ten in my squad," Albert said. "Two of us came home." He steered around a curve, and then another. Grassy hills rose on either side of the road. Raising a cheerful voice to Clayton, who sat in the back seat, he announced, "Here's something, lad. If you look out your window just ahead, you'll see the great chalk horse. On the hillside, to the left." He slowed, stopped the car on the grass verge. "There."

Carved out of living turf into the hill's chalk under-layer, a gigantic white horse lunged toward the skyline. Tiny head, elongated neck, legs as curved and taut as long-bows. An arc of joyous motion.

"It's huge," Clayton said.

"Very old, that is." Albert at the wheel. Car and driver idling. "Hundreds of years."

"Who put it there?"

"That I don't know, lad." Albert switched off the engine. Wind nudged against the car. "My father used to say it was cut to celebrate a victory during the time of King Alfred. But the old colonel said it was made as recent as the seventeen-hundreds. Either way, it's old. Every few years, the farmers hereabout pull up the weeds and trim up the sod. Traditional, that is. There's another horse in Oxfordshire they say is as old as Moses."

"Could I get out and take a picture of it?"

"'Course you can, lad."

As Clayton scouted around the car for the perfect angle, Albert allowed, "That's a good lad you've got there."

"I hope so."

"Most kids these days –" Albert shook his head.

"Yeah."

"When I was over there," Albert confessed, "you'd see these kids go down the shops and fetch things home for their mum, and you'd think butter wouldn't melt. An hour later, they'd be snarling at you with a rock or a bottle in their hands."

"Have you got any kids, Albert?"

"No. I was married for a time but – we didn't get on. I've got two nieces, though. Over in Swindon. My sister and her husband both work in computers. The girls are left on their own a lot. It's worrying."

Clayton climbed back into the car. His face was flushed. "I think I got some really good ones."

"Good man," Albert said.

An unpaved, winding lane through gnarled trees, and a weathered sign announced the place in faded letters. *The Lynch.* Cut through a copse of slender beech trees, the narrow drive ended abruptly at a low stone cottage, flanked at one end by a jungled rose garden, at the other, a tumbledown stone shed. A tall, raw-boned woman with lank grey hair and knuckled hands the shape of hockey gloves, stood in the driveway. She wore a raincoat, and her face was deeply creased as if it had been left out in all weathers. When Hendershot and Clayton stepped out of the car, she approached them. Smiled and extended an enormous hand.

"Mr. Rob." Her voice the youthful contralto from the telephone.

"Miss Weins." The contrast startled him. This aged, sinewy six-footer – candidate for a girls' school field hockey coach – had pure music in her voice.

"So good to meet you." Her big mitt smothered his. "And this is...?"

"I'm Clayton," the boy said shyly.

She pumped the kid's hand. "Well, Clayton, I hope Albert didn't bore you with his incessant and idle gossip."

At ease beside his car, Albert grinned.

"He showed us the great chalk horse," Clayton said.

"I thought he might." She shot Albert an approving look. "Well done."

The ex-soldier snapped to attention. "Thank you, sir."

"Irony, Albert," Miss Weins reminded him.

"Is not my forte, sir."

"But it's getting better."

"Yessir." Winking to Hendershot and Clayton, and turning to his car. "I'll leave you now."

"Thanks for everything," Hendershot said.

"You're welcome." Albert faced Miss Weins. "I leave you in *good* hands."

Miss Weins lifted an eyebrow. "Bordering on the personal, Albert."

"Won't happen again, sir. I'll be tackling the shed roof, if you need to find me."

As they crunched toward the house, Miss Weins said, "In his first year with us, Albert could go days without uttering a word." She turned to Clayton. "Have you heard the expression 'Loose lips sink ships'?"

"My granddad says it sometimes."

"With Albert," Miss Weins said, "loose lips were never in danger of sinking anything. When he first came to us, he rarely spoke. Oh, there was no rudeness intended. In those days silence was an absolute necessity to him. Something it has never been to me. Case in point, Clayton. Listen to me now. Chatter, chatter." She opened the wide front door. "Come in, come in" – and led them to a narrow foyer. A coat rack guarding an umbrella stand. A battered rosewood table set with pale yellow roses. A rubber mat holding a pair of high rubber boots.

Slipping out of her shoes, Miss Weins said, "Ms

Lowenstein is in the sunroom." She pulled on the rubber wellingtons. Smiled at Clayton, "You and I can take a walk along the top of the downs, while your dad and Ms L. have a chat. The weather's clearing, so we should be able to see right down to the plain. We're not far from Stonehenge, you know. And Old Sarum. And – although you might only see the top of the steeple – Salisbury Cathedral."

The mention of the cathedral gave Hendershot pause. Godless since he was eleven when his grandfather died from a prolonged and merciless cancer despite Hendershot's fervent prayers, he'd never been partial to religion, churches, or the Almighty. Never had been able to distinguish between destiny and dumb luck. Too close to call. Never seen Salisbury Cathedral, either. But when he saw Margaret rise from her chair in a room that was all plants and windows, something providential – or perhaps it was only the light – seized him by the throat.

37.

"He *was* guilty," Margaret assured him.

"At least we agree on that." Hendershot shifted in his chair. Rattan, once painted white, seat missing a few reeds. Creaked like a sailboat's rigging. In fact, the sunroom was a modern addition to the old cottage. Newer stonework and windows. Not big enough to be a conservatory, too big to be a sun porch. Without the plants, it could have been the poop deck on a pint-sized tall ship. Out there, the downs fell away to the plain like waves on the ocean. The heaving expanse left him perched vertiginously on the edge of his seat.

"Nice room," Hendershot said.

"1976," Margaret said. "I bought this place after the Tate purchased my little nude self-portrait."

"Lily Tarn," Hendershot remembered. "Margaret Naked in the Lake. Even my boy noticed that one."

"They took it as a feminist statement. I took it as manna from heaven." She waved her hand. "Connor did the stonework, free of charge. I think now that he might've been here to avoid the police."

"But he didn't make bombs."

"No, but he must have..." Uncannily, her eyes fixed on his. Still deep brown, but opaque. Glazed. He wondered what she saw. If anything.

"...he must have composed them," she said.

"Composed? What do you mean, 'composed'?"

"Imagined them into existence." Her sightless eyes slid

past Hendershot. "I didn't realize that until recently. And even then, I didn't want to believe he was involved in such brutality. He always had a sense of justice. Fair play, and all that. After all, he'd helped me many times when I'd needed it most. So that last year, when they accused him, I knew they must be wrong. Even if his name wasn't Connor Mack, as the police claimed, he couldn't have done what they said. He couldn't have."

"But?"

"But then I visited him in the lock-up. Before the trial. There was glass between us. Of course, I couldn't see it. I couldn't see him. Oh, at times, if I look sideways, I catch a certain...not light, really, but a memory of light. A shape. But not on that day. All I had was his voice. And as soon as I heard him say he was innocent, I knew he was lying. I heard it...saw it...clearly, in his voice."

"But you testified at his trial."

Her face collapsed. Blotched, puffy, old. "My evidence, of course, wasn't evidence at all. Promiscuous artist, blighted love affair, flagging career. The prosecution counsel had a marvelous time. Poor old fat blind thing, seeking publicity. That might be why Victory recently went up for auction. The terrorism market. Trailing a few clouds of notoriety, that might have added to its value."

He leaned forward. "Money doesn't stop it from being a good painting, Margaret."

"Well," she patted him, "you would say that, wouldn't you."

"What about Mister Green's notebook? When the cop came to see me in the hospital, I told him all about it."

"Ah, the notebook. There was some mention of it. But no evidence. It was reduced to a dead man's fiction. Apparently, after Mister Green died, the police searched his flat. All they found was an album full of newspaper clippings. The original investigators called it circumstantial. Most of them have retired or passed on since then."

He waited. "How did Connor compose bombs?"

"Not the bombs themselves, but the effects of the bombs. He knew his craft. He worked on the Tower of London. Look at the stones in this house."

"He did a good job."

"Connor never did things by halves." She folded her hands in her lap. "He told me once that some of the work on the Tower had been done by French masons brought over in the 14th century. The French sections, he said, were absolute rubbish. If they'd been bombed during the Blitz, all the walls at that end would have come down of a piece. He knew, you see. I think he could see where bombs could do the most damage. Where they could be placed to kill. He couldn't have composed all of them, of course. But there was an art to some of them. The prosecutors brought that out in the trial. But there was no overall pattern, you see, between where he went and where the bombs were placed. But he knew. He knew. And his knowing hurt me. It still hurts me. Because of his betrayal, I suppose. Not of me, of course. Who am I to speak of betrayals? But of his ... art. Yes, his art. You don't build things to be destroyed." She lifted her face to the window's light.

He smiled. "Fuzzing your eyes?"

She laughed softly. "You remember that?"

"I envied it."

"So do I, now." She paused. "I was so sorry when I learned about your leg. I ... couldn't face you. Your ice hockey."

"I'm used to it now. Besides, I got the money you left."

"I thought you wouldn't accept it."

"I wasn't going to. But I got greedy. Figured I was owed. Didn't take me long, as a matter of fact."

"And the nurse – your wife?"

"She's going to be somebody else's wife soon."

"But you have your son."

"Yes. We have him. Took three miscarriages and nine years, but we got him." And then, without meaning to, he told her everything. About Louise and Julian, Clayton and the knife, Franklin Burroughs and the charges that might be leveled against his son. When he was finished, he said, "So we're heading back to a real mess, Margaret. I'm not sure how it's going to play out. You got any tips for me?"

She cocked her head to one side as she used to, as though listening for – or looking at – something far away.

"Help me up," she said.

Following her instructions, he guided her into her studio, a cramped space of windows and clutter. Plastic bins lined the walls, each groaning with cast-offs: rags, machine parts, broken kitchen appliances, crockery, stones, driftwood, theatre posters, keys, fake fur, real fur, sandpaper.

"Albert finds and collects them," she said.

"It looks like a recycling centre."

"It is." Pleased, she tightened her grip on his arm. "The work table's in the middle of the room."

The table was littered with box-like frames, some of which contained strategically placed objects. The white skull of an animal, the innards of a clock, a spill of coins. Others were empty. One half of the surface held a stretched canvas, brushes, paint tubes and a palette.

Her hand clasped his forearm. As if her fingers were pleading with his very flesh. Her voice softened. "Lately, I've taken up painting again."

The canvas on the table was a blurred patchwork of riotous colour. A maelstrom of blobs, layers and fragments that exploded from the painting's bottom left corner and spattered toward the top right. The shadings were crude, thickly troweled. The dried brush strokes and palette-knife tracks as ragged as tree bark, as rough as unfinished cement. Layered higgledy-piggledy, black on yellow, blue on orange, green on purple, red on brown, the canvas was violent, disheveled, ugly.

"What do you think?" she asked.

"It's colourful, that's for sure."

"Abrasive," she said. "Unbalanced. Yes. So I've been told."

She felt across the table, rested her hand on the canvas's bottom edge. "Now. Can you make sure the curtains are drawn over the windows? When they are, turn off the light switch near the door."

The room was instantly black.

She said, "Walk straight towards my voice."

He stepped through the dark as though on a high, narrow ledge, until his leg bumped the table.

"Good," she said. In the dark, her voice was the only living thing. "Give me your hand."

She guided his fingers to the canvas. "Start at the bottom," she said. "Slowly."

He remembered, as in an old photograph, his hand on her bare flesh.

"Not so fast," she said.

At first, he felt only the paint's rough mountainous track, its dark-bouldered foundation, its lumpy rip-rap. His fingers tumbled into crevasses, bumped ridges, snagged cornices. Bending at the waist, he reached forward. His hands were lost in the painting's rubble for a time, and he paused to reorient himself.

"It's rough," he told her.

"I had to experiment," she said.

He continued to grope his way toward the top of the canvas. Closed his eyes without thinking. Ridges of paint led him on, turned him back, abandoned him, found him again. Time slowed, stalled, dissolved. His fingers opened pathways, climbed, stumbled, fell. They were trapped in ravines, then escaped along ledges; were boxed in canyons, then staggered up screes. As he held himself leaning forward, his knee ached, his back cramped.

"Keep going." She was beside him, shoulder touching.

Finally, valleys widened, ridges shrank and he was led, he thought, if not to a place of light, then at least to a high, nubbled smoothness, where layers glided beneath his fingertips, smooth as fish scales, as metal, as glass.

He was sweating. His hand curled over the top of the painting. "Ah, Margaret."

"At first I was going to call it Frozen Lake Crossing," she said. "Do you remember telling me?"

"That was a long time ago."

"But as it went along, it became more of a mountain."

"It's a good one."

"These things never turn out the way you plan." Finding his shoulder and tracing the length of his arm, her hand came to rest on his. "A bit obvious, I'm afraid."

They stood there in the dark and held each other, for longer than either of them had ever expected.

ACKNOWLEDGEMENTS

There are several people to whom I owe a debt in the writing of this novel:

– My maternal grandfather, now deceased, who, in story, led me to East London.

– Daryl Lipsey of the Swindon Wildcats, who shared with me the trials of a Canadian playing hockey in Great Britain.

– Gayle Freed-Sterne, whose art I saw and admired at the Emma Lake Artists' Colony.

– Chellie Dickinson, my wife, my love and my friend; and our children Luke, Paul and Alice, who gave their dad time to write.

– The staff at Coteau Books: John Agnew, publisher, for his kind observations, Nik Burton for his copyediting, Susan Buck for production, Tania Craan for the design, and especially Dave Margoshes, my editor, for his unstinting patience, persistence and encouragement.

ABOUT THE AUTHOR

Don Dickinson is the author of two short story collections, *Fighting the Upstream* (Oberon Press) and *Blue Husbands* (Porcupine's Quill); nominated for the Governor General's Award; winner of the Ethel Wilson Fiction Prize; and two novels, *The Crew* (Coteau Books; nominated for the Books in Canada First Novel Award) and *Robbiestime* (Harper-Collins). His stories have appeared in anthologies both in Canada and abroad.

For seven years he travelled widely, working at jobs as varied as labourer, fitness instructor and shepherd. He later taught high school and university English courses for over twenty years. Married with three children, he lives with his wife in Lillooet, British Columbia.

MIX
Paper from
responsible sources
FSC® C100212

Printed by Imprimerie Gauvin
Gatineau, Québec